ALSO BY JOHN BANVILLE

Long Lankin

Nightspawn

Birchwood

Doctor Copernicus

Kepler

The Newton Letter

Mefisto

The Book of Evidence

Ghosts

ATHENA

A NOVEL BY

JOHN BANVILLE

ALFRED A. KNOPF
NEW YORK
1995

to Anthony Sheil

My love. If words can reach whatever world you may be suffering in, then listen. I have things to tell you. At this muffled end of another year I prowl the sombre streets of our quarter holding you in my head. I would not have thought it possible to fix a single object so steadily for so long in the mind's violent gaze. You. You. With dusk comes rain that seems no more than an agglutination of the darkening air, drifting aslant in the lamplight like something about to be remembered. Strange how the city becomes deserted at this evening hour; where do they go to, all those people, and so suddenly? As if I had cleared the streets. A car creeps up on me from behind, tyres squeaking against the sides of the narrow footpaths, and I have to stop and press myself into a doorway to let it pass. How sinister it appears, this sleek, unhuman thing wallowing over the cobbles with its driver like a faceless doll propped up motionless behind rain-stippled glass. It shoulders by me with what seems a low chuckle and noses down an alleyway, oozing a lazy burble of exhaust smoke from its rear end, its lollipop-pink tail-lights swimming in the deliquescent gloom. Yes, this is my hour, all right. Curfew hour.

I

Three things the thought of you conjures up: the gullet of a dying fish into which I have thrust my thumb, the grainy inner lining of your most secret parts, ditto, and the tumescent throb in the throat of some great soprano – who? – on the third, held note of the second alleluia of Schubert's *Die junge Nonne* (O night! O storm!). Much else besides, of course, but these textures persist above all, I do not know why, I mean why these three in particular. (I apologise, by the way, for associating you with that fish; I caught it when I was a boy and never caught another, but I remember it, the poor creature hauled out of its element, shuddering as it drowned in air.) I hardly dare think what form of me you would recall: an eyed unipod heaving and slithering towards you across the floor, something like that, no doubt. Yet what a thing we made there in that secret white room at the heart of the old house, what a marvellous edifice we erected. For this is what I see, you and me naked and glistening in the mirror-coloured light of an October afternoon, labouring wordlessly to fashion our private temple to the twin gods watching over us. I remember Morden telling me the story of a builder of his acquaintance demolishing a folly down the country somewhere and finding a centuries-old chapel concealed inside the walls. *Tight as an egg*, he said. *Amazing.* And laughed his laugh. I thought of us.

We had our season. That is what I tell myself. We had our season, and it ended. Were you waiting all along to go, poised to leap? It seems to me now that even while I held you clasped in my appalled embrace you were already looking back at me, like one lingering on the brink of departure, all that you were leaving already fading in your glance, becoming memory even as it stood before you. Were you part of the plot, a party to it? I would like to know. I think I would like to know. Would we have been left free and undisturbed, left entirely to our own charming devices, as we were, had someone not decided it should be so? Before such little doors of doubt can open more than a crack my mind jumps up in panic and slams them shut. Yet reason with a scoffing laugh insists that you were in on it, as they say, that you must have been; but what does reason know except itself? Nowadays I prefer the murk and confusion of the lower brain, the one that used to go by the name of heart. Heart, yes; not a word you will have heard me employ very often up to now. I feel as I have not felt since I was a lovelorn adolescent, at once bereft and lightened, giddy with relief at your going – you were too *much* for me – and yet assailed by a sorrow so weighty, of so much more consequence than I seem to myself to be, that I stand, no, I kneel before it, speechless in a kind of awe. Even at those times when, sated with its pain, my mind briefly relinquishes the thought of you the sense of loss does not abate, and I go about mentally patting my pockets and peering absently into the shadowed corners of myself, trying to identify what it is that has been misplaced. This is what it must be like to have a wasting illness, this restlessness, this wearied excitation, this perpetual shiver in the blood. There are moments – well, I do not wish to melodramatise, but there are moments, at the twin poles of dusk and dawn especially, when I think I might die of the loss of you, might simply forget myself in my anguish and agitation and step blindly off the edge of the earth and be gone for good. And yet at the same time I feel I have never been so vividly alive, so quick with the sense of things, so exposed in the midst of the world's seething play of particles, as if I had been flayed of an exquisitely fine protective skin. The rain falls through me silently, like a shower of neutrinos.

The murders seem to have stopped. The police have not turned up a body now for weeks. I find this disturbing. The killings started about the time we met and now that you are gone they have come to an end. It is foolish, I know, but I cannot help wondering if there was a connection. I don't mean a direct link, of course, but could it be that we disturbed something with our wantonness, upset some secret balance in the atmosphere and thus triggered a misfire deep in the synapse maze of that poor wretch, whoever he is, and sent him ravening out into the night with his rope and knife? Foolish, as I say. I am convinced that I have seen him, the killer, without realising it, that somewhere in my prowlings I have stumbled across him and not recognised him. What a thought.

My headaches too have stopped. Pains in the head, murders in the night. If I tried I could connect everything in a vast and secret agenda. If I tried.

Aunt Corky left me all her money. (You see? – a lost love, a locked room, and now a will: we are in familiar territory after all.) There was a great deal more of it than I ever imagined there could be. Her last flourish, the sly old thing. I wonder if she thought it was her money I was after? I hope not. Sticking with her through all those long, last weeks of her dying was, I see now, the one unalloyed good deed I could point to in my life, the thing I thought might go some way towards balancing my account in the recording angel's big black book. Still, I won't pretend I am not glad to have the dough, especially as Morden despite his trumpetings about probity and fair dealing (and to think I believed him!) somehow managed to forget to recompense me for my troubles before he did a flit. My troubles . . . Funny thing, money; when you haven't got any you think of almost nothing else, then you get some and you can't understand why it ever seemed important. Aunt Corky at a stroke (to coin a phrase) has solved my life, or the getting and spending part of it, anyway. I feel light-headed and sort of wobbly; it is an odd sensation, like that flutter that lingers in the muscles when you put down a heavy load you have been carrying for a long time.

It's ironic, really: Aunt Corky was the one who was forever urging me to take up work and do something with my life, but now I have her money and will never again need to go out and earn a crust. What was she thinking of? I suppose it was me or the Cats and Dogs Home. 'You are a nogood,' she would say cheerfully in her deliberately fractured English, 'a no-good, yes, just as your father was.' She was given to such franknesses, they were not intended to wound – in fact, that mention of my father denotes rueful approval, for I know she had a soft spot for the old boy. What she meant was that he and I were wastefully dilettantish, even if to her eye we did have a certain style. She was not wrong, about the waste, I mean. I have frittered away the better part of my life. I did it all backways, starting out an achiever and then drifting into vagueness and crippling indecision. Now, becalmed in the midst of my decidedly unroaring forties, I feel I have entered already if not my second childhood then certainly my second adolescence – look at all this love stuff, this gonadal simpering and sighing; I shall break out in a rash of pimples yet.

Now that I think of it, it was largely Aunt Corky's workward urgings, as well, of course, as my own natural (or should that be unnatural?) curiosity, that led me to Morden and his hoard of pictures. I am still not sure exactly how he came to know of me, for I have changed my name (by deed poll: yes, there really is such a process), along with everything else that was changeable; it was his man Francie who ran me to ground in the end, by God knows what devious channels. Morden had a touching fondness for secrecy and sudden pouncings, I noticed that about him right away; he loved to lead . . . his victims, I was about to say; he loved to lead people on by a show of seeming ignorance and then reveal with a flourish that he had known all along all there was to know about them. For all his moneyed look and the sense of menace he gave off, there wafted around him a definite air of the mountebank. The occasion of our first meeting retains in my memory a sort of lurid, phosphorescent glow; I have an impression of a greenish light and dispersing stage smoke and the sudden swirl and crack of a cloak and a big voice booming out: *Tarraa!*

It was the first time I had been in that quarter of the city, or at least the first time I noticed myself being there. September, one of those slightly hallucinatory, dreamy afternoons of early autumn, all sky and polished-copper clouds and thin, petrol-blue air. The river still had a summery stink. How much larger, higher, wider the world appears at that time of year; today even the bellowing traffic seemed cowed by this suddenly eminent new season rearing above the clanging streets. I crossed out of sunlight at the entrance to Swan Alley, dodging a charging bus that mooed at me angrily, and found myself at once plunged in shadow thin and chill, like watered ink, and had to stop a moment to let my eyes become accustomed to the gloom. When I think of the place now I always see it caught like this in a sort of eclipse; even your presence in my mental picture of these little streets and cobbled alleyways cannot disperse the glimmering, subfusc atmosphere with which my memory suffuses them.

The house was in . . . what shall I call it? Rue Street, that sounds right. The house was in Rue Street. It looked derelict and I thought at first I must have the wrong address. Big gaunt grey townhouse with rotting windows and a worn step and a broad black door sagging on its hinges. I pressed the bell and heard no sound and knocked the dull knocker and imagined I could detect a muffled tittering from within. I waited, putting on that abstracted, mild look that waiting at doors always demands – or always demands of me, anyway. Next the obligatory ritual: step back, scan the upstairs windows, frown at the pavement, then scan the

6

windows a second time while slowly assuming a querulous expression. Nothing. On the left there was a fenced-off site with rubble and empty crisp packets and a flourishing clump of purple buddleia, on the right a dim little flyblown shop that seemed to have its shoulders hunched. I went into the shop. It smelled of cat and stewed tea. Do we really need all this, these touches of local colour and so on? Yes, we do. The usual crone peered at me over the usual bottles of boiled sweets, at her back a dim doorway leading down to hell. Before I could ask her anything there was a light, syncopated step behind me and I turned. This is how things begin. A blue cloud of cigarette smoke coming at me like a claw opening and behind his shoulder the honeyed sunlight in the street and a diagonal shadow by de Chirico sharp as the blade of a guillotine. Francie. Francie the fixer: an S-shaped, shabby, faintly grinning, glitter-eyed, limping character, tall-ish, thin, concave of chest, with scant reddish hair under a flat cap, face like a chisel, and a fag-end with a drooping inch of ash attached to a bloodless, hardly existent thin long line of lower lip. I had never set eyes on him before yet felt I had known him always; or at least – I can't explain it – that he had known me. 'Mr Morrow!' he said, in the tone of a hunter claiming his bag, pointing a finger pistol-wise at my breast. Morrow: yes, that is my name, now; have I mentioned it before? I chose it for its faintly hopeful hint of futurity, and, of course, the Wellsian echo. Finding a first name was more difficult. I toyed with numerous outlandish monikers: Feardorcha, for instance, which in our old language means man of darkness; also Franklin, the freeman, and Fletcher, a famous islander; Fernando, with its insin-uation of stilettos and the poison cup; and even Fyodor, though the overtones of that were too obvious even for me. In the end what I settled for seemed just the thing. But I confess I have not yet accustomed myself to this new identity – or identification, at least – and there is always a hesitation

7

when I am thus addressed. Francie I could see had caught that telltale lapse; Francie was a man who noticed such things. 'Come on along with me now, will you,' he said. I followed him out, and had a picture of the shopwoman standing there forever behind the counter with her pinched old face vaguely, patiently lifted, unable to stir, stricken into a statued trance for all eternity, waiting for the banal question I had left unasked.

On the sunny pavement Francie looked sideways at my legs and smiled with pursed lips as if something funny had occurred to him. 'We watched you from on high,' he said, pointing at the upper windows. 'I couldn't get down fast enough for you. Patience, they tell me, is a great thing.' The faint smile turned to a grin, his thin mouth seeming to stretch from ear to ear.

A large dog with bristling, shiny black fur and pricked-up, pointed ears had appeared from nowhere and was loping silently at our heels.

We stopped at the house and Francie flicked away his cigarette butt and produced a great key and jiggled it in the keyhole. He pushed open the sagging black door and waved me in with an elaborate sweep of his arm. High white shadowy hallway paved unevenly with sandstone flags. The door shutting produced a shiver of tiny echoes that fell plinkingly about us. Smell of distemper and ancient plaster and crumbling stone. A delicate staircase with a banister rail moulded into a sinuous, rising curve – I think of that part of your arm between the elbow and the wrist – ascended airily toward a soft glare of white light falling from tall windows high above. Echoingly we climbed. The dog, ignored, followed after us, claws clicking on the bare boards. 'These stairs,' Francie said, 'are a killer,' though I was the one who was panting. He turned suddenly and made a feint at the dog and roared merrily, '*Prince you bugger get out to hell out of that!*' The dog only looked at him adoringly and grinned, its pink-fringed, glistening jaws agape.

On the top floor we stopped under a peeling plaster dome. I could feel Francie eyeing me still with that expression of subdued mirth. I squared my shoulders and pretended interest in the architecture. There was a circular, railed balcony with white doors giving off it, all shut. I felt like the last Mrs Bluebeard. Francie walked ahead of me. That walk: a kind of slack-heeled, undulating lope, as if he belonged to a species that had only lately begun to go about upright. The limp seemed not to trouble him, seemed, in fact, to confer agility, less a limp than a spring in his step. He opened one of the white doors and again stood aside and waved me forward. 'Here we are, friend,' he said jauntily, and made an insolent, clicking noise out of the side of his mouth. *Now listen here, my man*, I said . . . No, of course I didn't. I stepped past him. I could sense the dog at my heels and hear its rapid breathing, like the sound of a soft engine hard at work. I do not like dogs.

There are certain moments in life when—

But no, no. We shall dispense with the disquisition on fate and the forked paths that destiny sets us upon and all such claptrap. There are no moments, only the seamless drift; how many times do I have to tell myself this simple truth? That day I could no more have prevented myself from stepping through that doorway than I could have made my heart stop beating or the lymph halt in its courses through my glands. I do not mean to imply there was coercion involved, that, fixed in Francie's amused, measuring gaze, I had been robbed of all volition; if it were so, how much easier everything would seem. No, what I mean simply is that I did not stop, did not turn aside, but went on, and so closed off all other possibilities. Things happen, therefore they have happened. If there are other worlds in which the alternatives to our actions are played out we may know nothing of them.

Even if I had felt a spider's web of foreboding brush against my face I would have been drawn irresistibly through it by the force of that linked series of tiny events that began the instant I was born, if not before, and that would bundle me however unceremoniously through today's confrontation, just as it will propel me on to others more or less fateful than that one until at last I arrive at the last of all and disappear forever into the suddenly shattered mirror of my self. It is what I call my life. It is what I imagine I lead, when all the time it is leading me, like an ox to the shambles.

The corridor in which I found myself was low and broad and cluttered with stuff. White walls again, the peculiar, tired, parched yellowish-white that was the overall no-colour of the interior of the house. Of the same shade and texture, at least in my first vague awareness of them, were the nameless things piled everywhere, the litter of decades – of centuries – resembling, to my eyes, big bundles of slightly soiled clouds or enormous, dried-up blobs of papier mâché. As I picked my way through them I had the impression that they were more than merely rubbish that had been dumped and left here over the years, that they were, rather, a kind of detritus extruded by the place itself, a solidified spume that the walls by some process of slow internal decomposition had spontaneously precipitated. And even later on, when I came to rummage through these recrements, they retained for me something of this desiccated, friable texture, and there were times when I fancied that I too from prolonged contact with them was beginning to moulder and would steadily crumble away until nothing remained of me but a shapeless heap of unidentifiable odds and ends. Behind me Francie swore lightheartedly and kicked a cardboard box out of his way. 'Heavenly Christ,' he said with a sigh, 'this place, this place.'

The corridor before me curved a little – the house was all bends and droops and sudden inclines, the result of subsidence, according to Morden, who managed to give the word an infernal resonance – and suddenly I came up against another door, this one open an inch or two. Doors standing ajar like that have always filled me with unease; they seem so knowing and somehow suggestive, like an eye about to wink or a mouth opening to laugh. A strange, intense white light was coming from behind it, spilling through the crack as if a great flare of magnesium were burning in the room beyond. It was only daylight, however, falling from two tall and, so it seemed to me at first, slightly canted, overhanging windows. The room, very high and airy, had the look of an atelier. A thing made of poles and pulleys, like a rack for drying washing, was suspended by ropes from the ceiling, and a large, dirty white sheet that seemed as if it had been stretched right across the room and had fallen down at one side was draped in a diagonal sweep from the corner of a window-frame to the floor, making a dramatic effect that was oddly and unaccountably familiar; the whole thing – the high room, the massed, white light, that cascading sash – might have been a background to one of Jacques Louis David's revolutionary group portraits. Morden followed my glance and said, 'The Tennis Court Oath eh?,' and threw me a sharp, ironical look, his great head thrown back. Thus at the very outset we had a demonstration of his divinatory powers. I took a step backwards, shocked, as if one of the floorboards had sprung up under my foot and smacked me bang on the nose. I could see he was pleased with himself. 'Yes,' he said, 'the place is that old, to the very year; amazing, isn't it?'

He had the look himself of a somewhat later vintage, less David's Robespierre than Rodin's Balzac, standing in the middle of the empty floor wrapped in his long coat with his arms folded high up on his massive chest and looking askance at me down his boxer's big, splayed nose. The eyes – ah, the eyes! That panther glance! I realised two things simultaneously, that he was younger than me by a good ten years, and that I was afraid of him; I did not know which of these two facts I found the more disturbing. I heard Francie moving about softly behind me and for a mad moment I had the notion that he was positioning himself to tackle me, like a henchman in the movies who will suddenly yank the victim's jacket back and pinion his arms so that the boss in his camel-hair coat and raked fedora may step forward smilingly at his leisure and deliver the hapless hero a haymaker into the breadbasket. After an interval of compressed silence Morden, still fixing me with that glossy black stare, seemed to come to a decision and nodded and muttered, 'Yes indeed, yes indeed,' and put on a look that was partly a grin and partly a scowl and turned and paced slowly to the window and stood in silence for a long moment contemplating the building opposite. That coat, though, he cannot have been wearing that greatcoat yet, the weather was still too warm; if I have got that detail wrong what else am I misremembering? Anyway, that is how I see him that day, posed there in the light under those beetling windows with his arms still folded and one leg thrust forward from the skirts of his coat, a big, deep-chested, brooding man with flattened features and a moneyed suntan and a lovingly barbered thick long mane of lustreless red-brown hair.

'So: here you are,' he said, as if to set aside what had gone before and start all over again. Already I felt out of breath, as if I were being forced to scramble after him back and forth across a steep incline. 'Yes, here I am,' I said, not knowing what else to say. Morden looked past me at Francie and raised his eyebrows and said, 'Hark: he speaks!' Then he fixed his level, measuring gaze on me once more. Behind me Francie laughed quietly. Another silence. Prince the dog sat in the doorway, tongue lolling, watching us attentively, its vulpine ears erect and faintly twitching.

I'm sure none of this is as it really happened.

'I think that you can help me,' Morden said briskly. 'I hear you are a man a man might trust.' He seemed to find that briefly amusing and turned aside a faint smirk. His voice was large, resonating in that big chest, and weighted with odd emphases, deliberately running on and falling over itself as if he wanted to make it known that he had not the time or patience to say all he had to say and therefore the words themselves must work overtime; a manufactured voice. He said he had lately acquired the house – I liked that word, acquired – and added, 'For development,' waving a beringed and strangely bloated, bloodless hand. 'Development, preservation, the two in one; big plans, we have; yes, big plans.' Now it was Francie's turn to smirk. Oh, they were having a rollicking time, the two of them. Morden nodded in happy satisfaction, contemplating the future and breathing deep through those wide nostrils as if he were snuffing up the heady smells of fresh-cut timber, bricks and mortar. Then he roused himself and turned from the window, suddenly, energetically cheery. 'And now, I think, a little toast,' he said. 'Francie?'

Francie hesitated and for a moment there was rebellion in the air. I turned and together Morden and I looked at him. In the end he shrugged and gave his side teeth a disdainful suck and slouched off with the dog following close behind him. Morden laughed. 'He's a bit of an artist himself, you know, is old Francie,' he said confidingly.

I felt something relax in me with a sort of creak, as if the pawl and ratchet of a suspended, spring-loaded mechanism in my chest had been eased a notch. Morden went back to his silent contemplation at the window. It was very quiet; we might have been in a lift together, the two of us, soundlessly ascending towards I knew not what. I could hear my heart beating; the rate seemed remarkably slow. Strange, the moments like that when everything seems to break free and just drift and anything might happen; it is not like life at all, then, but some other state, conscious and yet dreamy, in which the self hangs weightless in a sort of fevered stillness. Perhaps there is a kind of volition, after all (involuntary volition? – could there be such a thing?), and perhaps it is in intervals such as this one that, unknowingly, we make our judgments, arrive at decisions, commit ourselves. If so, everything I have ever believed in is wrong (belief in this sense is of course a negative quality). It is an intensely invigorating notion. I do not really credit it; I am just playing here, amusing myself in this brief intermission before everything starts up again.

Presently Francie returned with a bottle of champagne and three wine glasses greyed with dust. Morden took the bottle and removed the foil and the wire cap and gave the cork a peremptory twist; I thought of a hunter putting some plump, sleek creature out of its misery. There was an unexpectedly feeble pop and a limp tongue of froth lolled from the neck. The wine was pink and tepid. Francie got none. Morden clinked his dusty glass against mine. 'To art!' he said. I drank but he did not, only raised the glass to his lips in dry dumbshow.

We tramped up and down the house, Morden ahead of me swinging the champagne bottle by the neck and his coat billowing and Francie in the rear going along softly at his syncopated slouch with the dog loping close behind him. This forced march had something violent and at the same time faintly preposterous about it. I had a sense of impending, laughable collapse, as in one of those burlesque dreams in which one finds oneself scampering trouserless through a convulsed crowd of hilariously pointing strangers. Solemnly we processed through high rooms with flaking plaster and torn-up floorboards and windows below which the sunlight's geometry was laid out in complicated sections. Everywhere there was a sense of the place's mute embarrassment at being seen like this, in such disarray.

'. . . A person by the name of Marbot,' Morden was saying, 'Josiah Marbot, esquire, gent. of this ward. Great traveller, great builder, great collector, confidant to the King of Naples, guest of Marie Antoinette at the palace of Versailles (they say she had a clitoris as thick as your thumb, did you know that?). There are letters to him from Madame de Somebody, King Whatsit's mistress. He made his fortune early, in the linen trade: flax from Flanders, hemp from Ghent, weavers from Bayeux. He paddled around the Low Countries picking up whatever he could find; oh yes, a fine eye for a bargain. He never married, and left his fortune to the Anti-Slavery Society or somesuch. Quaker he was, I believe. A real eighteenth-century type.' He halted abruptly and I almost walked into him. He smelled of shaving balm and the beginnings of gum disease. He was still carrying his glass of champagne untouched. Mine he refilled. 'At the end, of course, he went peculiar.' He held the bottle tilted and fixed me with a beadily playful stare, his eyebrows twitching. 'Shut himself away here in the house, only a manservant for company, years and years, then died. It's all written up, I've read it. Amazing.'

While he spoke my attention was diverted to something behind him that he did not see. We had come to what seemed the dead-end of a corridor with a narrow, tall blank wall before us and no doors visible. The arrangement struck me as peculiar. The dead-end wall was a lath and plaster affair, and in one place, low down, the plaster had crumbled in a big, jigsaw-puzzle shape through which I could see to the other side: daylight and bare floorboards, and something black: black material, velvet, perhaps, which I took to be a curtain or a narrow screen of some sort until suddenly it moved and I glimpsed the flash of a stockinged leg and the spiked heel of a slender black shoe. The dog moaned softly. 'Now watch this,' Morden said, and turned to the blind wall, and, pressed his fingers to a hidden switch or something, and with a click the narrow wall turned into a door and swung open on creaking hinges. What a childish thrill it was to see it, a wall opening! I felt like one of RLS's plucky boy heroes. Beyond was a triangular room with a low, grimed window looking across the street to a brick parapet over the top of which I could see the city's domed and spiked skyline dusted with September sunlight. The furnishings consisted of a single spindle-backed chair left there by someone and forgotten, and a broad, prolapsed chaise-longue that presented itself to our gaze with an air of elephantine suggestiveness. Stacked against the wall and draped with a mildewed dustsheet were what could only be framed pictures, half a dozen or so (eight, in fact; why this coyness?). I peered about: no one, and nothing, save a tang of perfume that was already so faint it might have been only in my imagination. Morden walked forward with an impresario's swagger and whisked the dustsheet from the stacked pictures. Have a look, he said, gesturing at them with the champagne bottle, swinging it like an indian club. 'Just have a look!' While Francie leaned in the doorway with his hands in his pockets and winked at me, dropping with practised ease a lizard's leathery eyelid.

1. **Pursuit of Daphne** ca. 1680
Johann Livelb (1633-1697)

Oil on canvas, 26½ x 67 in. (67.3 x 170.2 cm.)

A product of this artist's middle age, the *Pursuit of Daphne* is a skilfully executed, poised yet vigorous, perhaps even somewhat coarse work with uncanny and disturbing undertones. The brooding light which throws the central figures into high relief and bathes the background distances in an unearthly glimmer produces a spectral and almost surreal quality which constitutes what some critics consider the picture's chief interest. The dimensions of the canvas, a lengthy rectangle, would suggest the painting was commissioned for a specific site, perhaps above a couch or bed; certainly the atmosphere of unrestrained though polished lewdness informing the scene supports the contention (cf. Popov, Popham, Pope-Hennessy) that the work was painted for the boudoir. As always, Livelb adapts his vision to the dictates of available form, and here has used the dimensions of his long, low panel to create a sense of headlong dash appropriate to the theme while yet maintaining a kind of ersatz classical repose, an enervated stillness at the heart of seeming frenzy. The action, proceeding from left to right, strikes the viewer as part of a more extended movement from which the scene has suddenly burst forth, so that the picture seems not quite complete in itself but to be rather the truncated, final section of a running frieze. The artist reinforces the illusion of speed by having the wind blow – and a strong wind it is – not in the faces of pursuer and pursued, as we might expect, but from behind them, as if Aeolus himself had come to urge Apollo on in the chase. Despite this following wind, Daphne's hair, bound in a purple ribbon, flows back from her shoulders in long, rippling tresses, a sinuous movement that finds an echo in the path of the river Peneus meandering through the distant landscape of the background like a shining, silver serpent. The figure of Cupid with his bow, hovering at the extreme left of the picture, has the aspect less of a god than of a gloating satyr, and there is in his terrible smile not only the light of revenge but also a prurient avidity: he intends to enjoy the spectacle of the rape that he believes he is about to witness. Apollo, love's bolt buried to the gilded fletching in his right shoulder-blade, cuts a somewhat sorry figure; this is not the lithe ephebe of classical depiction but, probably like the painter himself at the time, a male in his middle years, slack-limbed, thick-waisted, breathing hard, no longer fit for amorous pursuit (there have been suggestions that this is a self-portrait but no evidence has been adduced to support the theory). If Daphne is suffering a transformation so too is the god. We see in the expression of his eyes – how well the painter has captured it! – the desperation and dawning anguish of one about to experience loss, not only of this ravishing girl who is the object of his desire but along with her an essential quality of selfhood, of what up to this he believed he was and now knows he will not be again. His sinewed hand that reaches out to grasp his quarry will never find its hold. Already Daphne is becoming leaf and branch; when we look closely we see the patches of bark already appearing through her skin, her slender fingers turning to twigs, her green eyes blossoming. How swooningly the laurel tree leans over her, each fringed leaf (*wie eines Windes Lächeln*, as Rilke so prettily puts it) eager to enfold her in a transfiguring embrace. We could have done without that indecent pun between the cleft boughs of the tree and the limbs of the fleeing girl. Here as in so much of Livelb's work the loftiness of the classical theme is sacrificed for the sake of showiness and vulgar effects, and in the end the picture lacks that nobility of purpose and simplicity of execution that a greater artist would have brought to it. To quote the critic Erich Auerbach writing in a different context, what we have here is 'a highly rhetorical style in which the gruesomely sensory has gained a large place; a sombre and highly rhetorical realism which is totally alien to classical antiquity.'

Aunt Corky was not in fact my aunt but a cousin on my mother's side so far removed that by her time the bloodline must have become thinned to about the thickness of a corpuscle. She claimed to be Dutch, or Flemish when she thought that sounded fancier, and it is true, I believe, that her people originated in the same hunched hamlet in the Pays-Bas from which my mother's ancestors had emigrated centuries ago (I see it by Hobbema, of course: a huddle of houses with burnt-sienna roofs, a rutted road and a man in a hat walking along, and two lines of slender poplars diminishing into a dream-blue distance), but she had lived in so many places, and had convinced herself that she had lived in so many more, that she had become blurred, like a statue whose features time has abraded, her self-styled foreignness worn down to a vague, veiled patina. All the same, in places the original lines still stood out in what to me seemed unmistakable relief: she had the Lowlander's broad, bony forehead and high cheekbones (cf. Dürer's dauntless drawing of his mother, 1514), and her voice even had a faint, catarrhal catch on certain tricky consonants. When I was a child she was to me completely the continental, a product of steepled towns and different weather and a hotchpotch of impossible languages. Though she was probably younger than my parents, in those days she looked ancient to me, I suppose because she was so ugly, like the witch in a fairy-tale. She was short and squarely built, with a prizefighter's chest and big square hands with knotted veins; with her squat frame and spindly legs that did not meet at the knees and her always slightly crooked skirts she had the look of an item of furniture, a sideboard, perhaps, or a dining-room table with its flaps down. She carried off her ugliness with a grand hauteur. She was said to have lost a husband in the war; her tragedy was always referred to by this formula, so that I thought of him as not dead but misplaced, a ragged, emaciated figure with desperate eyes wandering amidst cannon-smoke through the great forests and shattered towns of Europe in search of my Aunt Corky (her real name, by the way, was an unpronounceable collision of consonants interspersed with i's and y's). She had suffered other things during the war that were referred to only in hushed hints; this was a matter of deep and strangely exciting speculation to me in my fumbling pre-adolescence, and I would picture her bound and splayed in the dank cellar of a barracks in a narrow street beside a canal while a troupe of swastikaed squareheads approached her and . . . but there, unfed by experience or, as yet, by art, my imagination faltered.

I am still not sure which one of Aunt Corky's many versions of her gaudy life was true, if any of them was. Her papers, I have discovered, tell another story, but papers can be falsified, as I know well. She lied with such simplicity and sincere conviction that really it was not lying at all but a sort of continuing reinvention of the self. At her enraptured best she had all the passion and rich inventiveness of an *improvvisatrice* and could hold an audience in a trance of mingled wonder and embarrassment for a quarter of an hour or more without interruption. I remember when I was very small listening to her recount to my mother one day the details of the funeral of the young wife of a German prince she claimed to have witnessed, or perhaps even to have taken part in, and I swear I could see the coffin as it was borne down the Rhine on the imperial barge, accompanied only by *seine königliche Hoheit* in his cream and blue uniform and plumed silver helmet while his grieving subjects in their thousands looked on in silence from the river banks. As so often, however, Aunt Corky went too far, not content until narrative had been spun into yarn: the barge passed under a bridge and when it came out the other side the coffin, bare before, was suddenly seen to be heaped with white roses, hundreds of them, in miraculous profusion. 'Like that,' she said, making hooped gestures with her big hands, piling imaginary blossoms higher and higher, her eyes shining with unshed tears, 'so many, oh, so many!'

How did she come to have all that money when she died? It is a mystery to me. She never had a job, that I know of, and had seemed to live off the charity of a network of relatives here and abroad. There was a prolonged liaison with an Englishman, a lugubrious and decidedly shifty character with a penchant for loud ties and two-tone shoes; he strikes me as an unlikely provider of wealth; rather the opposite, I should say. They married, I think – Aunt Corky's morals were a subject our family passed over in tight-lipped silence – and she moved with him to England where they travelled about a lot, mainly in the Home Counties, living in genteel boarding houses and playing a great deal of whist. Then something went wrong and Basil – that was his name, it's just come back to me – Basil was dismissed, never to be spoken of again, and Aunt Corky returned to us with another weight added to her burden of sorrows, and whenever there was talk of England or things English she would flinch and touch a hand to her cheek in a gesture at once tragic and resigned, as if she were Dido and someone had mentioned the war at Troy. I was not unfond of her. From those early days I remembered her curious, stumping walk and parroty laugh; I could even recall her smell, a powerful brew of cheap scent, mothballs and a dusty reek the source of which I was never able to identify but which was reminiscent of the smell of cretonne curtains. And cigarette smoke, of course; she certainly had the true continental's dedication to strong tobacco, and wherever she went she trailed an ash-blue cloud behind her, so that when I thought of her from those days I saw a startlingly solid apparition constantly stepping forth from its own aura. She wore sticky, peach-coloured make-up, and rouge, and painted her large mouth, always slightly askew, with purplish lipstick; also she used to dye her hair a brassy shade of yellow and have it curled and set every Saturday morning.

How pleasant it is, quietly turning over these faded album leaves.

I don't know why I allowed myself to go and to see her after all those years. I shy from the sickroom, as who does not, and so much had happened to me and to my life since those by now archaic days that I was not sure I would still speak a language comprehensible to this fading relic of a lost age. I had assumed that she was already dead; after all, everyone else was, both of my parents, and my . . . and others, all gone into the ground, so how should she, who seemed ancient when they were young, be surviving still? Perhaps it was merely out of curiosity then that I—

Ah, what a giveaway it is, I've noticed it before, the orotund quality that sets in when I begin consciously to dissemble: *and so much had happened to me and to my life since those by now archaic days* – dear, oh dear! Whenever I employ locutions such as that you will know I am inventing. But then, when do I not use such locutions? (And I said that Aunt Corky was a liar!)

She was living, if that is the way to put it, in a nursing home outside the city called The Cypresses, a big pink and white gazebo of a place set in a semi-circle of those eponymous, blue-black, pointy trees on the side of a hill with a sweeping and slightly vertiginous view of the sea right across to the other side of the bay. There was a tall, creosote-smelling wooden gate with one of those automatic locks with a microphone that squawked at me in no language that I recognised, though I was let in anyway. Tarmac drive, shrubs, a sloping lawn, then suddenly, like an arrow flying straight out of the past, the sharp, prickly smell of something I knew but could not name, some tree or other, eucalyptus, perhaps, yes, I shall say eucalyptus: beautiful word, with that goitrous upbeat in the middle of it like a gulp of grief. I almost stumbled, assailed by the sweetness of forgotten sorrows. Then I saw the house and wanted to laugh, so delicate, spindly and gay was it, so incongruous, with its pillared arches and filigree ironwork and glassed-in verandah throwing off a great reflected sheet of afternoon sunlight. Trust Aunt Corky to end up here! As I followed the curve of the drive the sea was below me, far-off, blue, unmoving, like something imagined, a sea of the mind.

The verandah door was open and I stepped inside. A few desiccated old bodies were sunning themselves in deckchairs among the potted palms. Rheumed yellowish eyes swivelled and fixed on me. A door with glass panels gave on to an interior umber dimness. I tapped cautiously and waited, lightly breathing. 'You'll have to give that a good belt,' one of the old-timers behind me said quaveringly, and coughed, making a squelching sound like that of a wellington boot being pulled out of mud. There was a pervasive mild smell of urine and boiled dinners. I knocked again, more forcefully, making the panes rattle, and immediately, as if she had been waiting to spring out at me, a jolly, fat girl with red hair threw open the door and said, 'Whoa up there, you'll wake the dead!' and grinned. She was dressed in a nurse's uniform, with a little white cap and those white, crêpe-soled shoes, and even had a wristwatch pinned upside down to her breast pocket (why do they do that?), but none of it was convincing, somehow. She had a faint air of the hoyden, and reminded me of a farm girl I knew when I was a child who used to give me piggyback rides and once offered to show me what she called her thing if I would first show her mine (nothing came of it, I'm afraid). I asked for Aunt Corky and the girl looked me up and down with an eyebrow arched, still grinning sceptically, as if she in her turn suspected me of being an impostor. A blue plastic tag on her collar said her name was Sharon. 'Are you the nephew?' she asked, and I answered stoutly that I was. At that moment there materialised silently at my side a plump, soft, sandy-haired man in a dowdy, pinstriped dark suit who nodded and smiled at me in a wistfully familiar way as if we were old acquaintances with old, shared sorrows. I did not at all like the look of him or the sinister way he had crept up on me. 'That will be all right, Sharon,' he murmured in a low and vaguely ecclesiastical-sounding voice, and the girl shrugged and turned and sauntered off whistling, her crêpe soles squeaking on the black-and-white tiled floor. 'Haddon is the name,' the pinstriped one confided, and waited a beat and added, 'Mr Haddon.' He slipped a hand under my arm and directed me towards a staircase that ascended steeply to a landing overhung by a broad window with gaudily coloured panes that seemed to me somehow menacing. I had begun to feel hindered, as if I were wading through thick water; I also had a sense of a suppressed, general hilarity of which I felt I was somehow the unwitting object. As I was about to mount the stairs I caught a flurry of movement from the corner of my eye and flinched as a delicate small woman with the face of an ancient girl came scurrying up to me and plucked my sleeve and said in a flapper's breathless voice, 'Are you the

26

pelican man?' I turned to Haddon for help but he merely stood gazing off with lips pursed and pale hands clasped at his flies, biding and patient, as if this were a necessary but tiresome initiatory test to which I must be submitted. 'The pelican man?' I heard myself say in a sort of piteous voice. 'No, no, I'm not.' The old girl continued to peer at me searchingly. She wore a dress of dove-grey silk with a gauzy silk scarf girdling her hips. Her face really was remarkable, soft and hardly lined at all, and her eyes glistened. 'Ah,' she said, 'then you are no good to me,' and gave me a sweetly lascivious smile and wandered sadly away. Haddon and I went on up the stairs. 'Miss Leitch,' he murmured, as if offering an explanation. When we reached the landing he stopped at a door and tapped once and inclined his head and listened for a moment, then nodded to me again and mouthed a silent word of encouragement and softly, creakingly, descended the stairs and was gone. I waited, standing in a lurid puddle of multi-coloured light from the stained-glass window behind me, but nothing happened. I became at once acutely aware of myself, as if another I, mute and breathing, had sprouted up out of the balding carpet to loom over me monstrously. I put my face to the door and whispered Aunt Corky's name and immediately seemed to feel another heave of muffled laughter all around me. There was no response, and in a sudden bluster of vexation I thrust open the door and was blinded by a glare of light.

By now I had begun seriously to regret having breached this house of shades, and would have been thankful if Mr Haddon or some other guardian of the place had come and stepped firmly in front of me and shut the door and ushered me down the stairs and out into the day, saying, *There there, it is all a mistake, you have come to the wrong place, and besides your aunt is dead.* I thought with panicky longing of the blue sea and the sky out there, those swaying, sentinel trees. That's me all over, forever stepping unwillingly into one place while wishing for another. I had the impression, and have it still despite the evidence of later experience, that the room was huge, a vast, white, faintly humming space at the centre of which Aunt Corky lay tinily trapped on the barge of a big high bed, adrift in her desuetude. She had been dozing and at my approach her eyes clicked open as if the lids were controlled by elastic. In my first glimpse of her she did that trick that people do when you have not seen them for a long time, thrusting aside a younger and now not very convincing double and slipping deftly into its place. She lay still and stared at me for a long moment, not knowing, I could see, who I was or whether I was real or a figment. In appearance she seemed remarkably little changed since the last time I had seen her, which must have been thirty years before. She was wrinkled and somewhat shrunken and had exchanged her dyed hair for an even more startlingly lutescent wig but otherwise she was unmistakably Aunt Corky. I don't know why this should surprise me but it did, and even made me falter for a second. Without lifting her head she suddenly smiled and said, 'Oh, I would not have recognised you!' Did I ever describe to you Aunt Corky's smile? She opened her eyes wide and peeled her lips back from a set of dentures that would have fitted a small horse, while her head very faintly trembled as if she were quaking from the strain of a great though joyous physical effort. A mottled hand scrabbled crabwise across the sheet and searched in space for mine; I grasped her hooked fingers and held her under the elbow – what a grip she had: it was like being seized on by a branch of a dead tree – and she hauled herself upright in the bed, grunting. I did the usual business with pillows and so on, then brought a chair and sat down awkwardly with my hands on my knees; is there any natural way to sit beside a sickbed? She was wearing a not very clean white smock with short sleeves, the kind that patients are made to don for the operating theatre; I noticed bruises in the papery skin of the crook of her arm where blood must have been put in or taken out. She sat crookedly with her mouth open and gazed at me, panting a little, her unsteady smile making it seem as if she were shaking her head in wonderment. Two big tears brimmed up in her eyes and trembled on the lower lids. As ever in the presence of the distress of others I found myself holding my breath. I asked her how she was and without a trace of irony she answered, 'Oh, but wonderful, wonderful – as you see!'

After that, conveniently enough, there are gaps in my memory, willed ones, no doubt. I suppose we must have talked about the past, the family, my so-called life – God knows, Aunt Corky was not one to leave any chink of silence unstopped – but what I best recall are things, not words: that white smock, for instance, bleached by repeated use (how many had died in it, I wondered), an overflowing tinfoil ashtray on the bedside table, the livid smear of lipstick she hastened to put on with an unsteady hand. She was a little dazed at first, but as the anaesthetic of sleep wore off she became increasingly animated. She was annoyed to be discovered in such a state of disarray, and kept making furtive adjustments – that lipstick, a dab of face powder, a rapid tongue-test of the state of her dentures – assembling herself in flustered stages, a prima donna preparing for the great role of being what she imagined herself to be. And as the physical she became firmly established so too the old manner strongly reasserted itself, as she sat there, fully upright now, smoking and complaining, at once haughty, coquettish and put-upon. Aunt Corky had an intimately dramatic relationship with the world at large; no phenomenon of history or happenstance was so momentous or so trivial that she would not see it as an effect directed solely at her. In her version of it the most recent world war had been an act of spite got up to destroy her life, while she would look out at a rainy day with a martyr's sorrowing gaze and shake her head as if to say, *Now look what they have sent to try me!* But a moment later she would shrug and gamely tip her chin (each whisker sprouting on it dusted with a grain or two of face powder) and flash that equine smile that never failed to make me think of the talking mule in those films from my childhood, and be her usual, chirpy self again. Always she bobbed up, pert and bright and full of jauntiness, a plucky swimmer dauntlessly breasting a sea of troubles.

But none of this was as I had expected it would be. After all, they had summoned me to what I had assumed would be a deathbed scene, with my aunt, a serene and quietly breathing pre-corpse, arranged neatly among the usual appurtenances (crisp linen, tweed-suited doctor, and in the background the wordless nurse with glinting kidney-dish), instead of which here she was, as talkative and fantastical as ever. She was frail, certainly, and looked hollow, as old people do, but far from being on her last legs she seemed to me to have taken on a redoubled energy and vigour. The Aunt Corky of my memories of her had by now dwindled so far into the past that I could hardly make her out any more, so vivid was this new, wizened yet still spry version before me. The room too seemed to diminish in size as she grew larger in it, and the glare of sea-light abated in the window, dimmed by the smoke of her cigarettes.

'Of course, these are forbidden,' she said, tapping the barrel of her fag with a scarlet fingernail, and added darkly, 'They are telling me all the time to stop, but I say, what concern is it of theirs?'

The bed, the chair, the little table, the lino on the floor, how sad it all seemed suddenly, I don't know why, I mean why at just that moment. I rose and walked to the window and looked down over the tilted lawn to the sea far below. A freshening wind was smacking the smoke-blue water, leaving great slow-moving prints, like the whorls of a burnisher's rag on metal. Behind me Aunt Corky was talking of the summer coming on and how much she was looking forward to getting out and about. I had not the heart to remind her that it was September.

'They are all so kind here,' she said, 'so good. And Mr Haddon – you have met him, I hope? – he is a saint, yes, a saint! Of course, he is trained for it, you know, he has diplomas. I knew the moment I saw him that he was an educated man. I said to him, I said, *I recognise a person of culture when I meet him.* And do you know what he did? He bowed, and kissed my hand – yes, kissed my hand! *And I,* he said, in that very quiet voice he has, *I, dear madam, I too recognise breeding when I see it.* I only smiled and closed the conversation; it does not do to be too much familiar. He sees to everything himself, everything. Do you know—' she twisted about to peer at me wide-eyed where I stood by the window '—do you know, he even makes out the menus? This is true. I complimented him one day on a particularly good ragout – I think it was a ragout – and he became so embarrassed! Of course, he reddens easily, with that fair colouring. *Ah, Miss Corky,* he says – that is what he calls me – *ah, I can have no secrets from you!'* She paused for a moment thoughtfully, working at her cigarette with one eye shut and her mouth pursed and swivelled to one side. 'I hope I do not go too far,' she murmured. 'Sometimes these people . . . But—' with an airy toss of the head that made the gilded curls of her wig bounce '—what can I do? After all, since I am here I must—'

The door opened with a bang and Sharon the child-nurse stuck in her carroty head and said, 'Do you want the pot?' Aunt Corky was scrabbling to stub out her cigarette. She shook her head furiously with lips shut tight. 'Right-o,' Sharon said and withdrew, then popped back again and nodded at the bristling ashtray and said cheerfully, 'I'm telling you, them things will be the death of you.'

When she had gone I returned to the chair beside the bed

and sat down. Aunt Corky, mortified, avoided my eye, breathing heavily through flared nostrils and casting about her indignantly with birdlike movements of her head. In the embarrassment of the moment I was holding my breath again; I felt like the volunteer in a levitation act, suspended horizontally on empty air and not daring to move a muscle. Aunt Corky with quivering hands lit another cigarette and blew a defiant trumpet of smoke at the ceiling. 'Of course,' she said bitterly, '*she* is nothing like *him*. She has I think no training, and certainly no feeling for things, no – no *finesse*. Where he got her no one can say.' I said vaguely, 'Well, she's young, after all . . .' Aunt Corky stared at me. 'Young?' she cried, a high, soft shriek, 'young – that one?' and began to cough. 'No, no,' she said impatiently, waving a hand and weaving a figure eight of smoke, 'not the nurse, I mean *her* – the wife.' A poisonous grimace. 'Mrs Haddon.' Whom, if I have the energy for the task, we shall be meeting presently. Aunt Corky got out her cartridge of lipstick again and with broad strokes moodily retouched the stylised pair of lips smeared over the ruined hollow where her mouth used to be, sighing and frowning; with the lipstick revivified she looked as if a tropical insect had settled on her face.

Was it on that visit or later, I wonder, that I told her about Morden and his pictures? Had I even gone to see him at that stage? See how you have loosened my grasp on chronology. I get as mixed up as a dotard. Things from long ago seem as if they had happened yesterday while yesterday itself grows ancient before today has waned. Once I used to date events from before and after the moment when you first confronted me on the corner of Ormond Street; then the day of your going became the pivot on which the eras turned; now all is flux. I feel as the disciples must have felt in the days of desolation between Calvary and the rolling aside of the sepulchre stone. (Dear God, where did that come from? Am I getting religion? Next thing I'll be seeing visions.) Anyway,

anyway, whatever day it was, that first or another, when I told her about my new venture, Aunt Corky went into raptures. 'Art!' she breathed, clapping a hand to her breast-bone and putting on a Rouault face. 'Art is prayer!' At once I was sorry I had mentioned the subject at all and sat and looked gloomily at my hands while she launched into one of her rhapsodies, at the end of which she reached out a shaky claw again and grasped my wrist and said in a fervent whisper, 'What a chance for you, to make of yourself something new!' I sat back and stared at her but she continued to gaze at me undaunted, still holding on to my wrist and nodding her head slowly, solemnly. 'Because, you know,' she said, with a sort of reproachful twinkle, 'you have been very naughty; yes, yes, very naughty.' I would not have been surprised if she had reached up and tweaked my ear; I may even have blushed. Somehow I had imagined she would know no more of my doings in the years since I had seen her than I knew of hers. Infamy, however, is a thing that gets about. Aunt Corky let go of my wrist and patted me on the hand and lit yet another cigarette. 'Death is nothing,' she said with vague inconsequence, and frowned; 'nothing at all.' She gave a fluttery sigh and sat for a moment looking about her blankly and then slowly subsided against the dented pillows at her back and closed her eyes. I stood up quickly and leaned over her in consternation, but it was all right, she was still breathing. I prised the cigarette cautiously from her fingers and crushed it in the ashtray. Her hand fell away limply and settled palm upward on the sheet. She began to say something but instead her mouth went slack and she suddenly emitted a loud, honking snore and her legs twitched under the bedclothes.

I am never at ease in the presence of sleeping people – that is, I am even less at ease with them than I am when they are awake. When I was married, I mean when I still had a wife and all that, I would have preferred to spend my nights alone, though of course I had not the nerve to say so. It is not so much the uncanny element of sleep that disturbs me, though that is disturbing enough, but the particular kind of solitude to which the sleeper at my side abandons me. It is so strange, this way of being alone: I think of Transylvania, voodoo, that sort of thing. There I sit, or, worse, lie, in the dark, in the presence of the undead, who seem to have attained a state of apotheosis, who seem so *achieved*, resting in this deeply breathing calm on a darkened plain between two worlds, here and at the same time infinitely far removed from me. It is at such moments that I am most acutely aware of my conscious self, and feel the electric throb and tingle, the flimsiness and awful weight, of being a living, thinking thing. The whole business then seems a scandal, or a dreadful joke devised by someone who has long since gone away, the point of which has been lost and at which no one is laughing. My wife, now, was a prompt if restless sleeper. Her head would hit the pillow and swish! with a few preparatory shudders she was gone. I wonder if it was her way of escaping from me. But there I go, falling into solipsism again, my besetting sin. God knows what it was she was escaping. Just everything, I suppose. If escape it was. Probably she was in the same fix as me, wanting a lair herself to lie down in and not daring to say so. To be alone. To be at one. Is that the same? I don't think so. To be at one: what a curious phrase, I've never understood exactly what it means. And I, what must I be like when I sleep, as I occasionally do? Something crouched, I imagine, crouched doggo and ready to spring out of the dark, fangs flashing and eyes greenly afire. No, no, that is altogether too fine, too sleek: more like a big, beached, blubbery thing, cast up out of the deeps, agape and gasping.

What was I . . . ? Aunt Corky. Her room. Afternoon sunlight. I am there. The cigarette I had crushed in the ashtray was still determinedly streaming a thin, fast, acrid waver of blue smoke. I waited for a while, watching her sleep, my mind empty, and then with leaden limbs and pressing my hands hard against my knees I rose and lumbered quakingly from the room and closed the door without a sound behind me. By now the patch of parti-coloured light from the big window on the landing had moved a surprising distance and was inching its way up the wall. It is odd how the exact look of that afternoon glares in my memory, suffused with a harsh, Hellenic radiance that is sharper and more brilliant, surely, than a September day in these latitudes could be expected to furnish. Probably I am not remembering at all, but imagining, which is why it seems so real. Haddon was waiting for me at the foot of the stairs, stooped and unctuous and at the same time sharply watchful. 'She is a handful, yes,' he said as we walked to the door. 'We were forced to confiscate her things, I'm afraid.' 'Things,' I said, 'what things?' He smiled, a quick little sideways twitch. 'Her clothes,' he said; 'even her nightdress. She had us demented, walking out of the place at all hours of the day and night.' I smiled what must have been a sickly smile and nodded sympathetically, craven as I am, and thought with a shiver, *Imagine, just imagine being him.*

It was a surprise, when I stepped out into the world again, how bright and gay everything seemed, the sun, the gleaming grass, those Van Gogh trees, and the big, light sky with its fringe of coppery clouds; I felt as if I had been away on a long journey and now all at once had arrived back home again. I legged it down the drive as fast as I could go, but when the gate had shut itself behind me I paused and pressed the bell again and the hidden speaker squawked at me as before. But I don't know what it was I had thought I would say, and after some moments of impatient, metallic breathing the voice-box clicked off, and in the sudden silence I felt foolish and exposed again and turned and skulked away down the hill road.

As I went along under the beneficence of the September afternoon's blue and deepening gold my heart grew calm and I felt another pang like the one that had pierced me when I smelled the eucalyptus at the gate. What paradisal longings are these that assail me at unconsidered moments when my mind is looking elsewhere? They are not, I think, involuntary memories such as those the celebrated madeleine is supposed to have invoked, for no specific events attach to them, no childhood landscapes, no beloved figures in rustling gowns or top-hats; rather they seem absences, suddenly stumbled upon, redolent of a content that never was but was only longed for, achingly. This mood of vague, sad rapture persisted even when I got back to the city and my steps took me unresisting and only half aware along the river and down Black Street in the direction of Morden's house. Some part of me must have been brooding on him and his secret trove of pictures stacked in that sealed room. The street was quiet, one side filled with the calm sunlight of late afternoon and the other masked in shadow drawn down sharply like a deep awning. The Boatman's double doors stood open wide and from the cavernous gloom of the interior a beery waft came rolling. A three-legged dog passed by and bared its sideteeth silently at me in a perfunctory way. Someone in an upstairs room nearby was listlessly practising scales on an out-of-tune piano. Thus does fate, feigning unconcern, arrange its paltry props, squinting at the sky and nonchalantly whistling. I stood on the corner and looked up along Rue Street at the house with its blank windows and broad black door. I was not thinking of anything in particular, just loitering. Or maybe in that impenetrable maze I call my mind I was turning over Morden's proposition, maybe *that* was the moment when I decided, in the dreamy, drifting way that in me passes for volition, to take on the task of evaluating and cataloguing his cache of peculiar pictures. (There it is again, that notion of volition, intention, decisiveness; am I weakening in my lack of conviction?) Suddenly the door opened and a young woman dressed in black stepped out and paused a moment on the pavement, checking in her purse – money? a key? – then turned and set off briskly in the direction of Ormond Street. I know you always insisted you saw me there, skulking on the corner, but that's how I remember it: the door, stop and peer into purse, then turn on heel without a glance and go, head down, and my heart quailing as if it knew already what was in store for it.

I am not naturally curious about people – too self-obsessed for that – but sometimes when my attention is caught I will go to extraordinary lengths to make the most banal discoveries about total strangers. It's crazy, I know. I will get off a bus miles before my own stop so I can follow a secretary coming home from the office to see where she lives; I will traipse through shopping malls – ah, those happy hunting-grounds! – just to find out what kind of bread or cabbages or toilet rolls a burdened housewife with two snotty kids in tow will buy. And it is not just women, in case some bloodhound's nostrils are starting to twitch: I follow men, too, children, anyone. No doubt a first-year psychiatry student could put a name to this mild malady. It's harmless, like picking my nose or biting my nails, and affords me a certain wan pleasure. I am saying all this in my defence (though who my accusers might be I do not know): when I set off that day in surreptitious pursuit of that young woman, a perfect (oh, perfect!) stranger, I had no object in mind other than to know where she was going. I am aware how strident and implausible these protestations of blame-lessness sound. Certainly someone observing us making our way along that street, she in sun and I slinking after her on the other, shadowed side, might well have pondered the advisability of alerting a policeman. She was dressed in a short-sleeved black dress and impossible high heels, on which she teetered along at a remarkably swift pace, her purse clasped to her breast and her slender neck thrust forward and her head bent, so that as she clicked along she seemed to be all the while peering over the edge of a precipice that was steadily receding before her. Very pale, with black hair cut short in page-boy style (my Lulu!) and high, narrow shoulders and very thin legs; even at this distance I could see her little white hands with their pink knuckles and ill-painted nails bitten to the quick. On this calm, bright day she looked odd in her black dress and those black silk seamed stockings and gleaming black stilettos; a new-made widow, I thought, off to hear the reading of the will. When she came to the corner of Ormond Street she paused again, daunted, it seemed, by the crowd and the noise and the stalled herds of rush-hour traffic throbbing in the sun. She glanced over her shoulder (*that* was when you saw me) and I turned away quickly and peered into a shop window, my throat thick with fright and gleeful panic, for this is how I get, all hot and fluttery, when I am in full pursuit and my quarry hesitates as if sensing a waft of my hot breath on her neck. After a moment I noticed that the shop I had stopped in front of was derelict and that the cobwebbed window in which I was feigning such interest was empty. When I turned to look for her again she was gone. I hurried to the corner but there was no sign of her. As always when the object of my morbid interest eludes me like this I felt a flattish sensation, a mixture of disappointment and not quite comprehensible relief. With a lighter step I turned to go back the way I had come – and there she was right in front of me, so close that I almost collided with her, standing motionless in a plum-coloured pool of shadow with her purse still primly clutched to her breast. She was older than I had at first supposed (her age, I have just counted it on the calendar, was twenty-seven years, four months, eleven days and five hours, approximately). The glossy crown of her head came up to the level of my adam's apple. Hair really very black, blue-black, like a crow's wing, and a violet shading in the hollows of her eyes. Identifying marks. Dear God. Absurdly, I see a little black pillbox hat and a black three-quarters veil – a joke, surely, these outlandish accessories, on the part of playful memory? Yet she did reach up to adjust something, a strand of hair or a stray eyelash, I don't know what, and I noticed the tremor in her hand and the nicotine stains on her fingers. With her small, pale, heart-shaped face averted she was frowning into the middle distance, and when she spoke I was not sure that it was me she was addressing.

2. The Rape of Proserpine 1655
L. van Hobelijn (1608-1674)

Oil on canvas, 15 x 21½ in. (38.1 x 53.3 cm.)

Although the grandeur of its conception is disproportionate to its modest dimensions, this is van Hobelijn's technically most successful and perhaps his finest work. The artist has set himself the task of depicting as many as possible of the elements of the myth of the abduction of Demeter's daughter by the god of the underworld, and the result is a crowded, not to say cluttered, canvas which with its flattened surface textures and uncannily foreshortened perspectives gives more the impression of a still life than the scene of passionate activity it is intended to be. The progression of the seasons, the phenomenon which lies at the heart of this myth, is represented with much subtlety and inventiveness. The year begins at the left of the picture in the vernal meadow by lake Pergus – note the opalescent sheen of water glimpsed through the encircling, dark-hued trees – where Prosperpine's companions, as yet all unaware of what has befallen her, wander without care amidst the strewn violets and lilies that were let drop from the loosened folds of the girl's gown when the god seized her. In the foreground the great seated form of Demeter presides over the fertile summer fields, her teeth like barley pearls (or pomegranate seeds?) and with cornstalks wreathed in her hair: a grotesque, Arcimboldo-esque figure, ancient yet commanding, the veritable mother of the mysteries. To her left, at the right of the picture, the trees that fringe the headlands above the narrow inlet of the sea have already turned and there is an autumnal smokiness in the air. Sunk here to her waist in the little waves the nymph Cyane, cursed by the god of death, is dissolving in her own bitter tears, while at her back the waters gape where Pluto has hurled his sceptre into the depths. On the surface of the water something floats which when we take a glass to it reveals itself to be a dark-blue sash: it is Proserpine's girdle, the clue that will lead her grief-demented mother to the underworld in pursuit of her lost daughter. The placing of the girdle in the sea is one of van Hobelijn's temporal jests, for when we examine the figure of Proserpine sus-pended above the waves we note that the girdle in fact has not yet fallen from her waist: in this painted world all time is eternally present, and redeemable. With what consummate draughtsmanship has the painter positioned in the pale, marine air the flying chariot with its god and girl. The arrangement of vehicle, horses and passengers measures no more than five centimetres from the flared nostrils of the leading steed to the tips of Proserpine's wind-rippled hair, yet we feel with overwhelming immediacy the full weight of this hurtling mass of iron and wood and flesh that is about to plunge into the gaping sea. With its sense of suspended yet irresistible violence the moment is an apt prefigurement of the rape shortly to take place in Tartarus. The god's swarth features are set in a grimace of mingled lust and self-loathing and his upraised arm wielding the great black whip forms a gesture that is at once brutal and heavy with weari-ness. Proserpine, a frail yet striking figure, intensely realised, seems strangely unconcerned by what is occurring and gazes back over her shoulder, out of the frame, with an air of languid melancholy, caught here as she is between the bright world of the living and the land of the dead, in neither of which will she ever again be wholly at home. Beyond her, in the background at the top of the picture, Mount Etna is spewing fire and ash over a wintry landscape laid waste already by the wrath of grief-stricken Demeter. We see the broken ploughshare and the starving oxen and the farmer lamenting for his fields made barren by the goddess in her rage at an ungrateful earth that will not give up to her the secret of her daughter's fate. And so the round of the seasons is completed. We think of other paintings with a seasonal theme, the *Primavera*, for example, but van Hobelijn is not that 'Botticelli of the North' some critics claim him to be, and his poor canvas with its jumbled perspectives and heavy-handed symbolism is utterly lacking in the poise, the celestial repose, the sense of unheard music sounding through its pellucid airs, that make of the Italian painter's work a timeless and inexhaustible masterpiece. However, *The Rape of Proserpine* wields its own eerie yet not inconsiderable power, fraught as it is with presentiments of loss and disaster, and acknowledging as it does love's destructiveness, the frailty of human wishes and the tyrannical and irresistible force of destiny.

I know now I should have told her who I was, should have admitted I had been to the house already, had met Morden and seen the pictures. In other words, I should have come clean, but I did not, and so the whole thing started off in a fog of ambiguity and dissimulation. On the other hand, you, I mean she (I must try to stick to the third person, which is after all what you turned out to be), she too it seems was less than candid, for although she treated me that day as if I were no more than an amiable stranger whose burden of solitude she was prepared to lighten for an hour, she insisted later that she had known very well who I was, or that at least – her version of the matter varied – she had known that I was someone who was involved with Morden and the house. Why else would she have accosted me on the street like that, she demanded, in the chalk-on-blackboard shriek by which now and then she betrayed herself; did I think she was in the habit of picking up strange men? I did not answer that but instead diffidently made mention of Cupid and his arrow, which caused her to snort. Anyway, if I had owned up that first day it would have destroyed the clandestine intensity of the occasion. I believe the tone of all that was to happen between us was set in that first encounter with its sustained, hot hum of mendacity and secret knowing.

It was odd to be shown the house for a second time in the same week. Everything was different, of course. This time the emphases fell on the off-beats. I followed her up the stairs through the cool stillness of afternoon and tried to keep my eyes off her narrow little rump joggling in front of me in its tight sheath of black silk; for reasons that were and continue to be obscure I felt it was incumbent on me not to acknowledge the possibilities of the situation. I think that despite everything I must be at heart a gentleman of the old school. I take this opportunity, before I have put both feet on the slippery slope and can still articulate a balanced sentence (there will be a lot of heavy breathing later on), to state that when it comes to what is called love and all that the word entails I am a dolt. Always was, always will be. I do not understand women, I mean I understand them even less than the rest of my sex seems to do. There are times when I think this failure of comprehension is the prime underlying fact of my life, a blank region of unknowing which in others is a lighted, well-signposted place. Here, in me, in this Bermuda Triangle of the soul, the fine discriminations that are a prerequisite for moral health disappear into empty air and silence and are never heard of again. I could blame the women I have consorted with – my mother, for instance – and of course my sometime wife, could accuse them of not having educated me properly, of not inducting me into at least the minor mysteries of their sorority, but to what avail? None. The lack was in me from the start. Maybe a chromosome went missing in the small bang out of which I was formed. Perhaps that's it, perhaps that's what I am, a spoilt woman, in the way that there used to be spoilt priests. That would explain a lot. But no, that is too easy; even if it should be the case, there is too much the possibility of exoneration in it. No, it is not the anima lost in me that I am after, but the ineffable mystery of the Other (I can hear your ribald snigger); that is what all my life long I have plunged into again and again as into a choked Sargasso Sea wherein I can never find my depth. In you I thought my feet at last would reach the sandy floor where I could wade weightlessly with bubbles kissing my shins and small things skittering under my slow-motion tread. Now it seems I was wrong, wrong again.

We stopped on the circular landing at the top of the house and she lit a cigarette. She kept frowning about her in a vague, vexed sort of way, as if she thought she had lost something but did not know what it could be. Abstract: that is the word I always associate with her: abstract, abstracted, abstractedly, and then the variants, such as absently, and absent-minded, and now, of course, in this endless aftermath, with the clangour of a wholly new connotation, just: absent. She smoked with a schoolgirl's amateurish swagger, dragging on the cigarette swiftly with hissing intakes of breath and puffing out big clouds of uninhaled blue smoke. Above us in the tall windows sunlight stood in blocks that looked as solid as blond stone. An aeroplane flew over, making the panes vibrate tinily, and as if in sympathy my diaphragm fluttered and with a faint shock I realised that what I was feeling most strongly was fear: not only of Morden and of being discovered here by him or his man or his man's black dog, but of her, too, and of the house itself – of everything. Yet I do not know if fear is the right word. Something less definite, then? Alarm? Apprehension? Whatever it was it was a not unpleasurable sensation; there was something of childhood in it, of games played with giddy girls in the groin-warm glow of firelit parlours on winter Sunday evenings long ago. Yes, this is what struck me that first time, this sense of having been transported back to some gropingly tentative, confused and expectant stage of life. For you see, I did not know what was happening, why she had brought me here or who she was or why she was dressed in these slinky, silken weeds (come to think of it, I never did discover the explanation for that outlandish costume; was it your seduction suit?), and I was as wary and uncertain as an adolescent, and as sweatily excited. No, I did not know what was going on, but being essentially a trusting type I was content to assume that someone did.

A., I shall call her. Just A. I thought about it for a long time. It's not even the initial of her name, it's only a letter, but it sounds right, it feels right. Think of all the ways it can be uttered, from an exclamation of surprise to a moan of pleasure or pure pain. It will be different every time I say it. A. My alpha; my omega.

Her manner was a mixture of curiosity and impatience and a kind of defiant offhandedness, like that of a spoiled, dissatisfied, far too clever twelve-year-old. She seemed to – how shall I say? – to fluctuate, as if we were engaged in an improvised dance my part in which was to stand still while she flickered and shimmered in front of me, approaching close up and at once retreating, watching me covertly from behind that black veil which my overheated imagination has placed before her face. Then the next moment she would go limp and stand gawkily with one foot out of her shoe and pressed on the instep of the other, gazing down in a sort of stupor and holding a bit of her baby-pink lower lip between tiny, wet, almost translucent teeth. It was as if she were trying out alternative images of herself, donning them like so many slightly ill-fitting gowns and then taking them off again and dispiritedly casting them aside. It was not the house she had been showing me but herself – herselves! – moving against this big, blank-white, sombre background, successive approximations of an ultimate self that would, that must, remain forever hidden. And now, blood thudding in my ears with a jungle beat and my clenched palms beginning to sweat, I was waiting for her to make the final revelation, to let fall the final veil, and take me into the secret room. For I knew it must have been she I had glimpsed through the crumbling wall the first time I came here. Would she open that last door and let me in? I saw myself standing there, suspended in the slanted sunlight at the top of the stairs, and everything was shifting and shaking and thrummingly taut, as if the house were a ship running before the wind with all sails spread. I was, I realised, embarked on an adventure, no less.

All this in my recollection of it takes place in a kind of ringing silence, but in fact she had kept a commentary going in her unfocused, smoky voice the whole way up through the house. I don't recall the words. Her tone was vague yet touched with an odd, displaced vehemence; always it was to be like this with her, everything she said seemed no more than a way of not saying what she was thinking. Does that make sense? It does to me. Now and then she would pause and stand listening intently, not to the sounds of the world about her but as if to a voice coming from a great distance inside her own head, telling her things, advising her, upbraiding her. I remember her saying to me one day – I think of it as much later, in another age, but it can only have been a matter of weeks – I remember her saying how sometimes she got frightened when she thought about her mind and how she could not stop it working. In the toils of lovemaking we had rolled from the lumpy chaise-longue on to the floor and were lying quietly now watching rain-clouds progressing like noble wreckage across the jumbled rooftops of the city. How sweetly poignant were those silent autumn afternoons with their quicksilver sheen and somehow friendly chilliness and the country smells of leaf and loam and wood-smoke that penetrated even here, in the depths of the city. She lay on her stomach with the moth-eaten blanket pulled to her shoulders and a cigarette trembling in her incongruously plump, pale fingers with their reddened knuckles. There was a smudge of lipstick like a fresh bruise at the corner of her mouth. What frightened her, she said, was the way it all kept spinning, just spinning and spinning, even when she was asleep, like a motor that could not be switched off even for an instant because if it was it would never start up again. She spoke as if she were alone in this predicament, as if it were only her mind that was perpetually in motion while the rest of us could turn ourselves into zombies whenever we felt like it. That was the way she conceived of everything to do with herself; all her experiences were unique. It wasn't egotism, I believe, or even the kind of rueful self-absorption that I so often lose myself in; she simply could not imagine that the rest of humankind lived as she was forced to do, in such solitude, locked inside this racing, unstoppable consciousness; if it were so, surely something would have been done about it long ago? For unlike me she was a great believer in progress, and was firmly of the opinion that everything was improving all the time – for others, that is.

Anyway, that first day, while we dawdled there on the landing, I convinced myself that I could sense her debating whether or not to betray what she must think was still Morden's secret and show me the white room and the stacked pictures, but in the end she turned, regretfully, so I imagined, and led the way downstairs again. I felt a sort of slackening then, a general relaxation of flesh and fancy, and all at once I was impatient to be away from her and from the house, to be alone again, to be on my own: always it is there, you see, the yearning for solitude, for the cell. Then like a blow to the temple it struck me: it was Morden, of course, who had set her on to me (I was wrong, he had not), had led her to one of these high windows and pointed me out to her as I was passing by in the street below, a foreshortened, waddling figure, and said to her, *Look, that's him, go down there and do your stuff*. Oh, the pander! Now in a rush I recalled him casually mentioning his wife, with an ironical twist of the lips (*My wife, you know, my beautiful wife!*), and chuckling. She, I told myself now, she was the final part of the deal, after the free hand and the cut of the profits he had offered me; she was the clincher. (Was he somewhere in the house even now, spying on us?) Oh, I had it all worked out in a flash. As I descended the stairs behind her, my gaze, heavy now with rekindled tumescence, fastened to the back of her neck with its straight-cut fringe and tapering wisp of dark down the shape of an inverted candle-flame, I was working up a fine head of indignation at Morden's wiliness (by now I had conjured up his big face with its Cheshire Cat grin suspended before us in the stairwell), while in another, altogether shadier part of the forest something that had drunk the magic bottle was getting bigger and bigger as my mind, by itself, as it were, speculated in dark excitement on how broad might be the brief that he had given her. But at the same time I kept telling myself it was all nonsense, a fantasy made up out of my head and one or two other areas of my ice-encased anatomy, a story to tell myself to light the drabness in which I was sunk; if she had known who I was it was probably just boredom, or curiosity, or an impulsive wish to meddle in Morden's affairs that had prompted her to address me there in the sun and shadow on that noisy street-corner where I stood dithering in gloomy, middle-aged dishevelment. Yet abruptly now, as if she had heard the rusty cogwheels of my long-disused libido squeakingly engage, she stopped and turned with one hand on the banister rail (I notice, by the way, that she has acquired elbow-length black gloves to match the little black hat and veil I have already imagined for her) and looked up at me from under her painted, soot-black lashes with a smile of complicity that fell upon those labouring meshed gears of mine like a warmed drop of amber oil, and it was as if it were we, and not Morden, who were the conspirators in some double double-cross too complicated to be grasped by my poor overburdened understanding.

'Come on,' she said, 'I want to show you something.'

How can I communicate the strangeness, the thrilling incongruity of that first hour with her? It was as if we were aloft on an ill-strung net which she was negotiating with careless ease while I was in danger of losing my footing at any moment and ending up in a hopeless tangle of trapped, flailing limbs. I kept waiting with foreboding for her to tell me why we were here and what it was she supposed we were doing (why, I wonder, did I assume that an explanation would inevitably mean disappointment?), but I waited in vain. She just went along in her flitting, abstracted way, pointing out this or that wholly unremarkable feature of the empty house, as if everything had already been understood and settled between us. She was half tour guide and half the bored madam welcoming an unprepossessing new client to this gaunt bordello. She made no mention of Morden (but then, did she ever speak of him directly, in so many words, in all the time I knew her?), didn't tell me her name or ask mine. *Did* she know who I was? Perhaps when I saw her through that hole in the false wall she in turn caught a glimpse of me and wondered who and what I was and determined to find out. How calmly I pose these questions, yet what a storm of anxiety and pain they provoke in me – for I shall never know the answers for sure, no matter how long I brood on it all, no matter how many obsessed hours I spend turning over the scraps of evidence you left behind. Anyway, for her purposes, whatever they were, probably someone else would have done just as well as I, some needy other who, I suddenly realise, from this moment on will always be with me, now that I have conceived of him, a hopeful phantom lingering just beyond seeing in the corner of my mind's jealous eye. I do not think she was lying, I mean I believe that as time went on she became convinced that of course she had known who I was, whether she had or not. (I am so confused, so confused!) Things like that got lost in her, dates, events, the circumstances of certain meetings, decisive conversations and their outcomes, they just dropped away silently into empty air and were gone; useless to dispute with her – if she believed something had been so then that was how it had been and that was that. Such conviction could make me doubt the simplest of simple facts, and when I had at last given in she would turn away, mollified, with a small, hard look of satisfaction. So now like an anxious naturalist unable to trust his luck I shuffled behind her down those endless, echoing stairs, watching the wing-cases of her shoulder-blades flexing under the brittle stuff of her dress, noting the fish-pale backs of her knees and the fine hairs pressed flat under her nylons like black grass splayed by rain, wincing at the state of her poor heels where those intolerable shoes had chafed them, and I felt myself carried off to other times and other, imaginary places: a spring day in Clichy (I have never been in Clichy), a hot, thundery evening on a road somewhere in North Africa (never been there, either), a great, high, panelled room in an ancient château with straw-coloured sunlight on the faded tapestries and someone practising on a spinet (though I have never seen a spinet or heard one played). Where do they come from, these mysterious, exalted flashes that are not memories yet seem far more than mere imaginings? You believed, you said, that we have all lived before; perhaps you were right. *Are* right; *are*. I cling to the present tense as to a sheer cliff's last hand-hold.

When we came to the ground floor she led me along the hall to the rear of the house. I thought she was taking me into the garden – in the barred glass of the low back door viridian riot was briefly visible – but instead she turned down yet another flight of stairs, this one narrow and made of black stone. I clattered after her. At the bottom was a dank, flagstoned basement passageway dimly illumined from the far end by a high lunette through which I could see the oddly mechanical-looking legs of people passing by outside in a sunlit street that from here seemed a place on another planet. The air was chilly and damp and smelled strongly of lime. In the suddenly attentive silence A. slipped her arm through mine and I felt with a soft detonation along my nerves her wrist's cool silkiness and the intricate bones of her elbow pressing against my ribs. Behind the spice of her perfume I detected a sharp, faint, foxy tang of sweat, and when she leaned her shoulder into the protection of my arm the low neck of her dress fell forward and revealed to me (picture an eyeball swivelling downward wildly, the bloodshot white showing) a glimmering pale slope of skin and a deckled edging of lace. I felt so large beside her, so unwieldy, a big, shambling, out-of-breath baboon. I imagined myself picking her up in my hooped, hairy arms and making off with her into the undergrowth, hooting and gibbering. We came to a door and she stopped, and a tiny tremor ran through her like the passage of an arrow through air, and she laughed softly. 'Here,' she whispered, 'here it is.'

All I saw was a cellar, long and low with a vaulted brick ceiling criss-crossed by a network of wiring from which were suspended a dozen or more naked light bulbs, which despite their profusion shed only a sullen, sulphurous glow that trickled away into corners thick with blackness and died. Along one wall there was a workbench with old wooden planes and mitre boxes and other such stuff, and a battery of powerful electric lamps, turned off, that struck me as vaguely minatory, leaning there ranked and hooded in an attitude of silent alertness. A. began to say something, too loudly, and stopped and laughed again and put a hand to her mouth as the echoes flittered up like bats into the vault of shadows above us. There was a smell, a mixture of sawdust and glue and pungent oil, that seemed familiar, though I could not identify it. Is it hindsight that has conferred on the place a pent-up, mocking air? I felt a silent breeze from somewhere on the back of my neck and I turned to speak to A. only to find that she was no longer there. I was about to call out to her when I heard the sound of clicking claws rapidly approaching along the passageway outside and my heart gave a sort of sideways lurch and then righted itself with a frightening thump. The clicking ceased and Prince the dog appeared soundlessly in the doorway and looked at me, jaws agape and red tongue softly throbbing. A moment passed. I spoke to the creature in a hoarse, high voice and put out a cautious hand. I felt an equal mixture of anger and alarm; how had I allowed myself to be lured into this trap? For this was what I had been expecting for the past half hour, to be discovered like this, caught in surprise and dismay and unaccountable guiltiness. A bead of sweat slid down between my shoulder-blades cold and quick as the point of a knife. Then Francie with his hands in his pockets materialised beside the dog and eyed me smilingly and sucked his teeth and said, 'Private view, eh?' He scanned the cellar with a swift, sharp glance and dog and master delicately sniffed the air: A.'s perfume; I could smell it too. Francie ambled forward and picked up a miniature hammer from the workbench and turned to me and—

Enough of this. I do not like it down here, I do not like it at all. A wave of my wand and *pop!* here we are magically at street level again.

Francie invited me to go with him to The Boatman for a drink, hunching his shoulders and looking away and smiling to himself. We walked along Fawn Street through the hazy, brazen light of early evening with the low sun in our faces. The dog kept close behind us, head down and sharp ears flattened along its skull. The office crowds were hurrying homeward; buses reared, bellowing, cars coughed and fumed. I thought of A., her pale face and vivid lips, the leaf-rustle of her silk dress. Spindly girls dressed all in black with stark white make-up passed us by, hanging on the arms of enchained, bristled young men; they glanced at Francie and nudged each other. He was in his usual outfit: threadbare tweed suit of a peculiar, gingery shade, a flat cap and collar-less shirt and cracked brown sharp shoes curling up at the toes. He had the look of one of those characters who used to appear now and then at our door when I was a child, itinerant knife-sharpeners, rag-and-bone men, tinkers selling cans: timeless figures of uncertain origin who went as silently as they had come, and who afterwards would appear along the margins of my dreams.

We turned into Hope Alley and came upon Quasimodo – remember him? – singing *The Green Hills of Antrim Are Calling Me Home* and waggling an empty plastic cup at pas-sers-by. I had been noticing him about the streets for some time, and took an interest in him. Down-and-outs have always appealed to me, for reasons that should be obvious. This was a new and fallen state for him; the last time I had seen him he was working as a signboard man for a jeweller's shop tucked up a laneway off Arcade Street. Those must have been his salad days, perched on a high stool at the sunny corner of the lane with flask of tea and mighty sandwich and the newspaper to read. His sign had borne the ambiguous legend, *The Bijou – Home of Happy Rings*, in front of which was painted a stylised hand with rigid index finger imperi-ously pointing up Tuck Lane. He was a little nut-brown fellow with curiously taut, shiny skin and a smear of oily black hair plastered to his skull as if he had just taken off a tight-fitting cap. His hump was not very pronounced, more hunch than hump, really; seen from the front, with his tor-toise's flattish head thrust forward and that fixed, worried grin that he always wore (was it a tic?), he seemed to be flinching from a playful blow constantly expected but never delivered. I felt proprietorial about him, and I was not pleased when Francie pointed at him now with his chin and snickered and said, 'He's come down in the world. It will be the knacker's for him next.' We drew level with the hunchback and Francie stopped and set himself squarely before him with hands in pockets, feigning enthusiastic appreciation, swaying his head in time to the poor fellow's tuneless bellowing. Quasimodo, alarmed by this unexpected attention, roared all the louder and looked rapidly from one of us to the other in mulish panic, showing the yellowed whites of his eyes. I was wondering where he lived, what hovel sheltered him, and thinking in that slow, amazed way that one does that he would have had a mother once. I tried to picture him as a suckling babe, but failed. At last the song warbled to a close and he wrapped himself in his old grey coat and sidled off, glancing back at us over his hump. Francie watched him go and said, 'Off for a bracer, I don't doubt.' We walked on. Francie was laughing softly to himself again and shaking his head. 'Have you heard this one? Raggedy old geezer staggers into a chemist's shop. *Bottle of meths, please, miss.* Girl brings the bottle, old boy feels it, hands it back. *Have you got one chilled, my dear? – it brings out the bouquet, you know.*'

I must say something about Francie's laugh, though I am not sure laugh is the right word. With eyes slitted and his upper lip curled at one side to reveal a wax-coloured canine, he would produce a low, rasping, squeezed-out sound in falling triplets, a sort of repeated nasal wheeze, while his shoulders faintly shook. It was a guarded, costive sort of laugh, as if he were enjoying too much the world's side-splitting ridiculousness to let others in on the fun and thus risk diminishing it for himself. Even when, as now, he told the joke himself there was the suspicion that it was only a blind and that what was really amusing him was something else altogether that only he was privy to. He gave the impression always of a sort of surreptitious squirming, of slipping and ducking in and out of view. He was like the trickster who comes up silently at your left shoulder and taps you on the right, and when you spin around you think no one is there until you hear his soft chuckle on the other side of you.

The Boatman was loud with nine-to-fivers released for the day, callow young men in cheap sharp suits and watchful girls with crinkled hair and baked-chicken skin. We sat on stools at the bar and Francie took off his cap and set it on his knee and leaned back against a partition with a mirror in it in which I could see reflected the two taut strings at the back of his neck and one of his uncannily flat ears; I was there, too, or half of me: an oddly startled eye and gloomy jowl and one side of a mouth fixed in a sort of rictus over which I seemed to have no control. I drank gin while Francie toyed with a glass of thin beer; he would suck up a mouthful and strain it back and forth through his teeth and then let half of it wash back fizzing into the glass, so that after a while a clouded, stringy deposit that I tried not to look at gathered at the bottom of the glass. One of my headaches was coming on. Even with his eyes fixed on mine Francie gave the impression of looking me up and down with a sort of muffled amusement.

'And you've got down to it already,' he said and gave a low whistle. 'Well, there's eager!' For a moment I thought he was talking about A. and I experienced a hot heave in the region of the solar plexus, sure he must have seen into my mind, where the image of her supple young silken back was still before me, climbing the steps of a steadily ascending scale of speculation. He was watching me with a narrowed eye, and I caught something, like the flash of a weasel's tooth down in the dark of the burrow. 'So what do you think?' he said.

A tall young woman with naked shoulders and extraordinary, glaucescent eyes bumped into me and apologised and immediately burst out laughing and passed on.

What did I think? I thought I should keep mum. Give him the slightest sign and next thing we'd be plotting to make off with Morden's pictures and split the take between us. Not such a bad idea, I suppose. The trouble with Francie was that he was not really real for me. He seemed made-up, a manufactured man, in whose company (if that is the word for what it was to be with him) credence was not required. And this air of fakery that he carried with him infected even his surroundings. Take this day, now. The whole thing had a contrived look to it, the pub, the girl with the grey eyes, the crowd of over-acting extras around us, that theatrically thick yellow beam of sunlight slanting down through the window and lighting up the bottles behind the bar, and Francie himself, sitting in the middle of it all with his cap on his knee, reciting his lines with the edgy, unconvinced air of an actor who knows he is not going to get the part. Why do I allow myself to become involved with such people? (I should talk; who is the real actor here?) I have – I admit it – I have a lamentable weakness for the low life. There is something in me that cleaves to the ramshackle and the shady, a crack somewhere in my make-up that likes to fill itself up with dirt. I tell myself this vulgar predilection is to be found in all true connoisseurs of culture but I am not convinced. I present myself here as a sort of Candide floundering amidst a throng of crooks and sirens but I fear the truth (the truth!) is different. I wanted Morden and his dodgy pictures and all the rest of it, even including Francie, longed for it as the housewife longs for the brothel. I am not good, I never was and never will be. Hide your valuables when I am around, yes, and lock up your daughters, too. I am the bogey-man you dream of as you toss in your steamy beds of a night. That soft step you hear, that's me, prowling the unquiet dark where the light of the watchfire fails. Your sentries are asleep, the guard at your gate is drunk. I have done terrible things, I could do them again, I have it in me, I—

Stop.

Francie was about to speak again but

Was about to speak again but then a change occurred, and he went still and sat at an angle looking at his drink with a fixed, unfocused smile.

Christ, look at me, I'm sweating, my hands are shaking; I shouldn't, I really should not let myself get so worked up.

When Morden arrived I did not hear but rather sensed him behind me. He leaned down to my ear and with mock-menace softly said:

'You're under investigation, you are.'

Today he wore an expensive, ash-grey, double-breasted suit the jacket of which was wrapped around and buttoned tightly under his big bull chest like a complicated sling, so that he seemed even more top-heavy than usual, set down on those thick, short legs and small, incongruously dainty feet. He was not tall, you know; big and wide, but not tall; I must have had at least a couple of inches on him. Not that it made any difference, I was still afraid of him (I know, I know, afraid is not the word, but it will have to do). It would always be thus, I realised, in an odd sort of musing way which must have been partly an early effect of the gin; even if I were to get the better of him in some worldly dealing I would still quail inwardly before him. He made me feel off-balance, as if in his presence everything were pitched at an angle and I must keep constantly at a tilt in order to stay upright. But then, that was the way I felt with all three of them, more or less. I was, I *was* Candide. I made my way amongst them in a daze of uncertainty, looking the wrong way and tripping over myself, picking my shaky steps, as in a panic dream, athwart the treacherous slope of their unnervingly knowing regard. What a dolt I was.

60

Morden must have loved me for it; I was his entertainment, his straight-man, his – what do they call it? – his patsy. Why do I not think more harshly of him than I do? Because – it has just come to me this moment – because he reminded me of myself. Well, that's a surprise; I shall return to it when I've given it some thought. Meanwhile he is standing in his Rodin pose with a hand in his pocket and his head thrown back, looking at me down the sides of his broad nostrils and smiling in his glintingly jovial way.

'Yes,' he said almost gaily, 'we're running a few checks on you. A few scans. Francie here thinks you may not be the thing at all. He thinks he's come across you somewhere before, in another life. Don't you, Francie? There's talk—' lowering his voice to a conspiratorial growl '– there's talk of serious misdemeanours, of grave misdeeds.'

And he laughed, still eyeing me merrily, as if it were all a grand joke. Francie said nothing and sat with lowered gaze, sucking his teeth and turning and turning his beer glass slowly in its own puddle on the bar top. I want you to see the scene: evening, the crowded, chattering pub, smoke and dust motes coiling in the last, thick rays of sunlight slanting down over the roofs of Gabriel Street, and the three of us there in that little pool of stillness, Francie and me facing each other perched on our stools with our knees almost touching and Morden standing at his ease between us with a hand in the pocket of his jacket as if he were cradling a gun, admiring his reflection in the flyblown mirror behind the bar. You were there too, of course, I could feel your presence vividly, the ghostly fourth of our quartet. Already, you see, I was carrying you with me, my phantom, my other self. And nothing else mattered very much.

'What do you say?' Morden said to Francie in the mirror. 'Is he the real thing or not? Because if he's not . . .' He took his hand out of his pocket and with finger and cocked thumb shot me silently and grinned. 'Bang. You're dead.'

61

I am always surprised and gratified by the composure I am capable of in the face of shocks and sudden perils. Morden in his menacingly playful way had brought my past, my buried past, sitting bolt upright out of its coffin, wide-eyed and hideously grinning, and there I was sipping my drink and looking at the ceiling with what I considered an admirable show of unconcern. It is not always thus, of course, but when it is it's wonderfully convincing, I believe. At least, I hope it is. Francie still had not spoken and Morden nudged me and said, 'Sherlock is silent.' He waved a hand in which a glass has suddenly appeared: mineral water – he does not drink, remember? 'Well, in that case, case dismissed,' he said and tapped the base of his glass gavel fashion on the bar. The dog is there too, lying on the floor beside its master's stool with front paws extended and ears pricked up, doing its Anubis impression. Francie scowls. Everything seems small and distant in the tremulous, gin-blue air. For no reason at all I felt suddenly, fatuously, cheerful. Morden put his gun-hand on my shoulder; extraordinary grip, have I said that already? 'Listen,' he said into my ear with mock-sincerity, 'don't worry, I like a self-made man.'

Now everything shifts again, the false panels and secret compartments slide this way and that with an oiled, surreptitious smoothness, and it is another day and we are somewhere else, and the sun is shining steadily as before but from a different angle and not thick but piercing in white-gold filaments through shutters, is it? or wooden blinds? We must be having an indian summer. Morning, I believe, calm and bright, with that clear-edged, headachy look to things as if they were exhibits set out under polished sheets of glass. We are in the lounge of one of those imitation grand hotels that had begun to spring up on the edge of the quarter, all chrome and honey-coloured wood and the woolly smell of expensive bad dinners. I was delivering a small, well-rounded lecture on the pictures, sitting with my hands clasped between my knees and frowning at the floor. Morden was in a restless mood and had begun to fidget, shifting massively in his chair and casting about him with impatient sighs. 'Yes yes,' he kept saying, trying to silence me, 'that's fine, fine,' and puffing on a vast cigar and clawing angrily at the smoke as though it were a tangle of cobwebs in front of his face. I kept on imperturbably, undeterred. It will not be news to you, I suppose, but I have come to realise that there is a strain of pedantry in me which I enjoy, in a quiet way. It dulls the senses, soothes the heart. It is satisfying to set out things just so, the facts on one side, speculation on the other, the strategies, the alternatives, the possible routes toward a desired conclusion. Perhaps there really is a scholar lost in me. (Need I add that I never believe a word I hear myself saying?) There in the flocculent hush of that hotel lounge I expounded on Josiah Marbot's bizarre collection in what used to be called measured tones, and was aware of a familiar calm descending on me at the centre of which there flickered a pilot-light of unemphatic happiness. And as I talked I listened to myself in mild surprise and admiration. It might have been another voice that was speaking for which I was only the medium. That is all I ever want, in a way, to be here and not here: a living absence. Sometimes in public places I fancy that if I were to stop and stand quite still people would be able to walk through me. I imagine them, that woman with the shopping bag, that girl on her bike, faltering for a second on the other side of me and frowning and giving an involuntary shiver, thinking someone had walked over their grave, while I, the invisible man, smile on them and hold my breath.

'Look,' Morden said, pressing his elbows down on the arms of his chair and squirming forward with knees splayed and ankles crossed, 'all we want to know is, are they genuine?' He waited, squatting before me like an ill-humoured frog. I paused for effect and then quietly pointed out, in my coolest, primmest tone, that the pictures were signed. He flexed an eyebrow; I could hear him breathing, a low, stertorous roar down those big nostrils. 'Which means,' I went on, 'that they are either genuine, or fakes.'

He opened his mouth and laughed, a short, sharp bark. 'What else would they be?' he said.

A large part of the pleasure of pedantry, I have discovered, is to pretend there is no pleasure in it at all. The low monotone, the neutral gaze, the faint edge of impatience and, of course, the touch of condescension, these are the things to cultivate. A picture done in the style of Vaublin, I explained slowly, even if it were a direct copy, does not pretend to be a Vaublin unless it is signed. 'For, you see, the signature –' I sketched a flourish on the air between us '– the signature is everything.'

He scowled. I found them odd and disconcerting, these looks of almost loathing he would fix on me. Now, of course, I suspect they were his way to keep from laughing. What a show it was, and what fun he must have had, playing the bluff businessman with an eye for beauty and all the rest of it, that whole travesty.

'No,' he said, hawking up the word like phlegm, 'I'll tell you what everything is: everything is when you go to flog a fake and *say* that it's the real thing.'

He kept his scowling stare fixed on me for a moment, nodding his big bull-head, then flopped back in the armchair and stuck the cigar in his mouth and studied a far corner of the room through a rich flaw of smoke.

'Anyway, I'll probably give them away,' he said carelessly. 'To some gallery, maybe.' At the thought of it a brief spark lit his sullen eye: The Morden Collection! 'It's just that I'm . . .' He gestured impatiently and took a sip of his mineral water – no, I mean a puff of his cigar. 'I'm just . . .' He scowled again. There was a wrathful silence. The dog

64

watched him keenly, expecting him, it seemed, to do something marvellous and mad at any moment.

'Curious,' Francie said flatly, and Morden and I turned and stared at him as if he were a foreigner who had suddenly spoken to us in our own language. He looked back at us with that air of boredom and wearied disenchantment, a cigarette dangling from his lip. Francie and his fags, his cap, his dog. Morden cleared his throat and said loudly, 'Yes, that's right, I'm curious.' He glared at me again as if he thought I might attempt to contradict him. 'I want to *know*, that's all,' he said. 'If they're fake they're fake.'

Did I believe him? It was a question that I used to put to myself over and over again, rolling on the floor of the prison cell of my anguish and shame, in the first days after the gimcrack edifice had all come crashing down. Futile, of course; it was never a matter of believing or disbelieving. Belief, trust, suspicion, these are chimeras that arise in hindsight, when I look back from the sad eminence of the knowledge of having been deceived. At the time I just tottered along as usual, like a drunk on a tightrope, trying to concentrate on the business in hand and not fall off despite the buzz of distractions around me, those trapeze artists whizzing past and the clowns cavorting down in the ring. Oh, of course, I must have known from the start that there was something fishy going on – but when is there not? Stick your nose into anything and you will get a whiff of brine and slime. I would catch one or other of them, even the dog, looking at me in what must have been incredulous wonderment, holding their breath, waiting for me to twig what was afoot. It was as if I had surprised them in the midst of a drunken carouse and now, sobered for a second, they were standing about and keeping a straight face, lips shut tight and cheeks bulging, trying not to catch each other's eye for fear of bursting out in guffaws. Sometimes, when I walked out of a room where they were, I would have an uneasy vision, which I would immediately dismiss, of them throwing their arms about each other's shoulders and collapsing into helpless mirth . . . But why do I torment myself like this, what does it matter any more? Is the loss of you not flame enough, that I must keep scorching myself over these embers? Yet I have nothing else, no packet of letters, no locket of bright hair, only these speculations that I turn over endlessly in my head like things on a spit. (*Ich brenne in dir* . . .) And I feel so foolish and pathetic, poor Mr Punch with his black eye and broken heart and his back humped with shame. I think of myself there in that hotel or wherever it was that day, talking about provenance and dating techniques and the history of oil-based pigments and the necessity for a detailed comparison of brushstrokes, and I squirm like a slug in salt. How could I allow myself to be so easily taken in? And the answer comes of course as pat as you please: because I wanted to be. Bang! go my fists on the cell floor, and bang! my forehead too, between them. Bang! Bang! Bang!

How I talked in those days; when I think back I am aware of a ceaseless background buzz that is the noise of my own voice going on and on. Guilt, I mean the permanent, inexpungible, lifetime variety, turns you into a kind of earnest clown. They speak of guilt as something heavy, they talk about the weight of it, the burden, but I know otherwise; guilt is lighter than air; it fills you up like a gas and would send you sailing into the sky, arms and legs flailing, an inflated Grock, if you did not keep a tight hold on things. For years now talk had been my tether and my bags of ballast. Once I got going on the autodidact's monody there was no stopping me. Art history, the lives of the painters, the studio system in the seventeenth century, there was no end to the topics at my command. And all for no purpose other than to keep suppressed inside me that ever-surging bubble of appalled, excoriating, sulphurous laughter, the cackle of the damned. That's why I was so easily fooled,

66

that's how I could be so easily taken in: because I was always thinking of other things, struggling inwardly with those big burdensome words that had I had the nerve to speak them would have made you stare first and then laugh. Atonement. Redemption. That kind of thing. I was still in hell, you see, or purgatory, at least, and you were one of the elect at whom I squinnied up yearningly as you paced the elysian fields in golden light.

Yet wait. That is not quite right, or not complete, at least, and gives altogether too worthy an impression. Those big words . . . Oh, leave it, I can't be bothered.

Suddenly, with a violent turn of the wrist, Morden crushed out his three-quarters unsmoked cigar and stood up briskly, startling the dog, and said, 'Come on, we'll go for a drive.' I looked at Francie but he only shrugged and rose with an air of weary resignation and followed Morden, who was already halfway across the lobby. The girl with the grey eyes gave me a distracted smile and turned away. Here is the door of the pub, I mean the hotel, the revolving door of the St Gabriel Hotel which with a violent sigh deposited me on the sunlit pavement in the middle of a crisp September morning.

Morden's car, a low-slung black beast, was parked on a double yellow line in a street behind the hotel loud with the archaic voices of delivery men. There was a parking ticket clipped to the windscreen. Morden crushed it in his fist and tossed it into the gutter, from where Francie dutifully retrieved it. This little exchange had the look of an established routine. 'I'll drive,' Morden said, and had the engine going before we were inside the car. I sat in the front while Francie lounged in the back with Prince beside him on the seat, ears up and breathing down the back of my neck. We travelled at high speed through the flashing streets. Morden drove with absent-minded violence, wrenching the wheel and stamping his foot furiously between the accelerator and the brakes. The river, then leafy avenues, then the canal, and then a broad cement road describing a long curve between acres of grim housing. Morden waved a hand. 'All this was fields in my day,' he said. We sped on in silence and sunlight over that sad, peopled plain under a high, thin blue sky. Behind me the dog moaned softly to itself, watching all that freedom flying past.

We were almost in the country when Morden slowed abruptly and turned into a drab estate. He negotiated a bewildering maze of streets at high speed and at last stopped at a place where the road dipped between a fenced-off terrace of identical houses on one side and on the other a stark grey school building fastened to a bleak field. A wind had sprung up and the sunlight had taken on a milky tinge. No one spoke. Morden, slumped in his seat, gazed out morosely upon the scene. Houses, and more houses, rank upon mean rank. The dog licked its chops and trembled in anticipation and at last Francie leaned over with a grunt and opened the door and the animal bounded out and was off across the school field, going at a swift lope with its nose to the ground. Morden got out too and stood squinting about him. I made to follow but Francie from the back seat put a hand on my arm and said, 'Hold on.' We sat and listened to the wind in the overhead wires and the jumbled crackle and thrum of a distant radio. Morden crossed the road and walked a little way along by the houses and stopped at one and went in at the garden gate and knocked on the narrow, frosted-glass door. The door opened immediately, as if by remote control. He glanced about him once and stepped inside. I got out of the car, unhindered this time, and stood as Morden had stood, shading my eyes against the light. The air hereabouts had that particular smell that poverty generates, a mingling of unwashed clothes and peed-on mattresses and sodden tea-leaves. On the other side of the road a toddler on a tricycle came to the edge of the footpath and toppled slowly, shakily into the gutter. An upstairs window opened and a raw-faced woman leaned out and looked at me with interest, challengingly. The infant in the gutter began to cry, producing a curiously detached, ratcheted little whimpering noise. Behind me Francie got out and lounged against the bonnet of the car with his arms and ankles crossed. The door where Morden had entered opened again and a short, hard-looking young man with Popeye muscles and bandy arms and legs appeared and ambled down the garden path. He had cropped red hair and a pushed-in face, and wore a vest and army trousers and lace-up boots and sported a single gold earring in the shape of a crucifix. He stopped at the garden gate and folded his stubby arms and gave me a cold stare. I turned away and went into the school yard. The gin had produced in me a fluctuating, tottery sensation. From within the school I could hear a class raggedly chanting the two-times tables. How affecting and lonely it is to loiter like that where children are at their lessons; nowhere emptier than a playground during school hours. The field rose before me, humped and high, the dark grass wind-bent and greyly burnished in the bruised sunlight. Far off I could see Prince ranging in wide loops, and farther off again a boy galloping bareback in slow motion on a piebald pony. Presently without a sound Morden appeared at my side – how quietly he could move, for all his bulk – and stood rocking pensively on his heels with his face lifted and nostrils flared as if to catch some faint fragrance, the smell of the past, perhaps. I asked him, for the sake of saying something, if this was the place where he was born. He stared at me and laughed. 'Here?' he said. 'No!' He laughed again, skittishly. 'I wasn't born anywhere!' And still laughing to himself he turned and set off back to the car with that curiously dainty, shuffling walk that he had, head down and hands in pockets, his trouser legs flapping in the wind. I lingered a while, gazing off across the field and thinking of nothing. The boy on the pony was gone. Behind me Francie gave a long, trilling whistle and the dog immediately ceased its circlings and came loping back, passing me by without a glance. A cloud covered the sun and a rippling shadow raced across the field towards me and all at once I was frightened, I don't know why, exactly; it was just the look of things, I think, the vastness of the world, that depthless sky and the cloud-shadow running towards me, intangible, unavoidable, like fate itself. It is not the big occasions that terrify me most, when the car goes out of control or a wheel drops off the aeroplane, but the ordinary moments, like this one, when suddenly I lose my hold on things and the ground drops away from under me and I find myself staring aghast into empty air, like a character in a cartoon film who runs straight off the edge of a cliff and does not fall until he notices there is nothing under his feet but the long plunge to the canyon floor far below. Hurriedly I turned back towards the car and was almost running by the time I reached it. The tough at the gate had been joined now by a fat, unhealthy-looking fellow got up outlandishly in pink carpet slippers and a sort of kilt and a tasselled shawl that was wrapped tightly around his big belly and slung over his shoulder like an ancient Roman's robe. He seemed to be studying me in particular, thoughtfully, with an eyebrow cocked, and as the car pulled away he drew a plump hand from under the shawl and lifted an index finger in a lax, ambiguous gesture, a sort of cautionary farewell, which neither Morden nor Francie acknowledged. 'Master of disguise,' Francie muttered and did his costive chuckle. I asked who was the fellow in the kilt but no one answered, and Morden glared at the space between his knees with an expression of angry boredom. The toddler sat beside its upturned tricycle, still whingeing.

This time Francie drove, with the dog on guard beside him and Morden and me in the back. Morden was silent, sunk in himself with his chin on his chest and his arms tightly folded as if he were strapped into a strait-jacket. What was I thinking now? Still nothing. Is that not strange? I never cease to wonder at my capacity for passive participation, if participation is the word. As if just being there were itself a force, a kind of inertial action requiring only my presence for it to operate. To make sense of this flow of happenings that was carrying me along like a leaf on the flood I would have had to stop everything and step out of the picture altogether and stand back on some impossible, Archimedean platform in space and view the spectacle as a completed whole. But nothing is complete, and nothing whole. I suppose that is why deep down I have never been able fully to believe in reality as it is described by the science of physics, with its moments of motionless and lucid insight, as if it could be possible to take a cross-section of the moving world and put it between glass slides and study it in perfect stillness and silence. No, no, flux and flow, unstoppable, that's all there is; it terrifies me to think of it. Yet more terrifying still is the thought of being left behind. Talk is one way of keeping up. Is that not what I'm doing? If I were to stop I'd stop.

On a newsagent's stand the noon editions, in headlines three inches deep, were announcing the first of the murders.

'Look at that,' Morden said and clicked his tongue. 'Terrible.' He sat back in the seat and let his gaze drift upward dreamily. 'Who was that chap,' he said, 'that stole that picture from Binkie Behrens and killed the maid when she got in his way?' A row of shops with delivery vans, dogs, defeated-looking women pushing prams; how little I know of what they call the real world. 'Ten or twelve years ago it was,' he said. 'Anyone remember?'

I kept my eyes on the passing streets. I have such a hunger in me for the mundane.

'Some name beginning with M,' Francie said and his shoulders shook.

'That's right,' Morden said. 'Montagu, or Montmorency, something like that.' He tapped me lightly on the knee. 'Do you recall? No? You were away, maybe – you've been away for a long time, haven't you?' He brooded, pretended to brood. 'A Vermeer, was it, or a Metsu? One of those. *Portrait of a Woman*. Lovely thing. Hit her on the head with a hammer, whack, like that.' He turned to me again. 'Ever been to Whitewater House, the Behrens place?' he said. 'Magnificent. The pictures! You should go. Take a day trip. Do you good.' He heaved himself up until he was sitting sideways on the seat and examined me critically. 'You're very pale, you know,' he said. 'Cooped up too much, that's your trouble.'

I began to talk about Aunt Corky, her history and present status, the nursing home, the Haddons. Babblebabblebabble. Why Aunt Corky? I have few topics, when all is said and done. Morden let me go on and when I had straggled to a stop he sat up and rubbed his hands and said he wanted to meet her. 'Francie,' he cried, 'turn the car, turn the car!' He waved aside my weak-voiced protests. He was enjoying himself. Soon we were bowling northwards along the coast road. The tide was out and the sun was resplendent on the mudflats and the verdant algae. A heron stood on a rusted spar with wings spread wide. 'Flasher,' Morden said and laughed. Presently his mood turned again and he became lachrymose. 'I have no family, you know,' he said. 'I mean real family: aunts, uncles, brothers, that kind of thing.' He turned and to my alarm seized me by the wrist and peered searchingly into my eyes. 'Have you a brother?' he said. I looked away from him. Yes, just like me, a sentimentalist and a bully. This was awful. Francie rolled down the window and leaned out his elbow and began to whistle. The car climbed the hill road and at last we were pulling up at the gate of The Cypresses. 'This it?' Morden said, peering. I was picturing Mr Haddon's face as Morden strode in shouting for Aunt Corky. But Morden had lost interest in my aunt and had already plunged back into himself again and sat looking off, dead-eyed and frowning. Then as I was starting to get out of the car he reached forward quickly and caught me by the wrist again and again demanded to know if I had a brother. No, I told him, eager to be away, no, I had no family. Searchingly he gazed into my eyes. 'A sister?' he said. 'No one?' He slowly nodded. 'Same as me,' he said; 'an orphan.' Then he let go of me with a wave and I stumbled out on to the road and the car roared away. I stood blinking. I felt as if I had been picked up and shaken vigorously before being tossed negligently aside.

Aunt Corky had got religion. In her hospital clouts she sat up in bed in her big room and talked ecstatically of God and salvation and Father Fanning (I suppose we shall have to meet him, too, before long). I did not mind. Her voice was a soothing noise. I wanted to crawl under the covers with her and beg her protection. I was shaky and breathless and my legs felt wobbly, as if I had scampered the last few yards of the tightrope and were clinging now to the spangled pole in a sweat of rubber-kneed relief with the vast, dusty darkness yawning beneath me; presently I would have to retrace my quaking steps, back, back to where Morden stood waiting for me in his tights and his acrobat's boots, grinning his dare-devil grin; but not yet. Aunt Corky's breakfast tray was on the bedside locker: a porridge bowl with bent spoon, a smeared cup and mismatched saucer, a charred crust of toast. When she stopped talking I hardly noticed. How tired I was suddenly. She peered at me closely, frowning. 'You,' she said, and poked me in the chest, 'what is the matter with you? You look as if you have seen a ghost.' She was right; an all too familiar revenant, the ghost of an old self, had risen up before me again. If only there were a deed poll by which past deeds might be changed.

3. **Pygmalion** (*called* **Pygmalion and Galatea**) 1649
Giovanni Belli (1602-1670)

Oil on canvas, 23 x 35 in. (58.4 x 89 cm.)

Belli is unusual in that he represents a reversal of the tra-
ditional direction of artistic migration, being an Italian who
moved north. Born in Mantua, he is known to have studied
for a time in Rome as a young man, probably as a pupil of
Guido Reni (1575-1642), whose influence – less than benign
– is clearly detectable in the works of the younger painter.
We next hear of Belli in the year 1640 in a catalogue entry
by the dealer Verheiden of The Hague, where he is referred
to as '*Joh. Belli ex Mantova, habit. Amstelodam*'. Why this
quintessentially Italian (southern, Catholic, death-obsessed)
painter should have settled in the Low Countries is not clear.
Certainly, from the evidence of his work, with its highly
worked, polished textures and uncanny, one might almost
say macabre, atmosphere, it seems it was not admiration for
the serene genius of Dutch painting in the Golden Age that
drew him northwards. He is an anachronistic, perhaps even
faintly absurd figure, displaced and out of step with his
time, an exile in an alien land. His work is marked by the
inwardness and isolation of a man who has distanced himself
from the known, the familiar, and betrays a hopeless yearning for all that has been lost and abandoned. His concern

with the theme of death – or, rather, what one critic has called 'life-in-death' – is manifest not only in his characteristically morbid choice of subject matter but in the obsessive pursuit of stillness, poise, and a kind of unearthly splendour; a pursuit which, paradoxically, imparts to his work a restless, hectic quality, so that the epithet most often applied to it – inaccurately, of course – is 'Gothic'. This constant effort of transcendence results in a mannered, overwrought style; what Gombrich summarises as critical attitudes to Guido Reni might also be applied to Reni's pupil, that his work is 'too self-conscious, too deliberate in its striving for pure beauty'. In the *Pygmalion* this self-consciousness and desire for purity, both of form and expression, are the most obvious characteristics. We are struck at once by the remarkable daring of the angle at which the couch is placed upon which Pygmalion and his awaking statue-bride recline. This great crimson parallelogram lying diagonally across the painting from the lower right to upper left corners gives a sense of skewed massiveness that is almost alarming to the viewer, who on a first encounter may feel as if the room in which he is viewing the picture has tilted suddenly. Against the blood-hued brocade of the couch the ivory pallor of the awaking statue seems a token of submissiveness: here 'Galatea' (the name does not occur in any version of the myth in classical literature and in this context is probably an invention of Renaissance mythographers) is more victim than love-object. How strikingly this figure displays itself, at once demure and abandoned, sprawled on its back with left knee flexed to reveal where the smooth ivory of the lap has dimpled into a groove, and the right arm with its still bloodless, slender hand flung out; is it the goddess's inspiration of life that is convulsing these limbs, or are these the paroxysms of fleshly pleasure that the half-incarnate girl is experiencing already and for the first time? And is Pygmalion leaning over her the better to savour her sighs, or is he drawing back in consternation, appalled at the violence of this sudden passion he has kindled? The shocking gesture of his hand seizing upon the girl's right breast may as easily be a token of his fear as of his desire. Likewise, the gifts of shells and pebbles, dead songbirds, painted baubles and tear-shaped drops of ambergris that lie strewn in a jumble before the couch seem less 'the kind of presents,' as Ovid says, 'that girls enjoy' than votive offerings laid at the altar of an implacable deity. With what obsessive exactitude has the artist rendered these trifles, as if they are indeed a sacrifice that he himself is making to Venus, whose great, smooth, naked form hovers above the two figures on the couch, dwarfing them. In this portrayal of the goddess – impassive, marmoreal, lubriciously maternal – can clearly be seen the influence of the mannerists, in particular the Bronzino of such works as *Venus, Cupid, Folly and Time*. The overall tone of ambiguous sexuality is slyly pointed up by the triple dancing tongues of flame rising from the sacrificial pyre that burns on the little moss-grown mound visible in the middle distance in the upper right-hand corner of the scene. However questionable they may be in terms of taste, it is in such subtle touches rather than in the larger gestures of this phantasmal and death-drunk work that, to quote Gombrich again, Belli's 'quest for forms more perfect and more ideal than reality [is] rewarded with success.'

What affects me most strongly and most immediately in a work of art is the quality of its silence. This silence is more than an absence of sound, it is an active force, expressive and coercive. The silence that a painting radiates becomes a kind of aura enfolding both the work itself and the viewer as in a colour-field. So in the white room when I took up Morden's pictures and began to examine them one by one what struck me first of all was not colour or form or the sense of movement they suggested but the way each one suddenly amplified the quiet. Soon the room was athrob with their mute eloquence. Athrob, yes, for this voluminous, inaudible din with which they filled the place, as a balloon is filled with densened air, did not bring calm but on the contrary provoked in me a kind of suspenseful agitation, a tremulous, poised expectancy that was all the more fraught because there seemed nothing to expect. As I worked I talked to myself, only half aware that I was doing so, putting on voices and playing out dialogues under my breath, so that often when I finished for the day my head resonated with a medleyed noise as if I had been since morning in the company of a crowd of garrulous, mild lunatics. The room too was disorienting, with its cramped wedge shape and single, disturbingly square window and invisible door. It's a wonder I did not go off my head in that first period of solitude and unremitting concentration (perhaps I did?). I could have worked elsewhere in the house, for the place had many big empty airy rooms, but it never occurred to me to shift. I had Francie help me (he was less than gracious) to carry up an old pine table from the kitchen on which I set out my reference books, my powders and potions and glass retorts (I exaggerate), and unfolded on their green oilskin cloth the tools of my craft: the tweezers, scrapers, scalpels, the fine sable brushes, the magnifying glass and jeweller's monocle; some other time, perhaps, I shall essay a little paean of praise to these beautiful artefacts which are an enduring source of quiet pleasure and consolation to me. So see me at play there just as in the days of my glowing if not quite gilded youth when it pleased me to pretend to be a scholar. Then it was science, now it is art.

I have considered many things since your going, and I have come to some conclusions. One is, that I was lost that radiant Florentine morning in the infancy of the *quattrocento* when the architect Brunelleschi disclosed to his painter colleagues the hitherto unrealised laws of perspective. Morally lost, I mean. The thousand years or so before that epochal event I think of as a period of deep and dreamless slumber, when everything moved in enfolding curves at a glacial pace and the future was no more than a replay of the past; a long, suspended moment of stillness and circularity between the rackety end of the classical world and the first, fevered thrashings of the so-called Renaissance. I picture a kind of darksome northern Arcady, thick-forested, befogged and silent, lost in the glimmering, frost-bound deeps of immemorial night. What calm! What peace! Then came that clarion dawn when the architect threw open his box of tricks and Masaccio (known to his contemporaries, with prescient and to me gratifying accuracy, as Clumsy Tommaso) and his henchmen clapped palms to foreheads in disbelief at their own short-sightedness and got down to drawing receding lines and ruined everything, spawning upon the world the chimeras of progress and the perfectibility of man and all the rest of it. Illusion followed rapidly by delusion: that, in a nutshell, is the history of our culture. Oh, a bad day's work. And as for the Enlightenment . . . ! How, fed on these madnesses, could a man such as I be expected to keep his head?

Anyway.

In the first days in that secret room I was happier than I can remember ever having been before, astray in the familiar otherwhere of art. Astray, yes, and yet somehow at the same time more keenly aware, of things and of myself, than in any other of the periods of my life that have printed themselves with particular significance on my memory. Quick, is the word: everything, myself included, was quick with import and intent. I was like some creature of the so-called wild poised on open ground with miraculously refined senses tuned to the weather of the world. Each painting that I lifted up and set under my enlarging glass was a portent of what was coming. And what was coming, though I did not know it yet, was you, and all that you entailed.

Or did I know? Perhaps when I peered into those pictures what I was looking for was always and only the prospect of you, a speck of radiance advancing towards me from the vanishing-point.

At heart I am a hopeless romantic: I wished to believe in Josiah Marbot, that staid adventurer and beady-eyed snapper-up of unconsidered treasures. As I got to know the pictures I was convinced I was coming to know him, too (perhaps it was with him my phantom dialogues were conducted?), his bitter sense of humour, his taste for the grotesque, the diffident manner masking the ruthlessness of the dedicated collector. I could almost see him, a thin old tall figure in frock-coat and stock making his slow way up through the house at nightfall, leaning on a pearl-handled cane, one arm behind him with fist pressed to the small of his bent back, the arthritic fingers curled. His rheumed eyes are still sharp, the corners of his mouth turn down (the teeth are long gone); his nose is thin and pointed and bloodlessly white, dry white, like these desiccated walls. He pauses at a window, his man with candle going on ahead capered about by shadows, and looks down into the narrow street; drizzle greases the cobbles; a carriage clops and creaks past, the nag's head hanging; he is remembering an alleyway on the Ile de la Cité thirty years before, the darkness coming on as now, and a half-drunk fat dealer under a low, smoke-blackened ceiling bringing out a package wrapped in dirty rags and crooning and kissing bunched fingers as if it were one of his daughters he was offering the rich milord: *Vaublin, m'sieur – un vrai Vaublin!* I thought of his passion for pictures, or at least for collecting them, as somehow indecent, a secret vice. I imagined him haunting the showrooms, as he might have the great brothels of the time, in a subdued fever of longing and shame, stammering out his desire for something different, something special . . . Certainly his taste was for the louche and the deformed, yet the sports he possessed himself of looked perfectly proper – I mean, insofar as technique was concerned – like so many humpbacked, threebreasted whores tricked out in silks and crinolines.

But what exactly did I make of these paintings, what exactly did I feel for them? (I am sitting here, by the way, with a pitying half smile on my face, like a magistrate listening to a doltish accused stumbling through his earnest and self-condemning testimony.) How can I say for certain what I felt or did not feel? The present modifies the past, it is a continuing, insidious process. That time, though it is only a little while ago, seems to me now impossibly distant, a prelapsarian era bathed in a tawny light and filled with the slow music of solitude. Did I give myself to the pictures with that sensation of inward falling that great art is supposed to provoke? Probably I did. True, I found them uncanny; they stared at me from across the room, remote and motionless, like a row of propped-up catatonics. But you see, I had never before been in such proximity to works of art, had never been allowed such freedoms, had never been permitted to take such liberties. It was like suddenly breaking through to a different version of reality, a new and hitherto undreamed-of dimension of a familiar world. It was like – yes, it was like what they seem to mean when they talk of love. To place one of these extraordinary artefacts before me on the little table in the white room and go to work on it with my tweezers and my magnifying glass was to be given licence to enter the innermost secret places of a sacred object. This was the surface the painter had worked in, I kept telling myself, these were the brushstrokes he had set down; still lodged in the paint would be a few stray atoms the creator had breathed out as he leaned rapt before his canvas three and a half centuries ago in a leaky garret on some back street of Antwerp or Utrecht under a sky piled high with gigantic clouds. That was how it seemed to me, that was how I thought; no wonder when I stood back and rubbed my eyes I could not focus on what was before me. I was like a lover who gazes in tongue-tied joy upon his darling and sees not her face but a dream of it. You were the pictures and they were you and I never noticed. All this I understand now – but *then*; ah, my dear, *then!* You see my difficulty: a grotesque among grotesque things, I was content there and wanted nothing but that this peaceful and phantasmally peopled solitude should continue without disturbance; content, that is, until you became animate suddenly and stepped out of your frame.

Here is what happened. This is what happened, the first

time. Not the first first time but the first time that you that I that we . . . Here it is.

And yet, what did happen? Nothing, to speak of, nothing that can be spoken of, in words, adequately. Morning. The autumn was really under way by now, with sunlight the colour of brass on the faces of the houses and the sense of a silent, continuous slippage in the full, still, shining air. Very quiet, too, only the odd blare of a bus engine revving on the quays and, farther off, a tipsy jangling of bells from the cathedral where what must have been an apprentice campanologist was practising his scales. I am at my table, poring over my catalogue of the big Vaublin show in Washington, the pages lying open at a rather muddy reproduction of the *Flaying of Marsyas*: peasants having a carouse in the foreground while the bad business is done in miniature in a bosky grove off in the middle distance. I have a headache, it is beating away in there, a slow, soft, silent pounding. I lift my gaze. A great chubby silver-white cloud by Magritte is standing upright in the window in front of me, opening its arms. You appear out of silence. That is how I think of it, as if the silence in the room had somehow materialised you and given you form. I felt you there before I heard your step. A sort of shift occurred, as if an engine somewhere had shunted silently, enormously, into another gear, and I looked up, puzzled. It is said that in the instant before lightning strikes you can feel the rocks and trees around you buzzing. You were wearing . . . what were you wearing? A light dress of linen, or cotton, with tiny flowers printed on it, tight-waisted with a full skirt; what was called in my day a summer frock, the weather was still just warm enough for it. And pumps, black pumps with a little pressed black satin bow on each instep. No make-up today, or none that I could detect, so that her features had a shimmery, ill-defined quality, as if I were seeing her through a fine, bright mist. What was surprising was that we were not surprised. We might have been meeting here like this every morning for months. When she leaned down at my shoulder I could hear the faint soft rasp of her breathing. And I could smell her. That was the first thing, really the first thing, her smell: at once staleish and tart, with a tang in it like a tang of nettles that made my saliva glands tingle. She smelled of childish things, of seasides, of schoolrooms, and of something else, I don't know, something chafed and raw – just flesh itself, maybe – and I thought at once, with a sort of startled, swollen avidity, of sunburn, and chilblains, and the delicate, translucent pink rims of your nostrils when you caught that cold and would not let me touch you for three days (I know, I know, this is all out of sequence). Occasionally even still I am reduced on the spot to a state of slack-jawed inanity by an afterbreath of that mingled, carnal savour; there must be a whiff of it lodged somewhere in the caverns of my skull. If only I could isolate that trace, some fiendish savant might be able to culture out of it a genetic model of you perfect in every detail – except, that is, the only one that matters. She wanted to know what was happening in the picture on the page before me and when I told her she squared her mouth in disgust and made a retching noise. Poor Marsyas; they sing Apollo's praises but give me Dionysus any day. She walked to the window and put her face close to the glass and peered off sideways at something only she could see. That stillness, that feline concentration: where had I seen some other loved one stand in just that pose? Then she turned and sat down on the sill, leaning forward with elbows locked and the hollows of her arms turned inside out (those delicate blue veins, my God!) and her hands braced at her sides and one balletic toe pressed to the floor, while she slowly swung the other leg which at the apogee of each swing bared itself to glimmering mid-thigh. I cannot see a Balthus, any Balthus – those autumnal tones, that character-istic air of jaded lewdness – without thinking of A. sitting there that day, lips parted, faintly frowning, gazing into herself with that irresistibly vacant expression her face always took on in repose. What was I thinking now, what was I feeling? I was waiting, I did not know for what exactly, while the pendulum of that hypnotically swinging leg marked off the slow, swollen seconds. How pale she was. Her hair at the side hung away from her canted cheek like a cropped black gleaming wing. I could not see her face clearly with the light behind her. Had her gaze shifted, was she looking at me now? Time passed. We must have talked, or at least exchanged remarks, we cannot have sat in silence all that while, but if so I don't remember. I recall only the look of things: her print dress, that hanging wing of hair, the triangular shadow lengthening and contracting along her inner thigh as she swung her leg, the polar blue in the window behind her and that ogreish cloud at her back still stealthily spreading its icy arms. Or is it just that I want to linger here in this moment when everything was still to come, to preserve it in the crystal of remembrance like one of those little scenes in glass globes that I used to play with as a child, cottage and tree and robin redbreast on a twig and all swirled about with snowflakes? (I could weep a blizzard if I once got started.) Her face was unexpectedly cool under my hand. With a fingertip I traced the line of her jaw, her chin. She did not lift her head. Her leg had stopped swinging. How had I got from table to window? I imagine a great soft bound, a sort of slow-motion kangaroo hop that landed me grinning and atremble before her. I felt shaky and impossibly lofty, as if I were balancing precariously on stilts and ogling down at her with a clownish, protuberant eye. She was very still, a sleek, warm, watchful creature poised in wait for whatever was to happen. I took a deep breath that caught in my gullet and became a gulp, and in the would-be no-nonsense voice of a workman rolling up his sleeves to tackle a tricky but attractive job I said, 'Well, this chance won't

86

come again,' and unaccountably the taste of blackberries flooded up from the root of my tongue. She began to say something rapidly, I did not catch the words, and she laughed breathily into my mouth and I felt her lips slacken and slide sideways under my ill-aimed, glancing kiss. We kept our eyes wide open and gaped swimmingly at each other in a sort of amazement, then she drew her face away quickly, looking at once pleased and scornful, and made a circle of her lips and said softly, 'Poh!' A very long moment of absolute immobility, and then I have the impression of a complicated, awkward untangling, with clearings of throats and muttered apologies and the threat of ruinous laughter hanging over all. Then I swung about and walked to the table, stumping along on my invisible stilts, hot with thrilling terror and keeping my back firmly turned to her. I picked up something from the table, I don't know what, and began to discourse on it in a laughable attempt at nonchalance. And when I looked again she was gone.

That kiss. Well. The effect of it was to last for days – for weeks. I felt like something that had been shattered and yet was still of a piece, all run through with hairline cracks and fissures and rocking on my base, as if I were an effigy carved from ice and she had come running at me with a hammer and delivered me a ringing blow. I brooded ceaselessly on that brief contact in a state of gloomy joyfulness and misgiving, turning the memory of it this way and that, scrutinising it from every possible angle. At times I got myself into such a state of finicking speculation that I doubted it had happened at all. It was so long since I had kissed a woman I hardly knew how it should feel, and anyway I was always old-fashioned in these matters. Nowadays young people (I still thought her much younger than she was) seemed to kiss each other at the drop of a hat. Everywhere I looked they were at it, in the street, in motor cars, on bicycles, even. And it was not the demure, stiff-backed grappling of my day, but the real thing, open-mouthed, groin-grinding, noisy. I know. I watched them. (It is a wonder I wasn't arrested.) And of course I could not believe it had meant as much to her as it had to me; the tongue of flame that had licked my middle-aged flesh and made it sizzle would hardly register, surely, on her hot young hide. Probably she was being kissed all the time and thought nothing of it. Yes, I would tell myself sternly, it was nothing at all to her, she hardly noticed it, and I would give myself a vigorous shake, like a dog out of water, and go on about my business, only to fall again immediately, with redoubled frenzy, into tormented, mad-eyed, hopeless speculation. Ice, did I say I was like shattered ice? – a mud pool, more like, hot and heaving, and the thought of her a bubble rising and steadily swelling and then breaking the surface and bursting with an awful plop while down in the depths another bleb of turbid speculation was already forming itself.

I should say that A. herself was almost incidental to these swoony ruminations, which at their most concentrated became entirely self-sustaining. After all, what did I know of her? This was only the second time I had seen her, not counting the jigsaw-puzzle glimpse through the crumbling plaster of the false wall that first day I entered the house, and even after I had kissed her I could not summon up her face in my memory except in a general way. I know what I am saying here, I know how thoroughly I am betraying myself in all my horrible self-obsession. But that is how it was, at the start: as if in an empty house, at darkest midnight, I had stopped shocked before a gleaming apparition only to discover it was my own reflection springing up out of a shadowy, life-sized mirror. It was to be a long time before the silvering on the back of that looking-glass began to wear away and I could look through it and see her, or that version of her that was all she permitted me to see.

I felt such a fool. I seemed to myself an absurd figure,

something like a village idiot, sad and laughable and yet in a way pathetically endearing. My ribs ached from the effort of holding in check a constantly incipient cheer. The city opened like a rose under the steady radiance of my newfound euphoria. I found myself talking to people in the streets, complete strangers; I might have done anything, ordered drinks on the house in The Boatman or clapped Quasimodo on his hump and dragged him off to the St Gabriel to share a bottle of bubbly with me. And she was everywhere, of course, or phantom images of her, at least: a fleeting face in the crowd, a figure disappearing around a corner, or lone and motionless on the top deck of a bus and being borne away from me down the grey wastes of a broad, windy, leaf-strewn avenue. My powers of misrecognition were prodigious. I remember one occasion in particular, when in the street I ran up panting and clapped a hand on a black-clad shoulder I was certain was hers, only to find myself a moment later confusedly apologising to a short, fierce gentleman of military aspect with a waxed moustache. What strikes me now is how little of thought there was in all this. By thought I don't mean deep and sober consideration, a weighing of matters upon the balance, that kind of thing, but just ordinary, everyday thinking, the half-conscious drone of instruction and admonition that seems an echo of the voice of a parent long ago teaching me to stand, to walk, to talk. My mind now had become a quaking marsh where if I tried to wade out over what seemed the shallowest margins I would promptly sink up to my crotch. And this, mark you, all this on the strength of a single and wholly ambiguous kiss. Oh, yes, what a fool!

And yet you, she – both of you! – must have been in something at least of the same elated, twittery state of adolescent expectation and surmise that I was. Surely you were. Don't say it was all false, or even if it was, say it was only so at the start and became real later. Please, do not deprive me of my delusions, they are all I have.

Three days passed. I think of them as somehow glazed, the things and events in them fixed, unreal, glossily distinct, and me set down in their midst, stiff-gestured and madly, unstoppably smiling, a manikin in a shop-window display. (Ah, this plethora of metaphors! I am like everything except myself.) I was waiting for A. There was no sense of hurry, everything was proceeding at the heart's excited but steady pace under a mysterious and ineluctable influence working on us in secret, a kind of aerial geometry that would bend us inevitably toward each other like lines of light in space. I basked in this time out of time as in one of those long Saturday mornings of childhood. She would come. We would be there together. Everything would happen.

What came instead, however, was Aunt Corky.

In fact, now that I think of it, it was a Saturday morning when I got the call. It was early and I was bleared after a fitful night and at first I could not understand what was being said. 'This is Mrs Haddon at the home,' a stranger's shrill voice kept repeating, with a rising inflection of annoyance. All I could do was stand on the cold lino of the hall and nod dumbly into the receiver, as if it were the phone itself that was hectoring me. The letter box in the front door behind me opened with a clack and spat a sheaf of bills on to the mat; Hermes was having a busy morning. '*Hello hello, can you hear me!*' the voice cried. '*Your auntie has taken a turn!*' In the background I could hear a swooping, ululating noise, and the image came to me of Aunt Corky twirling like a dervish in that black-and-white tiled hallway at The Cypresses, her cerements flying. 'She's asking for you,' Mrs Haddon said stridently. 'She says she'll only talk to you.' The keening noise intensified and drowned her words; she seemed to be saying something about the sun. 'Sharon,' she shrieked, '*Sharon*, turn off that bloody thing!' and the noise stopped abruptly. 'I'll come,' I said, sounding to myself like a sulky child who has been summoned from play. 'Well, I think you had better,' Mrs Haddon said, in a bridling, head-tossing tone, as if to let me know she had the right to expect considerably more from me than mere acquiescence.

She was a darting, nervy woman, oddly formed: thick and rounded in the middle but with thin arms and unexpectedly shapely legs that suggested tennis parties and pleated skirts and pink gins on the lawn. Her face was sharp and pale with a curiously moist sheen, and her washed-blue eyes were prominent and faintly fishy, which gave her something of the goggling look of one of Fragonard's pop-eyed, milky-skinned ladies. While she talked she looked away fixedly and kept chafing her wrist with a finger and thumb as if she were giving herself a chinese burn. She met me in the glassed-in porch with an air of angry reproach, and although I had come with all speed I found myself mumbling apologetically about traffic and the infrequency of the hill bus. 'She's a terror,' she said, cutting me off. 'We don't know what to do with her. And of course when she starts she gets the rest of them going. They're like children, the lot of them.' All this was delivered in a distracted mutter with her face firmly averted and her sharp white nose aquiver. She was so pale and unpronounced that she seemed to lack a dimension, and I had the impression that if she turned to me head-on she would contract into a vertical line, like a cardboard cut-out. She led me into the hall, where I spotted her other half, the ghostly Mr Haddon, heavy-jowled, stooped and circum-spect, loitering in the shadows by a potted palm; he pretended not to see me and was in turn ignored by his wife. 'You are the son,' she said to me; it sounded more like an accusation than a question. When I denied it she tightened her lips, in deprecation, it seemed, not only of me but of my entire irresponsible and unsupportive family. 'Well,' she said with a sniff, 'she has been talking non-stop about him.'

That Aunt Corky had a son was news to me. As far as I was aware she was without issue, and the image of her dandling on her knee a small, male reproduction of herself smacked, I am afraid, of the comic. That day, however, what with the dizzy-making earliness of the hour and my mood of adolescent exaltation (that kiss still!), the notion seemed wonderfully piquant and right, somehow, and with a sort of bleary brightness I said, 'Yes, well well, her son, I see!' all the while grinning and nodding and making a sort of humming noise under my breath. Mrs Haddon, walking ahead of me up the stairs, threw back a dark and disapproving glance that landed in the region of my knees. As we reached Aunt Corky's room the door opened and an untidy young man slipped out; seeing us he hesitated and looked about him wildly, ready it seemed to take to his heels. This was Doctor Mutter – I never did catch his name. He need not detain us here, we shall be meeting him again. He reminded me vaguely of a character out of *Alice in Wonderland*, the Rabbit, perhaps, or the Mad Hatter. Mrs Haddon gave him a hard glare of dismissal and with an awkward nod he sidled off, evidently much relieved.

Aunt Corky was lying so still and flat on her big bed that at first I thought she was under restraint. She seemed perfectly calm, with her eyes closed, breathing lightly. Red-headed Sharon, today looking about twelve years old, sat beside the bed on a metal chair with her raw knees splayed, reading a comic-book (I caught a glimpse of the open page: slack blood-dark mouth and a big tear and a voice-bubble in the shape of a fat apostrophe: *Oh Darren . . !* – such are the things gimlet-eyed Mnemosyne records). As I approached on tiptoe Sharon looked up at me and grinned and winked, and I noticed with a sharp tender shock my aunt's hand like a big bundle of withered twigs resting in the girl's extended, fat little paw. I must have looked like the smiling undertaker himself, with my pouched and shadowed eyes and deathbed leer and my mackintosh folded on my arm like a shroud. I leaned over the bed and at once, as on my first visit, Aunt Corky's elasticated eyelids snapped open and she sat up in her white habit like the Bride of Frankenstein (come to think of it, she did bear a passing resemblance to Elsa Lanchester) and cried, 'Oh, I've seen him, I've seen him!' and clutched at me wildly with one hand while the other twitched agitatedly in Sharon's clasp. It was a scene for one of the Victorian sentimentalists: *The Dream*, by Sir Somebody Somebody-Somebody: the stark old woman leaning forward in distress in her disordered bed and supported on one side by the smiling child-nurse, on the other by the ageing and faintly disreputable nephew, whose shabby coat and less than perfect linen bespeak an interest in the whereabouts of the will, while in the background hovers whey-faced Mistress Death. 'She's seeing things,' Sharon confided to me cheerfully, and gently rattled Aunt Corky's hand and shouted, 'Aren't you, love?' My aunt ignored her and dug her dry old fingers into my arm. 'He came to me,' she whispered in a stricken voice, 'he came to me and stood just there where you are standing now and looked at me. Oh, how he looked at me, with those eyes, his father's eyes!' There was a pause then, and something, a sort of shimmer, passed through the room, as if a light-reflecting surface somewhere had been tilted inwards suddenly. 'You were only dreaming,' Mrs Haddon shouted, and then, more loudly still, '*I say, you were only dreaming, that's all!*' Aunt Corky gave her the merest glance and looked at me again and shrugged. 'Of course it was a dream,' she said with airy disdain, and letting go of my hand she reached for her cigarettes on the bedside locker and brazenly lit up, releasing into the air in Mrs Haddon's direction a big, bold balloon of rolling smoke.

Yes, yes, there had been a child, so she insisted, a little boy. The story was confused, the details vague. He did not seem even to have had a name, this *Wunderkind*. She had lost

93

him, she said. I took this to be a euphemism for another violent though unspecified removal such as had befallen her husband, but no, she meant it literally. One day, one terrible day in the midst of the exigencies of war, she had just lost him, his hand had slipped from hers and he was gone. 'Such things happened, then,' she said. 'Such things happened.' We were silent for a long moment, listening to the raucous cries of gulls and the soft, gastric gurgling of water in the radiator under the window. Sharon and Mrs Haddon had been dismissed so that Aunt Corky might make her confession in confidence. She sat before me wreathed in cigarette smoke with her face turned aside and the light of morning playing on her gilded wig, while I wrestled with the tricky question of how much, if anything, it might be possible to believe of this latest instalment in the convoluted tale of tragedy and loss that she claimed was her life. Would she, even she, invent such a tale? But then I thought, why not? I was in a tolerant mood; I felt positively parental. This was one of the effects that infatuation (for now, I shall put it no more strongly than that) was having on me, this feeling of being fully grown-up at last, an adult called in to deal with a world of children. Aunt Corky might have been a daughter whose cries in the night had summoned me to her bedside, so softly solicitous was my manner. I squeezed her hand, I smiled at her soothingly and nodded, letting my eyelids gravely fall and pursing up my lips, in a travesty of sympathy, full of self-regard. Yes, self-regard, for as usual it was I who was the real object of all this attentiveness, the new-made, sticky-winged I who had stepped forth from the cocoon that A.'s kiss had cracked. Half-heeded, meanwhile, poor Aunt Corky was pouring out the story of her little lost boy. I could see him, all alone on a cratered road under a hare's-pelt sky in his ragged coat and too-big peaked cap, clutching a cardboard suitcase in his frightened hand. Those eyes, looking at me out of Europe. 'The dead do not forgive,'

94

Aunt Corky said, shaking her head sadly and sighing. And then she smiled at me sweetly. 'But you know that, of course,' she said.

Mrs Haddon was waiting for me outside the door, her white hands clasped under her bosom. I wondered if she had been listening at the keyhole. With her prominent, shiny eyes fixed on my adam's apple she said in a flat voice, 'She's very bad.' I did not know in what sense she was using the word and could not think how to frame the question, and so I just nodded vaguely and put on a troubled expression. In fact, in all those weeks with Aunt Corky I never did find out exactly what it was that ailed her. I think she was just dying of herself, if I can put it that way. I walked with Mrs Haddon in solemn silence down the stairs. I could feel her wrestling with something and at last she brought it out, though in a roundabout fashion. 'Have you a family?' she said. I was being asked that question with remarkable frequency these days. I shook my head vigorously, half realising, I suppose, what was coming. 'Your auntie needs a home,' she said, in the restrained tones of a great hostess whose patience is being sorely tried by a no longer welcome but distressingly tenacious house-guest. 'You wouldn't want her to die here.' This was a shock in more ways than one. It was the first time I had heard it said in so many words that the old girl was dying; if it was true, and these were her last days, I could not decide what was more significant for me, that it increased the burden of my responsibility or promised a quick release – for me, I mean. I said nothing. I had begun seriously to take fright. What had seemed a harmless indulgence on my part had sprouted tendrils that were already wrapped around my ankles. I wanted to say that I could think of no more fitting place to die than this, but instead I muttered that I was living alone, that I had very little space and few facilities for an invalid, and that really I could not think of, I could not manage to, it would be impossible for . . . I'm sure I was blushing, my face felt as if it were on fire and there was a horrible thickening in my throat.

Amazing how the world keeps on offering new opportunities for betrayal. I had thought I was finished with everything: desire and duty, compassion, the needs of others – in a word, life – yet here I was, mooning after a girl and lumbered with a dying relative, up to my oxters again in the whole bloody shenanigans. No wonder I was in a funk. Slope-shouldered in his funereal dark suit Mr Haddon was waiting for us at the foot of the stairs with a carefully detached look in his eye. Beside me his wife called out to him grimly, 'I was just saying to Mr Morrow that his auntie is in need of a home.' He glanced at me with what seemed a melancholy hint of fellow-feeling; we were both afraid of this woman with her pale fish-eyes and candle-grease skin and air of screwed-down hysteria. I trotted out for him the same set of excuses I had given her, and plunged for the door, talking over my shoulder and fighting my arms into my mackintosh as if it were a pair of recalcitrantly flaccid wings I was trying to put on.

Outside it was a silver day. My heart lifted, as it always did when I made good my escape from that place, but beneath that momentary exaltation I was still upset. There were things I did not want to think about. Aunt Corky's story had stirred the murky waters of remembrance. That's how it is, you tie a rock to things and sink them in the depths and then the first autumn storm breaks and they come bobbing up again with bloated limbs and filmed-over eyes that stare straight through you into eternity. But I did not blame her. Why should she not people her world with dramatic figments, if they brought her comfort, or amused her, or helped to pass the time? I am done with blaming people for their weaknesses. I am done with blaming anyone for anything. Except myself, that is. No, no end to that.

Home, after that unsettling venture into the haunted landscapes of Aunt Corky's past, was suddenly a tricky proposition, so when I got off the bus I found myself turning,
inevitably, in the direction of Rue Street. A Saturday quiet
reigned in the quarter. Outside the house, on the opposite
pavement, a man was loitering. He had a large, smooth,
globular head, and was dressed in a buttoned-up tweed jacket
and too-tight trousers and very shiny black brogues; he
reminded me of those glossy wooden peg-shaped toy soldiers I used to be given to play with as a child. As I
approached he shot me a peculiar, underhand sort of smile,
as if he knew me, and turned away. I had a key by now and
could let myself into the house. I shut the front door behind
me and stood for a moment in the lofty silence of the hall.
Immediately, as if I had entered a decompression chamber
of the heart, the thought of A. came bubbling along my
veins and everything else fell away.

But what does it mean, what does it signify, to say: the
thought of A.? Was it her I was thinking of, or the idea of
her? That is another of the questions that torment me now.
For, even when she was still here, still with me, if I summoned her to mind it was not she who came but only the
vague, soft sense of her, a sort of vaporous cloud through
which her presence gleamed like the sun unseen gleaming
through a mist at morning. Only once or twice, towards
the end, when she was in my arms, did I seem to penetrate
that cloud of unknowing and find what I told myself must
surely be the real she. I know, I know the objections, I have
read the treatises: there is no real she, only a set of signs, a
series of appearances, a grid of relations between swarming
particles; yet I insist on it: she was there at those times, it was
she who clutched me to her and cried out, not a flickering
simulacrum foisted on me by the stop-frame technique of a
duplicitous reality. I had her. I don't care about the deceit
and the cruel tricks that were played on me, I don't care

about any of that. I had her, that is the thing. And already I am forgetting her. Oh yes, that is another torment. Every day she decays a little more in my memory as the ever-returning tides wash away steadily at her image. I cannot even remember exactly what colour her eyes were, are. This is part of the price I must pay: in order to have had her I must lose her. Something amiss with the tenses there, I think. What would I do to divert myself if I had not language to play with?

I felt her presence in the house before I heard her. I climbed the stairs silently, rising in spirals like a suppliant soul making its slow ascent to Heaven. The secret door stood open and I could see her moving about in the room. I lingered in the corridor, watching her. It occurs to me that this moment of covert surveillance was the first, unacknowledged token of what was to come; do I imagine it or did I feel an anticipatory flick of pleasure's flame, as I skulked there, bloodshot and breathless, wrapped in my dirty old mac? We were well matched, the watcher and the watched. Perhaps she in turn knew that I was there, perhaps that was what gave her the idea of the spyhole (which will open its amazed eye presently). She was busy at something, walking in and out of my field of vision, her high heels clicking. Quicksilver noon in the window behind her and the first murmurs of rain on the glass. What shall I dress my dolly in today? Black, as usual, a black silk blouse and those stretched trousers that I disliked – in my day they were called ski-pants – that hooked under her heels and made her legs look rubbery and kneeless, tapering sharply from hip to ankle. I shall have to look into this matter of clothes, learn the styles and so on, the names, remember not to call a skirt a dress, that sort of thing. (And what exactly, by the way, is a frock?) That will be another diversion, a harmless one. In a drapery store the other day I saw a quietly distraught, haggard young man at the knickers counter in earnest consultation with a surprisingly tolerant female shop assistant. Certainly times have changed – in the old days that chap would have got himself a cuff on the ear or even have been put into the hands of the police. A. was indulgent in this regard. Once when we were lying together and I got up the courage to ask her shamefacedly not to take off a last, flimsy covering, and mumbled an apology, she laughed her throatiest laugh and said she had always wanted to have a fetishist for a lover. Happy memories. Meanwhile I am loitering in the corridor as the soft rain of September comes on and A., bless her dear and on occasion shockingly practical heart, is making up a bed for me (for us, in the fullness of time) on the old, lumpy, uncomplaining and ever accommodating chaise-longue that thoughtful fate or the exigencies of art had placed at our disposal in that white room.

At length my knees began to tremble from the strain of keeping still and I coughed with theatrical loudness and sidled into the room, trying to look abstracted, as if I had not noticed her. If she was surprised to see me she did not show it, just gave me a glance and put a pillow into my arms and said, 'Hold that.' She was being quite the little home-maker, all bustle and frown. She wanted to know if I thought the couch was all right where it was, opposite the window. 'And I must get curtains,' she said, measuring the casement with a slitted eye. Oh yes, curtains, by all means, and a rocking chair and a cat, and slippers and pipe for me, and presently a cradle in the corner, too, why not? I stood with the pillow clasped to my chest and a simpleton's smile on my face, trying to decide which was more absurd, what she was doing, or me behaving as if it were the most natural thing in the world to come upon her in the empty house on a Saturday lunchtime turning this grim little room into a love-nest. That was the last moment when I might have come to my senses, the final, clear-eyed recognition that what was happening was ridiculous, impossible, fraught with unspeakable perils. I would only have to tell her who and what I really was, I thought, and she would back out the door shaking her head with eyes like saucers and her mouth working in silent horror and disbelief. But I said nothing, only stood smiling and nodding like a brand-new hubby drunk on love, and when she briskly plucked the pillow from my embrace and bore it like a plump white baby to the bed I let my hands fall helplessly to my sides and realised that I was lost. I remember wondering, with stupendous irrelevance, if she dyed her hair, it was so glossy and black against the white of her brow, her virginal neck. Have I mentioned her paleness? There was nothing enervated or sickly about it. She was luminous, she shone within the taut, transparent sheathing of her skin. At times, at the start, when I held her naked in my arms I fancied it was a false covering that I touched, a sort of marvellously fine and supple carapace within which another, unreachable she lay in hiding. Did I really, ever, manage to break through that gauzy membrane?— Oh for Christ's sake, stop! It's always the same question, I am sick of it! And anyway I know the answer, so why keep asking? The rain on the window whispered to itself, agog to know what we would do next. The smell of fresh linen made me think, incongruously, of childhood. A. held the pillow tucked under her temporarily doubled chin and was shrugging it into its case. I stepped towards her as if wading through oil, walking my fingers along the edge of the work-table like a squad of quaking soldiers. She threw the pillow on to the bed and turned her head sideways and watched me approach, with a faint, calculating smile, as if she were counting the paces diminishing between us, her eyes narrowed. For a moment I was afraid she was going to laugh. I seemed to have at least three arms, all of them superfluous. I began to say something but she put a finger quickly to my lips and shook her head once. I took her hand in both of mine and remembered a bird once that I had caught and held like this; it must have been sick; it must have been dying. 'You are cold,' I said to her. This is not the theatre, these are the banalities that spring to the most eloquent lover's lips on such occasions. 'Oh no,' she answered, 'oh no, I'm not.'

Of all our sweet occasions of sin, I think this one, preliminary and practically blameless, is the one I recollect most vividly, with the sharpest and acutest pangs of pain. I remember that unwavering small smile with which she held me as slowly she undid the buttons of her blouse. She was sitting on the edge of the couch now, with me standing over her, still in my raincoat, mouth agape, I suppose, and breathing laboriously, like a staggered old bull. I remember the dips of shadow in the hollows of her shoulders, and her shoulders themselves, shapely and high, the right one stamped with a curved patch of eggshell sheen from the window, and her odd little knobbled breasts with their swollen, bruise-coloured aureoles, that always made her look, God forgive me, as if she were holding her upraised clenched fists pressed against her chest. The waistband of her ski-pants was hidden under a fold of pale flesh the line of which I wanted to trace with my tongue. She had kicked off her shoes and unhooked the heel-straps of her pants, and the elasticated material clung to her legs now like deflated balloon skins. Her miniature. feet were of a reddish hue, and curiously splayed at the toes, betokening a barefoot childhood spent in some gaudy, aquatic region of mud and magnolia and bright, shrieking birds. Oh, my Manon, where are you? Where are you.

From below came a knock at the front door. (Perhaps this *is* the theatre, after all.) What a change it brought. We stared at each other, two guilty children caught doing naughty things, and I noticed the gooseflesh on her arms and her puckered nipples and the mauve strap-marks scored into her shoulders. Came another knock, not loud, and oddly diffident, though all the more imperative for that. My heart joggled, rearing on its tethers. 'Don't answer it,' A. whispered. She seemed more thoughtful than alarmed, frowning towards the window and gnawing on a thumbnail; this noise off had not been in the stage directions as she knew them. Absently she began to put her clothes back on. Despite my fright I admired with a sort of tumid wonderment the deft, clambering shrug with which she fitted her joggling breasts into their skimpy lace sling and then dived stiff-armed into her blouse, and as I turned and blundered from the room, rabbit-eyed and wiping the back of a hand across my dried-up mouth, I was in such a swollen state I thought I might have to negotiate the stairs on all fours. All fives.

The front door as I approached it across the hall had a pent-up, gloating aspect, as if it were just dying to fly open and unleash on me a shouting throng of accusers. What prophetic intuition was it that provoked in me such dread? When I opened the door (how eagerly it swung on its snickering hinges!) my first reaction was an inward whinny of relief, though who or what it was I had expected I don't know. On the step, tilted at an apologetic angle and with raindrops glistening on his already shiny brow, was the fellow with the big smooth head I had seen earlier loitering on the pavement opposite – remember him? His hand was lifted to knock a third time; hastily he let it fall and smiled beatifically and cleared his throat and said:

'Ah, Mr M. – the very man.'

4. Syrinx Delivered 1645
Job van Hellin (1598-1647)

Oil on canvas, 23⅝ x 31½ in. (60 x 80 cm.)

This painter, as is well known, served in the busy studio of Peter Paul Rubens for some ten years before the Flemish master's death in 1640; indeed, it is possible that sections, some of them large-scale, in Rubens's greatest paintings are in fact the work of van Hellin, who was one of the finest technicians in the Flanders of his day and seems to have enjoyed the complete trust of his teacher and mentor. In his letters van Hellin speaks of his deep respect for the older painter, and certainly in the pictures of his final years the influence of Rubens is clearly apparent, particularly in the vigorous brushwork and the painterly richness of their execution. However, as *Syrinx Delivered* attests, there is in van Hellin a coolness of approach – a coldness, some critics would say – which sets him apart from the majority of Rubens's pupils and followers. Here, a remoteness and classical stillness are reminiscent more of Poussin or Claude Lorrain than of the fleshly immediacy characteristic of the school of the great Flemish master. The statuesque repose – so at variance with the violent subject – that is achieved in this picture, along with the pastoral simplicity of the landscape with its wandering flocks and feathery, evanescent distances, are the marks of a more temperate, less Italianate style than that of his teacher; van Hellin was a Catholic in Catholic Flanders, yet in his mature work we detect what, with licence, we may call a Protestant restraint that seems to indicate the painter's consciousness of the political and religious tensions of the time. The landscape depicted here is not the Arcady of rock and olive tree and harsh, noonday light, but a peaceable northern plain untouched by the riotous passions of gods and heroes yet over which there hangs an atmosphere of indefinable unease. Mount Lycaeus shimmers in a blue miasmic mist, and the brown, somehow bulging surface of the river Ladon has a menacing sheen. Placed in the middle distance, the figures of god and nymph, caught in their little drama of desire and loss, seem almost incidental to the composition, which could easily stand without them as a self-contained landscape. The temple buildings on the right, tall and pale and set amongst dense greenery which in places is almost black, lend an air of solemn calm to the scene. They are the portals to that other world where the invisible Olympians sit in silent contemplation of the mortal sphere that fascinates and baffles them. Here, in this green and golden world, on this tawny afternoon, their black sheep Pan disports himself; with what skill the artist has depicted this figure, making it at once numinous, comic and terrifying. The god seems to run and dance at the same time, in mad pursuit of the nymph already lost to him amongst the leaning reeds. This Syrinx, who, with her white robe gathered above her knee, might be taken for Diana the huntress, is expressive both of great sorrow and a kind of languorous yearning for release from the human sphere that has become wearisome to her; she seems to long for that transfiguration into the world of nature that is imminent. The wind that blows against her, bending the reeds in the river's shallows and drawing out her long yellow hair, is indeed the wind of change. (What a pity the painter has seen fit to set so delicate a figure amidst these swarming and frankly phallic bulrushes.) She is the pivot of the picture, the fulcrum between two states of being, the representation of life-in-death and death-in-life, of what changes and yet endures; the witness that she offers is the possibility of transcendence, both of the self and of the world, though world and self remain the same. She is the perfect illustration of Adorno's dictum that 'In their relation to empirical reality works of art recall the theologumenon that in a state of redemption everything will be just as it is and yet wholly different.' I haven't even a reed pipe to play on in commemoration of you.

Always it comes back. I think of it as another story altogether but it is not. I delude myself that I have sloughed it all off and that I can walk on naked and unashamed into a new name, a new life, light and gladsome as a transmigrating soul, but no, it comes back dragging its boneless limbs through the muck and rears up at me grotesquely in the unlikeliest of shapes. Such as this fellow, for instance, with his extruded head balanced perilously on top of that cylindrical trunk – all three buttons of his tweed jacket were fastened – like a stone ball set on the pillar of a gate. I have never come across another such almost perfectly spherical head. The effect was emphasised by the oiled black hair parted just above his left ear and fanned out sideways across the dome of his bald skull like a tight-fitting, patent-leather cap. His eyes, also black, were very small and set very close together and slightly out of alignment, the left one higher than the right, which gave to his expression a quizzical cast I found both comic and disturbing. His smile, which he did with lips pressed shut and turned up at right angles at the corners, seemed less a mark of pleasure than discomfort, as if he were wincing at a twinge of indigestion or the pinching of a too-tight shoe. I had the impression of exceptional, fanatic cleanliness: he shone; he fairly glowed. I pictured him of a morning at a cracked sink in vest and drawers, vehemently ascrub, buffing himself to this high sheen. I knew straight away what, if not who, he was, and I felt a sort of soundless shock, and a shiver ran through me, as if I had been cloven clean in two from poll to fork by a blade of unimaginable fineness. Fright always has a flash of pleasure in it, for me.

He told me his name was Hackett. 'Do you not remember me?' he said, seeming genuinely crestfallen.

'Of course I do,' I said, lying.

Now, it is a curious thing, but really, I did not know him at all. My recollections of that time of crisis and disaster in my life – what is it, twelve, thirteen years ago? – have become blurred in certain aspects. No doubt memory, selective and indulgent record-keeper that it is, has seen fit to suppress this or that detail of my case, but I do not see how it could have erased entirely from the admittedly crowded picture of those fraught weeks a figure so memorable as Detective-Inspector Ambrose Hackett. Yet one of us was misremembering and it did not seem to be him. We stood in uncomfortable silence for a moment and he inserted a finger under his shirt-collar behind the fat knot of his tie and turned his head to the left with a quick little painful jerk, one of the many tics he had and which if I had already encountered them I would surely not have forgotten. Some more moments passed, marked by heartbeats. Among the few things I have learned over the years is that there is no occasion, no matter how weighty or terrible the circumstances, that is not susceptible to a merely social awkwardness. In my time I have known lawyers to go mute with embarrassment, judges to avoid my eye, jailers to blush. Surely it says something for our species, this sudden, helpless floundering when the universal code of manners fails us; surely the phenomenon bespeaks the soul's essential authenticity? Here we were, the detective and myself, caught in an impossible situation, me proprietorial at the door of someone else's uninhabited and unfurnished house, with a half-naked young woman upstairs eager for my imminent return, and him coatless on the step getting rained on and waiting with a wistful demeanour to be asked in.

I said that I had been doing some work; it was all I could think of that would be vague and businesslike at once. It sounded preposterous. My voice was abnormally loud and unconvincing, as if I were speaking for the benefit of some concealed eavesdropper. Hackett nodded in a thoughtful way. 'Yes,' he said, 'that was what I wanted to have a word about.'

This was a surprise. I had thought he was just another of the functionaries the authorities like to send periodically to remind me that I am not a free man (*life means life*: how often has that deceptively tautological-sounding caution rung in my ears).

I invited him to step into the hall and wait while I fetched my coat.

A. was gone from the room. I stood a moment gazing about the place in helpless distress, panting, then clattered down the stairs again, in a panic that Hackett would have started nosing about the place, though I'm sure I don't know what I feared he might uncover; his kind can turn the most trivial of things into a clue to a crime you were not even aware of having committed. I need not have worried, though; he was the soul of punctiliousness. I found him standing to attention in the hall with his hands clasped behind him, blamelessly smiling, like a big gawky schoolboy waiting at the side of the stage on prize-day.

We walked in the direction of the river. Hackett turned up the collar of his jacket against the drizzle. 'Forgot my mac,' he said ruefully; he had a way of injecting into everything he said a note of humorous apology.

I was in a strange state, unable fully to acknowledge the alarming potentials of this encounter. On the contrary, still swollen and hazy with the thought of A., I seemed to bounce along, like a dirigible come loose from its moorings and softly, hugely adrift, puffed up on heedless bliss. And there was something else, another access of almost-pleasure, which it took me a while to identify: it was relief. To harbour a secret is to have power, says the philosopher, but it is a burden, too. I had not realised, or had forgotten, that the effort of pretending to be someone other than I was was a great, an intolerable weight, one that I was glad to be allowed to put down, if only for a brief while, and by one who claimed to have been amongst those who had loaded it on to my back in the first place. When I told him I had changed my name he smiled indulgently and nodded. 'Oh, I know,' he said. 'But I don't mind that. Leopards and spots, Mr M., leopards and spots.'

The rain was intensifying, big drops were dotted like pearls on his glossy crown.

I suggested we might go for a drink, or was he on duty? He took this for a joke and laughed appreciatively, crinkling up his eyes. 'Still a card, I see,' he said.

His motor car, a dented red Facade with a nodding plastic dog in the back window, was parked up a narrow street behind the cathedral close. Hackett opened the door for me and we got in. Inside it smelled of pine air-freshener, synthetic leather, sweat; I have travelled many times in the back seats of cars like this, pinned between big, tense, heavy-breathing men in blazers and blue shirts. At once the sheep-stink of our wetted clothes overpowered the tang of pine and the windows began to fog up.

'Terrible about that murder,' Hackett said. 'Stabbed her through the eye and cut her diddies off. Like some sort of a ceremony. He'll do it again, I'd say. Wouldn't you?'

'Wouldn't I what?' I said.

'Say he'll do it again. They always do.'

'Not always.'

'Ah.'

After that brief skirmish something that had been standing rigidly between us sat down and folded its arms. I have nothing against the police, you know. I have always found them polite and attentive, with a couple of notable exceptions. One of the first things that struck me about them, at the time when I had to deal with them in the plural, so to speak, was their remarkable curiosity. They were like schoolgirls crowding round one of their number who has finally managed to lose her virginity. Details, they wanted all the dirty details. How they sweated, leaning over me and softly snorting, their nostrils flared, as I recklessly embroidered my squalid little tale for their delectation. *But hold on there*, they would say, laying a blunt paw softly but urgently on my arm, *the last time round you told it different*, and I would have to revise practically the entire plot in order to accommodate whatever new twist it was that my imagination, working in overdrive, had just dreamed up. And always at the end of the session there was that rustling and creaking as they sat back on their plastic chairs with a wistful, faraway look in their bruised and pouchy eyes; and then that release of breath, a soft, drawn-out *ahh* with a grace-note in it of what I can only think was envy. It is true, what has been said, that we get to know a man most intimately when he represents a threat to us. I believe I knew my interrogators better than their wives did. All the more strange, then, that I could not place Hackett. 'I was there the first time they brought you in,' he said. 'Do you not remember?' No, I did not remember, and to this day I do not know whether he was telling the truth or making it up for some shady and convoluted purpose of his own. I took him for a fool at first; it is one of my failings, that I judge people by appearance. He had, as I would discover, a way of playing with things that made me think of a big, slow, simple-looking cat toying with a captured mouse. He would approach a subject and then take a soft jump back and turn and pretend to fix his attention elsewhere, though one restraining paw remained always extended, with its claws out.

'Them paintings,' he said dreamily, frowning out at the rain. 'What do you think of them?'

The very tip of a thin blade of panic pricked my inflated consciousness and the last of the gas hissed out of the balloon of my euphoria and I came to earth with a bump.

'What paintings?' I said, too quickly, I'm sure, my voice quivering.

He laughed softly and shook his head and did not look at me. For a moment he said nothing, letting the silence tighten nicely.

'Tell me this,' he said, 'did you recognise them, at all?'

At that he turned his head and gave me a straight look. At least, it was as near to straight as he could manage, for his nose was pushed somewhat aside (early days on the beat, perhaps, scuffle outside a pub, a punch from nowhere, stars and blood), and that, along with his mismatched, pinhead eyes, made me think of those moon-headed stick figures with combined full-face and profile that Picasso in old age drew on the walls of that château of his at Cap d'Antibes or wherever it was. I almost laughed for fright.

'Recognise?' I said shrilly. 'What do you mean, recognise?'

His face took on a distant, unfocused expression, like that of a very old tortoise, and he sat for a long moment in silence tapping the rhythm of a tune with his fingertips on the steering-wheel. The light inside the fogged-up car was grainy and dense, as if the sky had descended on us. The rain ticked on the roof.

'They say,' Hackett said at last, pensively, 'that lightning never strikes the same place twice. But it does. And it has.' He chuckled. 'You were the first flash, so to speak.' I waited, baffled. Inside the silence small, tinny things seemed to tinkle. He glanced at me and grinned slyly and the tip of a purplish tongue appeared between his teeth. 'You wouldn't have heard,' he said softly. 'The insurance crowd asked us to keep it quiet for a while.' He paused, still grinning; he seemed to be enjoying himself hugely, in his quiet way. 'Whitewater House was robbed again,' he said.

I turned away from him as if I had been slapped. Breathe slowly. With my sleeve I wiped the window beside me. Three laughing girls with linked arms passed by in the rain. Above the street there was a tightening in the air and the great bell of the cathedral produced a single, reverberant dark stroke. I lowered my eyes in search of shadows and rest. The toes of Hackett's shoes gleamed like chestnuts. Twill; I had not seen a pair of twill trousers in thirty years. I went to school with the likes of Hackett, farmers' sons bent on bettering themselves, tough, shrewd, unloquacious fellows with an affecting streak of tentativeness, not my type at all. I treated them with indifference and scorn, but in secret I was made uneasy by them, daunted by their sense of themselves, the air of dogged authenticity they gave off. Real people: I am never at ease in the presence of real people.

'Half a dozen or more this time,' Hackett said, 'frames and all. They backed a van up to the side of the house and handed them out through the window. Knew what they were after, too.' He pondered the matter briefly and then glanced at me sideways and did his circus clown's smile. 'Must have had the help of an expert.' I was thinking of the Three Graces laughing in the rain. 'We know who they were, of course,' he said, thoughtful once more. 'They as good as left their calling card. It's a question now of . . . evidence.' He paused again, then chuckled. 'Oh, and you'll be interested in this,' he said. 'One of them gave the security guard a belt of a hammer and damn near killed him.'

A country road and a big old car weaving from side to

side and veering to a halt in the ditch. The scene is in black and white, scratched and jerky, as in an old newsreel. All is still for a moment, then the car rocks suddenly, violently, on its springs and a voice cries out in agony and anguish. Welcome to my nightmares. I am always outside the car, never in it. Is that not strange? Hackett was watching me with quiet interest. I experienced then a flash of that old malaise that seizes on me now and then in moments of stress and extremity, bringing with it a dizzying sense of dislocation, of being torn in two; for a second I was someone else, passing by and glancing in through the window of my self and recognising nothing in this other's commonplace and yet impenetrably mysterious surroundings.

'Has he a wife?' Hackett said. I looked at him blankly. 'Morden,' he said gently and tapped me once smartly on the knee with his knuckle.

The rain stopped with a sort of swish.

'I don't know,' I said. It was the truth.

Suddenly then, and inexplicably, I experienced a sort of mild, mournful elation. Very strange. Hackett brightened too. In rapid succession he passed a finger under his shirt-collar, grinned, and plucked convulsively at the knees of his trousers. Three tics in a row: somehow I had hit the jackpot.

We parted then, as if we had settled something between us and for the moment there was nothing left to say. 'Toodle-oo now, Mr M.,' Hackett said, 'and good luck to you.' As I was getting out of the car he leaned across the seat and laid a hand on my arm. 'We'll have a talk again,' he said. 'I'm sure we will.'

I walked back slowly to the house through the shining streets. A molten rip had appeared in the clouds low above the roofs but the rain had started up again and fell about me in big awkward drops like flashing spatters of steel. There are times when I feel drunk though I have not touched a drop for days; or rather, I feel as if I have been drunk and now have begun to sober up, and that the fantasias and false perspectives due to inebriation are about to clear and leave me shocked and gulping in the face of a radically readjusted version of what I had taken the world to be. It never quite arrives, that state of pluperfect sobriety, and I stumble on baffled and deluded amidst a throng of teetotallers who turn from me coldly, tight-lipped, sweeping their skirts aside from my reeling path. As I walked through the rain now my mind raced throbbingly on a single thought. The thought was you. You had the power to push everything else aside, like an arm sweeping across a littered table-top. What did Morden and his pictures, or Hackett and his evidence, what did any of that matter, compared with the promise of all you represented? You see? – you see how I was lost already, careless even of the prospect of the dungeon once again?

As always, you had left your mark on the house, it resonated with your absence like a piano slammed shut. I climbed to the room, which already I thought of as *our* room, and sat on the chaise-longue in my wet mac with my knees apart and hands drooping between my thighs and gazed through the window for a long time at the rain spattering raggedly across the rooftops. Have I described the view from our eyrie? Spires and curlicues and beautiful rusted fire-escapes, and a big green copper dome that always reminded me of a cabbage; directly below, on the other side of the road, behind a hoarding and hidden from the street, was a vacant site with flourishing greenery where sometimes, at twilight, a fox appeared, stepping delicately over the rubble with brush down and snout up; beyond that there was a large, stately building, a church or meeting-house or some-thing, foursquare and imposing, that I never could manage to locate when I was at street level. I was cold. Draggingly I turned myself about, a stone statue turning on its plinth, and walked with granite tread to where the pictures were stacked. Of course I had recognised them. I could close my eyes and see the walls of Whitewater House where they had hung, interestingly gapped now in my mind's eye, like a jigsaw puzzle with half a dozen pieces missing. I had recognised them and at the same time I had not. Extraordinary, this knack the mind has of holding things, however intimately connected, on entirely separate levels, like so many layers of molten silt. I turned and went to the couch and got between the sheets, wet coat and shoes and all, and lay on my side curled up with a hand under my cheek and felt my eyelids fall as if ghostly fingertips had closed them. Gradually the cold seeped out of my bones and I lay swaddled in my own fug, breathing my own smell, a mixture of wet wool, flesh, sweat and damp shoe-leather.

And here memory, that ingenious stage director, performs one of its impossible, magical scene-changes, splicing two different occasions with bland disregard for setting, props or costumes. It is still Saturday afternoon, it is still raining, there is still that rent in the clouds bright as a magnesium flare, and I am still lying between the smooth new crackly sheets on the chaise-longue, but now I have been divested of my clothes, and A. is in my arms, naked also, or nude, I should say, for she was never merely naked, my pearly, damp darling. That was the first time, as they say; very chaste it was, I can think of no better word, and almost absent-minded, as if we were outside ourselves, half looking away from this strange, laborious act in which our bodies were conjoined; looking away and listening in a kind of subdued astonishment to the far, small noises of a no longer quite recognisable world. The first time, yes, and in a way the last: never again that luxurious, doomed sense of something final, complete, done.

What do I remember? Tears at the outer corners of her eyes, her sticky lashes; the little hollow at the base of her spine, with its dusting of burnished, fair hairs; the hollow of her throat, too, a tiny cup full of her that I drank to the dregs; the sudden flash of her thigh, fish-belly white, with its thick, lapis-blue artery through which her very life was pulsing. She muttered things under her breath, words I could not catch, and I had the eerie sensation of there being a third with us for whose benefit she was keeping up a breathless running commentary. And once she said *No*, very loud, not to me but to herself, and went rigid, with her eyes screwed shut and teeth bared, and I waited in alarm, holding myself poised above her on arms quivering like bent bows, and slowly whatever it was went out of her and she gave a hoarse, falling sigh and clung to me, grinding her moist brow against mine. Then she fell asleep.

Once more I am lying on my side, facing as before towards the window and the dwindling rain, cradling her in my arm now as she snuffles and twitches, and my arm has gone numb but I will not shift it for fear of disturbing her, and besides, I feel heroic here, young Tristan watching sleepless over his *Irisch Kind*; heroic and foolish, unreal, anxious, exultant. And slowly there unfolded in me a memory from the far past, when as a child one summer afternoon on a holiday at the seaside I stepped out of a tin-roofed cinema expecting rain, fog, boiling clouds, and found myself instead standing in the midst of rinsed and glistening sunlight with a swollen cobalt sea before me upon which a boat with a red sail leaned, making for the hazed horizon, and I felt for once, for one, rare, mutely ecstatic moment, at home in this so tender, impassive and always preoccupied world.

The rain stopped altogether and the rent in the clouds turned into a broad sash of marian-blue sky and A. woke with a start and frowned as if she did not know who I was. 'Look,' I said to her softly, 'look what we have done to the weather!' She peered at me closely to see if I was joking and, deciding I was not, laughed.

If ever I get round to writing that work of philosophy which I am convinced I have in me, curled up in the amnion of my imagination with its thumb in its mouth, it will be on the subject of happiness. Yes, happiness, believe it or not, that most mysterious because most evanescent of conditions. I know there are those – the mighty Prussians, for instance – who say it is not a condition at all, in any positive sense, holding it to be nothing more than the absence of pain. I do not fall in with this view. Don't ask me to compare the state of mind of two animals one of which is engaged in eating the other; the happiness I speak of has nothing to do with nature's fang and claw, but is exclusive to humankind, a by-product of evolution, a consolation prize for us poor winded runners in the human race. It is a force whose action is so delicate and so fleeting we hardly feel it operating in us before it has become a thing of the past. Yet a force it is. It burns in us, and we burn in it, unconsumed. I cannot be now as I was then – I may recall but not experience again the bliss of those days – yet I must not be led by embarrassment and sorrow and pain to deny what I felt then, no matter how shaming or deluded it may seem to me now. I held her to me, this suddenly familiar stranger, and felt her heart beating and listened to the rustle of her breathing and thought I had come at last to my true place, the place where, still and at the same time profoundly stirred, feverish yet preternaturally calm, I would at last be who I was.

Here she is, the moving mirror in which I surprised myself, poor goggle-eyed Actaeon, my traitorous hounds already sniffing suspiciously at my heels. Five foot two in her bare, her heartbreakingly bare, red little feet. Bust, thirty-four inches, waist . . . but no, no, this is no good. In the long-ago days when I took an interest in the physical sciences it was mensuration that gave me the most trouble – philosophically, that is – for how could anything in this fluctuant world be held still for long enough to have a measuring rod applied to it? (Have I said this before? I don't care.) And even if it were possible to impose the necessary stillness, would the resulting measurements have any meaning outside the laboratory, the dissecting room? Old What's-his-name was right, all is flux and fire wherein we whirl. Even the dead move, as they crumble and drift, dreaming eternity. When I think of A. I see something like one of those dancing, multi-limbed figures from an oriental religion, all legs and slender, S-shaped arms, her face alone always turned towards me, even as she spins and shimmers. She is the goddess of movement and transformations. And I, I am bowed down before her, abject and entranced, my forehead pressed to the cold stone of the temple floor.

I have a handful of images of her, fixed in my memory like photographs. When I summon one of them up a spasm of mingled pain and pleasure goes off in me like a flashbulb. The tones range from platinum-white through glass-grey and nickel to silky blacks, with in places a pale sepia wash. Here, look at this one, look: I turn from the window and you are lying on your front amid the tangled sheets, wearing only a short, satin vest, facing away from me propped on your elbows and smoking a cigarette – ash everywhere, of course – your knees apart and feet in the air, and with stopped breath I stand and gaze at the russet and pink crushed orchid between your thighs and, above it, the tight-furled little bud with its puckered aureole the colour of pale tea. You feel my eyes on you and turn your head and squint at me over your shoulder and smile the smile of a debauched child, wriggling your toes in a derisively jaunty salute. Or here, look, here is another one, do you remember it? This time you are at the window. You are barefoot and your skirt I mean your dress is unbuttoned. You stand with eyes closed and head leaning back against the frame and one leg flexed with a heel hooked on the low sill, your arms folded tightly, crushing your breasts outwards like pale, offered fruit. I say your name but you do not hear me, or hear me and pay no heed, I don't know which, and suddenly, as if summoned, a seagull, bigger than I would have thought possible, descends out of the sky on thrashing wings and hangs suspended for a second just beyond the glass in the bronze light of the October afternoon and seems to peer in at us, first with one agate eye and then the other, and sensing its annunciatory presence you turn to the window quickly just as the bird, screeching, with beak agape, goes on its way, downward into the shadowed chasm of the street.

At first in the weeks after she had gone I used to torture myself with the thought that I had not observed her closely or carefully enough, that when I still had the opportunity I had not fixed her sufficiently firmly in the frame of memory, but now that I am calmer (am I calmer?) I cannot believe that anyone ever can have been subjected to such unwavering, demented attention as I devoted to you. Every day when you arrived in the room (I was always the first one there, always) I turned on you a gaze so awed, so wide with ever-renewed astonishment, beseeching in its intensity, that I thought you must take fright and flee from me, from such need, such fear, such anguished happiness. Not that you so much as flinched, of course; my poor haggard glare was never fierce enough to dazzle you. All the same I insist that I looked harder at you and deeper into your depths than anyone ever did before or will again. I saw you. That was the point of it all. I saw you. (Or I saw someone.)

We had no night; it was always daylight when we met. Oh, the stillness of those pewter-coloured afternoons, with the muffled hum of the city below us and the sibilance of rain on the window and our breath white as thought in the motionless and somehow waiting air under that cranium-coloured ceiling. She did put up curtains, brown, hairy things that hung in lumpy folds like hides, but we never drew them. I wanted to look at her in the harshest light, to see the pores and blemishes and the little dark hairs that stood erect under my caresses; especially I treasured those times when, exhausted, or half asleep, she would lie sprawled across the couch, flaccid and agape, beached in forgetfulness of herself and of me; then I would sit by her side with my legs drawn up and arms clasped about my knees and study her inch by inch, from her gnawed fingernails to her splayed, unsettlingly long toes, devouring her slowly, minutely, in an enraptured cannibalism of the senses. How palely delicate she was. She glimmered. Her skin had a grainy, thick texture that at times, when she was out of sorts, or menstrual, I found excitingly unpleasant to the touch. Yes, it was always there, behind all the transports and the adoration, that faint, acrid, atavistic hint of disgust, waiting, like pain allayed, waiting, and reminding. This I am convinced is what sex is, the anaesthetic that makes bearable the flesh of another. And we erect cathedrals upon it.

I believe that she did not much like the thing itself, the act, as it is interestingly called, or not as we performed it, anyway; no, I believe it was the accompanying ceremonial that interested her, the eager play, the games of consequences, the drugged post-coital exchanges. Perhaps it is only in the bitterness of hindsight that I look back now and see a certain briskness always at the end. She would push me aside and sit up and reach for her cigarettes, as though she were folding up some item of everyday use, a deckchair, say, or an ironing board, and putting it away so that the real business could start. I remember once after the final paroxysm when I lay on her breast gasping like a jellyfish she squirmed out nimbly from under me and picked up a half-eaten apple from where she had set it down on the floor beside the couch and set to work on it again as carelessly as an interrupted Eve. I would not have been greatly surprised, or greatly displeased, for that matter, if I had looked up one day from my endless, vain attempt to burrow myself bodily inside her (I think of an actor trying to struggle into a marvellously wrought but too-small costume) and found her idly smoking a cigarette, or flipping through one of those glossy magazines in the pages of which she lived yet another of her flickering, phantom lives. I must not give the impression that she was indifferent or that she played her part with anything less than enthusiasm; it is just that she was, I believe, more interested in the stage directions than the text. But speeches, she was certainly interested in speeches. Talk was the thing; she loved to talk. Endless discussions. She would detach herself from my panting, pentapus embrace and sit up and wrap herself in the sheet, securing it under her curiously plump armpits with a deftness surely learned from the cinema, and demand that I tell her a story. 'Tell me things,' she would say, the tip of her sharp little nose turning pale with anticipation, 'tell me about your life.' I was evasive. It did not matter. She had enough fantasies for two.

She lied to me, of course, I know that, yet the things she told me (as distinct from the things that she did not) I think of not as lies but inventions, rather, improvisations, true fictions. The tales she spun had been breathed on and polished so often that the detailing had become blurred. There was the story of her family, and of her mother in particular. This mysterious woman – whom A. could not mention without narrowing her eyes and pursing up her lips as if to spit – though she was still malignly and, I suspected, exuberantly alive somewhere, was dead to her daughter. 'I don't want to talk about her!' she would declare, turning aside her head and holding up a hand with its fuming cigarette canted at a trembling angle, and then proceed in a tight-throated drone to enumerate yet again the lengthy list of maternal enormities. The first time I heard of Mother she had been born in America, in Savannah, or Louisiana, or some other homonymous bayou of the Deep South, into a family of ancient lineage; in subsequent accounts, however, the birthplace shifted to Mississippi, then Missouri, and once even, if my ears did not deceive me, to Missoula, which, my atlas tells me, is a town in the Rocky Mountains in the northerly state of Montana, to where I, Melmoth the Bereft, shall journey on that circumferential pilgrimage I intend one of these days to undertake in search of my lost love. But Missoula! – where on earth did she get that from? Her father, she said, was Swiss. He had been – I heard it coming before she said it – a diplomat in the foreign service, and she had been brought up all over the place; and indeed, in her sleep she often spoke in what seemed to me foreign languages. (By the way, why is it, I wonder, that I always take up with restless sleepers?) About Daddy ominous hints were dropped; I pictured a dark, sleek-haired *gentilhomme*, sinisterly handsome – see his skier's tan, his chocolate-dark eyes, his multi-jewelled watch – idly fondling a pale little girl perched in his lap.

Did I believe her? Did it matter? Lolling there on our makeshift narrow bed in a daze of happiness I would listen to her for hours as she spun out her stories, and smoked her cigarettes, and picked at the callused skin along the side of her feet, now and then glancing at me sidelong, cat-eyed, gauging her effect, wondering how far she could go. In the early days, before I knew better, I would sometimes diffidently draw her attention to this or that discrepancy in whatever tale she was spinning and immediately she would retreat into a sullen silence outside which I would be left to stand, puzzled and repentant, with my nose pressed to the cold glass. I believed you, I believed you – how could you doubt it? Oh, my sweet cheat, I believed every bit of it.

Certain of her more outlandish claims retain for me even still a distinct tinge of authenticity at their core, even if the details were shaky. 'My trouble is,' she said one day, frowning as if into dark inner distances, 'there is only half of me here.' At first she would not explain, but sat with her arms clasped about herself, rocking back and forth and mutely shaking her head. At last, though, I got it out of her: she was the survivor of a pair of twins. Her double had come out dead, a tiny white corpse whose blood fierce little embryonic A. had leached from her to ensure her own survival.

A.'s mother let it be known that in her opinion the wrong twin had died. When as a child A. misbehaved, the Monster of Missoula, that Pasiphäe of the Plains, would chide her with the memory of little P. (a name had been chosen, a second christening gown had been bought). A. had grown up in a state of permanent, vague bereavement. She was a survivor, with the survivor's unshakeable sense of guilt and incompleteness. When she had finished her story she turned on me a strange, solemn stare. 'Maybe,' she said, 'maybe you too had a twin that died, and they didn't tell you.' We held hands and sat side by side in silence for a long time, clinging to each other like children who have frightened themselves with stories of hobgoblins.

There were other ghosts. I recall . . . dear Christ, some-times I falter. I recall one stormy late afternoon, it must have been at the beginning of November, when the first real autumn gales were blowing. The buffeted house shuddered in its depths and there was a thrilling sense of things outside – top hats, toupées, wrecked umbrellas – flying and falling in the scoured, steel-grey air. It was such weather as makes me think always of the far past, as if my childhood had been one long, tempestuous twilight. We were in the draughty bathroom on the second-floor return, the only one in the house that had water and a lavatory that flushed. The pipes banged and the linoleum was buckled and often the flame in the coffin-shaped geyser above the bath would extinguish itself spontaneously with a frighteningly understated *whump*. The wind that day leaked sighing through the window-frame and the keyhole and under the door, and the air was gritty with steam that swirled in the waxy effulgence from the bare lightbulb that must have been there since electricity first came to Rue Street. I was washing A.'s hair; we liked to play house like this (and, afterwards, mammies and daddies). She was in her slip, leaning over the big old chipped handbasin and cling-ing white-knuckled to the rim of it as if for dear life. I can see her there, the pink tips of her ears, the dark comma of wetted hair at the nape of her neck, the pale taut skin of her shoulders stretched on their intricately assembled ailettes of moulded bone, the slippery, silken slope of her back bisected along the dotted line of vertebrae. She liked to have her hair washed. It gave her the jitters, she said. She would squirm and shiver, and stamp from foot to foot, mewling in protest and cringing pleasure. As I crouched over her, with a crick in my back and my jaw clenched, I suddenly saw my son. It must have been the shape of her head in my hands that conjured him. I used to wash his hair, too, bending over him awkwardly like this on brumous evenings long ago when he was a child and I was still his father. My hands must have remembered the contours of his skull, brittle and delicate as a bird's egg, with those hollows at the temple as if a finger and thumb had pressed him there, and the bumpy little dome at the back where his hair was always tangled from the pillow. I shut my eyes and a wave of something, some awful burning bile, rose up in me and I tottered and had to sit down on the side of the bath.

A. must have felt that charge of grief pass through me, it must have crackled out of my fingertips into her scalp. She turned without a word, her hair in dripping rats'-tails, and took my head in her hands and pressed it to her breast. There was a scrawny, freckled place between her sternum and her collarbone that I found pitifully endearing, and there I nestled my ear and listened to the oceanic susurrus of her inner organs at work. I felt breathless and hiccuppy, as if I were at the end and not the beginning of a bout of tears. For I wept. Oh, yes, I am still a weeper, though I do not cry so often or so lavishly as of old. Was a time when hardly a day passed, or a night, that I did not shed my scalding quota. There is a barrier, a frontier of the emotions, where one must surrender – what is it: self-possession? dignity? grown-upness? – in exchange for the giddy and outlandish pleasure of abandoning oneself wholly to grief. It is not a crossing I often make. I weep, yes – but there are tears and tears. On the other side of that final boundary the ground drops clear away and one topples slowly, helplessly, into oneself, with nothing to break the fall and nothing to grasp except armfuls of empty air. She led me back upstairs (my God, if we had met Morden then, or his man!) and we sat on the couch and she held my hands in hers while I sobbed my heart out. Plump hot tears fell on our knuckles, each one printed with a tiny, curved image of the window in which the raucous grey day was rapidly dying. I recall the noise of the wind, a huge, hollow trumpeting high up in the air, and leaves and bits of twigs blowing against the panes, though that cannot be right, for there are no trees in the vicinity; perhaps they were fragments torn from the buddleia bush down in the waste site beside the house? We had a double-barred electric fire, an antique affair she had salvaged from somewhere, which burned now at our feet with what seemed to me a baleful, gloating redness that reminded me of the coke fires of my childhood. Often nowadays I toy with the notion of breaking into the house – I'm sure everything there is much as it was – and rescuing something for a keepsake, that fire, or a smeared wineglass, or a tuft of lint, even, from between the floorboards, perhaps with one of her hairs tangled in it; what I really want, of course, is the chaise-longue, but even in my worst throes I have to laugh at the image of myself, sweating and swearing like a cattle drover, bumping that recalcitrant big brute down endless flights of stairs. All the same, what would I not give to be able to throw myself down on my face upon it now and breathe deep its fusty, exhausted, heartbreaking smell.

My memory is up to its tricks again, conflating separate occasions, for now as I sit there weeping with A. beside me it is I who am undressed, under the cheap bathrobe that she had bought for me, while she is got up for outdoors in one of her expensive black suits and a pair of those needle-sharp high-heeled shoes the sound of which on bare wooden floors still tick-tocks in my dreams, always, always receding. I have the impression of a certain impatience, of exasperation, even, on her part; the tears of others, no matter how heartfelt, can be hard to tolerate. I was embarrassed myself, and even as I sobbed I had that hot, panicky feeling you get when the passenger beside you on a crowded bus begins to rave and curse. It was a long time since I had heard myself cry like this, so simply, so unaffectedly, with such heartfelt enthusiasm.

'I lost him,' I said, the words coming out in jerks and weepy plops. 'He just slipped out of my hands and was gone.'

A. sat with her gaze fixed on the floor beside my bare feet and said nothing. Disconcerted I suppose by her silence I peered at her anxiously through the mica-glitter of tears; she had the glumly patient air of someone dutifully waiting for a familiar and not very interesting story to end. I suppose I needed to impress her then, to do in words the equivalent of taking her by the shoulders and giving her a good shake. Besides, I had to live up to those extravagant tears. So I sat swaddled in my robe, swollen and blotched, with my hands bunched in my lap, like a big, bruised baby, and told her of my poor boy who was born damaged and died, and of my wife, that by now archaic, Minoan figure, with whom long ago I wandered the world until one day we found we had used up world and selves, and I left her, or she left me, and I went into free fall.

I wonder if she believed my tale, my tall tale?

But how good it felt, telling her. The crepuscular light, the silence all about, and her beside me with her face half turned away. I have made her wear her veil again; how like a grille it looks: the confessional, of course. Oh, absolve me!

Down in the street the newsboys were crying the evening editions.

'I know a man,' I said, 'who killed a woman once.'

She was silent for a moment, looking off from under lowered lashes.

'Oh yes?' she said. 'Who did he kill?'

'A maid in a rich man's house.' How quaint it sounded, like something out of the Brothers Grimm. The bad thief went to the rich man's mansion to steal a picture and when the maid got in his way he hit her on the head and killed her dead. 'Then they took him away,' I said, 'and locked him up and made him swallow the key.' And from that durance he is still waiting for release.

Such stillness.

But why am I in my bathrobe, when obviously she has just come in from outside? I could feel the little slivers of chill air that fell out of the folds of her jacket (three bright black buttons, cutaway pockets, a narrow velvet collar: see, I remember everything) as she stood up and walked tick-tock tick-tock to the window and stood looking out with her arms folded and her face turned away from me. Sometimes I seem to glimpse it through another's eyes, that simpler place, that Happy Valley of the heart where I long one day to wander, if only for an hour, hand in hand, perhaps, with my dead.

Day fails before the advancing dusk. I am there again, as if the moment cannot end. The wind bellows mutedly in the street and the window shudders, great indistinct dark clouds are churning like soiled sea-waves above the huddled roofs. My tears have dried, my face feels like glass. In the tin-coloured light at the window A. was turning to shadowed stone and when she spoke it was with a sibyl's unreal voice. She began to tell me the story of how when she was a schoolgirl in Paris she had run away from the convent and spent a night in a brothel, going with anyone who wanted her, twenty or thirty faceless men, she had lost count. She had never felt so real and at the same time detached, floating free of herself, of everything. She lifted her hand and made an undulant gesture in the dusk's dimming glow. 'Like that,' she said softly. 'Free.'

128

5. Capture of Ganymede 1620
L.E. van Ohlbijn (1573-1621)

Oil on copper, 7¾ x 7 in. (19.2 x 17.8 cm.)

Although he is not best known as a miniaturist, van Ohlbijn puts his skills, modest though they may be, to finest use when working on a small scale, as we can see from this charmingly executed little scene, a curiosity among this curious collection. What strikes us first is the artist's determination to avoid sentimentality – a determination the true result of which, some commentators believe, is a complete absence of *sentiment*, surely not the effect that was intended: a case, we may say, of throwing the bath-water out with the baby, or boy, in this instance. That doesn't sound right. Van Ohlbijn has combined in this work the homely skills of the Dutch genre painter that he was, with some scraps of learning brought back with him from a winter spent in Venice and Rome in the early 1600s. We detect influences as disparate as Tintoretto, in the dash and dramatic pace of the piece, and Parmigianino in the curious elongation of the figures, while the almost vertiginous sense of elevation and dreamlike buoyancy anticipates the skyborne works of Gaulli and Tiepolo. There is evidence also, in the softness of textures and the diaphanous quality of the paint surface, that van Ohlbijn on his Italian journey studied with application the work of Perugino and Raphael. The figure of Ganymede is admirably fashioned, being both an individual, wholly human boy (the painter is said to have used his son as a model), and an emblematic representation of ephebic beauty. How affecting is the conjunction of the creatural grace and delicacy of this young male, with his Phrygian cap and his mantel thrown back over his shoulder, and the ferocity and remorseless power of the feral bird that holds him fast in its terrible talons. In the eagle's muscled upward straining, its fierce eye and outstretched neck and flailing, bronzed wings, are manifested the power and pitiless majesty of the god. This is not our Father who is in Heaven, our guardian in the clouds; this is the *deus invidus* who kills our children, more Thanatos than Zeus Soter. Although the boy is bigger than the bird we are in no doubt as to which is the stronger: the talons clasped upon the narrow thighs are flexed with a peculiar delicacy yet we can feel their inescapable strength, while Ganymede's outflung arm communicates a deeply affecting sense of pain and loss and surrender. The gesture is at once a frantic appeal for help and a last, despairing farewell to the mortal world from which the boy has been plucked. In contrast, the attitude of the boy's father, King Tros, standing on the mossy pinnacle of Mount Ida, seems overstated and theatrical. His hands are lifted in impotent pleading and tears course down his cheeks. We do not quite credit his grief. He has the air of a man who knows he is being looked at and that much is expected of him. Why, we wonder, has the artist's judgment failed him here? Has he allowed an access of anxiety or personal sorrow to guide his hand into this overblown depiction of paternal distress? Those tears: he must have painted them with a brush made of a single sable hair. Remember how I showed them to you through the magnifying glass? Your breath forming on the picture, engreying the surface and then clearing, so that the scene kept fading and coming back as if appearing out of a mountain mist. There was a tiny mole on your cheek that I had not noticed before, with its own single hair. 'Why would he bother?' you said. So that one day, my love, you and I would lean with our heads together here like this in the quiet and calm of a rainy afternoon and be for a moment almost ourselves. Hebe in the clouds looks on as the boy is borne towards her in her father's claws. Does she see in him the usurper who will take her place as cupbearer to the deathless ones? She holds in her hands the golden bowl the god will take from her, his daughter, and give to the mortal boy. Everyone loses, in the end. Some little time after completing this painting van Ohlbijn, in grief at the loss of his beloved son and, so it is said, abandoned by a mistress, drank poison from a gilded cup and died on the eve of his forty-eighth birthday. The gods have a sense of humour but no mercy.

More immediately alarming to me than any of my own ghosts were the living phantoms who haunted the house. I was in constant fear that someone would click open the secret door some afternoon and discover us cavorting on the couch or sprawled steaming and exhausted on the floor with our limbs in a tangle. I am still amazed it never happened. Or maybe it did? Maybe Francie did get in one day when we were too absorbed to notice him – I believe that man could slip through a crack in a wall – and quietly withdrew again, pocketing our secret. He seemed to be always about, clambering up and down the house with that lopsided gait. He had an unnerving way of materialising silently out of doorways or on shadowed landings: a hand, an eye, that smile, and then that clicking noise that he produced out of the side of his mouth as if he were geeing up a horse. He had a little mocking salute that he would give me, lifting two fingers to his forehead and letting them fall lazily sideways. It amused him to feign large surprise when he came upon me, halting in his tracks with an exaggerated, wide-eyed stare and dropping open his mouth in a silent exclamation of mock amazement and delight. One day I met him with Gall the painter at the turn of the corridor outside our room. I had thought it was A. approaching and had been about to call out her name (ah, the eager gaiety of brand-new lovers!). He must have seen the alarm in my face. He stopped and grinned. Gall, slouching along in his wake, almost collided with him, and swore and gave me a bilious stare. Gall was a squat, bearded person with a big, unlikely-looking belly, as if a couple of cushions were stuffed inside his paint-stained pullover. He had very small, dark, sharp eyes and a clown's red nose. He carried himself stiffly, gasping a little and listing to one side, as though he were strapped too tightly into his clothes. This tense, leaning stance gave him an air of resentfulness and barely restrained hostility. (How I love them, these incidental grotesques!) I had the impression, even at a distance of yards, of unwashed flesh and under-garments badly in need of changing. 'Who's this?' he growled. Francie made elaborate and sardonic introductions. ' . . . And this is Gall,' he said, 'artist and, like yourself, Mr Morrow, a scholar.' Gall gave a snort of phlegmy laughter and turned away, making an ill-aimed kick at Prince the dog, which stood at point on the landing with glistening snout delicately uplifted, seeming as always to be peering this way and that over the backs of a milling pack of its fellows. I was hot with anxiety, picturing A. hurrying up the stairs with her head down in that way she had and stopping dead at the sight of us. Francie was studying me with quiet enjoyment. 'You're looking a bit agitated,' he said. 'Are you expecting a visitor?' Gall had started down the stairs. 'Are we right, for Christ's sake?' he called back angrily. Francie touched my arm. 'Come on and have a drink with us,' he whispered. 'Gall is gas.'

We went down to the big empty room where I had first met Morden. The trestle or whatever it was still hung by its frayed ropes from the ceiling and the soiled white sheet was still draped from the high corner of a window. Frail sunlight of late autumn was arranged in trapezoids on the floor. We sat down on dusty bentwood chairs that cracked and groaned under us in geriatric complaint. Gall had a stone jug with a handle at the neck through which he hooked his thumb and hoisted the jug to his shoulder and drank a deep draught, his adam's apple bobbing.

'Ach!' he said and grimaced, and wiped his mouth with the back of his hand.

'Good stuff, eh?' Francie said.

Gall offered me the jug. His eyes were watering. 'Poteen,' he said hoarsely. 'The missus makes it in the back shed.'

Francie laughed. 'Champagne is Mr Morrow's tipple,' he said.

They watched with interest as I took a tentative slug, trying not to think of Gall's wet little pursed-up mouth on the rim. No taste to speak of, just a flash of silvery fire on the tongue and then a spreading burn.

'Mind the backwash now,' Francie said gaily.

I passed the jug to him and he shouldered it expertly and drank. Now my eyes were watering.

'Spuds,' Gall said with satisfaction. 'You can't beat the spuds.'

As I think I began to say elsewhere, I have always had a distressing weakness for the low life. It is a taste that sits ill with what I consider otherwise to be a dignified, not to say patrician, temperament. In the old days, the days of my travels, I could sniff out the worst dives within an hour of arriving in this or that new place. The lower the haunt and more disreputable its denizens the better I liked it. Something to do with danger, I think, that thrilling, fluttery feeling under the diaphragm, and with transgression, the desire to smear myself with a little bit of the world's filth. For I never felt that I belonged in those squalid places – quite the opposite, in fact. I would sit on a high stool with an elbow leaning on the bar and a misted glass of something ice-blue and toothsomely noxious in my hand and watch for whole afternoons (daytime was always best) with admiration and a certain wistful enviousness the doings of people who in their small-scale wickednesses were more natural, more authentic, than I knew I could ever manage to be. They had, some of them, the men especially, a nervous elegance and an air of hair-trigger alertness that seemed to me the characteristics of the true grown-up, the real man of the world. Then there was the other type, of whom Gall was a fine example, all resentment and sullen self-absorption and bottled-up rage. Which kind would I be, I wonder? A mixture of the two, perhaps? Or something altogether other, and far worse. The jug came back to me and this time I took a good long fiery gulp and passed it on to Gall and grinned and with what was intended to be irony called out 'Cheers!'

They were discussing a painter of their acquaintance whose name was Packy Plunkett.

'He's only a piss-artist,' Gall said, 'that's all he is.'

Francie nodded thoughtfully.

'He can do the business, though,' he said, and winked at me.

Gall's pocked brow darkened.

'A piss-artist!' he said again, clawing violently and audibly at his straggly beard that looked like a species of lichen that had taken hold of his face.

The jug returned. How swiftly it was circulating. I recalled stories of wild men of the west driven mad by poteen, their brains turned to stirabout and their tongues rotted in their heads. It all seemed very funny.

I drank to their health again and said, 'Cheers!' more loudly this time, and laughed.

Gall gave me a sour look. '*Sláinte*,' he said with heavy emphasis, and turned to Francie and jerked a thumb in my direction. 'What is he,' he said, 'some sort of a West Brit, or what?'

Presently I noticed that the light was taking on a thickened, sluggish quality and somewhere at the heart of things a vast pulse was slowly thudding. I wanted to leave but somehow could not think exactly how to stand up; it was not a physical difficulty but rather a matter of mental organisation. This predicament was more interesting than distressing, and greatly amusing, of course. I felt like a rubber ball trapped out at the end of an elastic that stretched, fatly thrumming, all the way up the stairs to the secret room where I pictured A. waiting for me, squatting on the end of the couch, a cigarette smouldering in the corner of her mouth and one eye shut against the smoke, with her chin on her knees and clutching her cold feet in her hands, my monkey girl. I wonder if when you were with me you too experienced those swings between desire and tedium that I found so disconcerting. On occasion, even as I pressed you in my arms I would find myself longing to be somewhere else, alone and unhindered. (Why am I talking like this, why am I saying these things, when all I really mean to do is send up a howl of anguish so frightful and so piercing you would hear it no matter where you are and feel your blood turn to water.) There was a sort of trickling sensation in my sinuses and I realised with a faint start of surprise and, mysteriously, of satisfaction, that I was on the point of tears.

'The thing about my stuff is,' morose Gall was saying, 'the best of it is not appreciated.'

Francie chuckled. 'You can say that again,' he said, and the dog, lying at his feet, looked up at him with its head held at what seemed an admonitory tilt.

Gall's jackdaw eyes were filming over and his pitted nose had turned from cherry-red to angry purple.

I enquired, in a tone of grand accommodation, snuffling up those unshed tears, what kind of painting it was that he did (I think at that stage I still thought he could only be a house-painter). He threw me another soiled glance but disdained to answer.

'Figurative!' Francie cried, lifting his hands and moulding rounded shapes out of the air. 'Lovely things. Woodland scenes, girls in their shifts.' He clapped a hand on my knee. 'You should have a look at them, I'm telling you: right up your alley!'

Gall glared at him. 'Shut the fuck up, Francie,' he said in a slurred voice.

I began to tell them about my encounter with Inspector Hackett. It seemed to me a very droll tale, which I illustrated with large gestures and what struck me as a particularly witty turn of phrase. 'Is that so?' Francie kept saying; he was having trouble keeping his eyes in focus, and when he tried to light a cigarette he fumbled and let the whole package spill on to the floor, and Gall laughed loudly. When Francie had got his smoke going he sat nodding to himself and gazing blearily at my knees.

'Hobnobbing with the rozzers, eh?' he said, and we all laughed at that, as if he had cracked a fine joke.

The next moment, so it seemed, and to my large surprise, I found myself walking briskly if erratically up Rue Street, swinging my arms and breathing stertorously. The pavement was remarkably uneven and the flagstones had a tricky way of rising up at the corners just as I was about to step on them. I had no idea where I was going but I was going there with great determination. The sunlight glared and had an acid cast to it. At the corner of Ormond Street, near the spot where A. had first spoken to me, there was parked a very large, old-fashioned American motor car of a pale mauve shade with tailfins and a stacked and complicated array of rear lights. As I approached, the driver's door swung open and with a swift, balletic, corkscrew movement a heavy-set young man leaped lightly out and placed himself in my path. I halted, snorting and heaving.

'The Da wants a word,' he said.

It took me a moment to recognise him as young Popeye, the one who had stood at the garden gate and glared at me the day Morden had taken me with him on that drive into the suburbs. There was something about him I seemed to know – I had seen it that other day, too – as if under the crustaceous accretion of rock-hard muscle there lurked a different, more delicate version of him, a ghostly Sweet Pea with whose form I was somehow familiar. Today he was dressed in an expensive, dark wool suit inside which despite his muscles he seemed lost, as if it were a hand-me-down from his big brother. Beads of sweat glittered in the nap of his close-cropped red hair. He bunched his fists and a nerve in his jaw danced.

'Your *father*?' I said with interest.

He opened the rear door of the car smartly and jerked his head at me. I leaned down. Sitting in the back seat like a stone idol was the pasty-faced fellow who had come in his kilt and shawl to join young Popeye at the garden gate and watch us that day as we drove away. He was enveloped this time in a vast overcoat with a broad fur collar on which his big, pale, pointed head with its lardy jowls sat as if it had been placed there carefully and might tumble off at the slightest movement. Very small eyes, soft-boiled in their puckered sockets, swivelled and took me in and a hand emerged from the folds of the coat and offered itself to me.

'How are you getting on?' he said; it was not a greeting but a question. I said I was getting on very well. His hand was soft and moist and cool; he shook mine slowly, solemnly, studying me the while. 'I'm the Da,' he said. 'Do you not know me? I know you. Get in and we'll have a chat.'

The springs in the seat twanged under me and I sank so low my knees were almost at the level of my shoulders. There was a strong smell of mothballs, from the greatcoat,

I presumed. The sun in the windows was all spikes and sheer edges. Young Popeye slipped behind the wheel and started up the engine but we did not move; I was childishly disappointed; I would have liked a spin in this big crazy car. Popeye turned a knob and a fan came on and blew a blast of hot, metallic air in our faces. 'I suffer terrible from the cold,' the Da said. 'I have to have the heat and then I get the chilblains. It's fucking awful.'

So our conversation began. We discussed the climate and ways of coping with its vagaries, the provenance of his motor car, the incidence of spontaneous combustion among elderly ladies in the city in recent years, Morden's character ('Is he dependable, would you say?'), the stupidity of policemen (despite the fact that he was a notorious criminal, as he admitted with quiet pride, they had not managed to get him into jail since he had been a teenager, and then only for six months for shoplifting), the pastimes that make prison life bearable, the state of the picture market, the nature of art. I found all this perfectly agreeable and interesting. He was originally, he told me, a butcher by trade, although he had not practised for a long time, being in a different line of work nowadays. I nodded, saying of course, of course, one serious man of the world to another. I'm sure he explained many more things to me but if so I forgot them instantly. The hot breeze from the heater and the glitter of sunlight in the windscreen gave a sense of headlong movement, as if we were swishing smoothly down the boulevards of some great humming metropolis. After a time the Da ventured to unbutton his greatcoat and I noticed that he was dressed as a priest, with a full soutane and an authentically grubby collar.

He wanted me to tell him about art. He said he had just gone into the art business – Popeye in the front seat snickered at that – and he needed the advice of an expert.

'That one, now,' he said, 'that *Birth of what-do-you-call-her*, why would that be so special?'

I did not hesitate. 'Scarcity,' I told him, in a strong voice firm with conviction. My face, however, had a rubbery feel to it and I had some trouble getting my arms to fold.

'Scarcity, eh?' he said, and repeated the word a number of times, turning it this way and that, nodding to himself with his fat lower lip stuck out. 'So it's like everything else, then,' he said.

'Yes,' I answered stoutly, 'just like everything else, a matter of supply and demand, what the market will bear, horses for courses, and so on. There are not,' I said, 'very many Vaublins in existence.'

'Is that so?' the Da said.

'Yes, indeed. Scarcely more than twenty in the world, and few of them of such quality as the *Birth of What's-her-name.*'

In my mind I saw Morden's big surly face and through the murk suddenly I had a glimpse of the far-off state of sobriety and a shimmer of unease passed over me like a gust of wind passing over the surface of a still pool; dark, fishy forms were down there, nosing about. The Da pondered in silence for a while, his chin sunk on his breast and his hands playing together like piglets in his lap. Then he roused himself and put an arm around my shoulder and gave me a quick squeeze. 'Good man,' he said, as if I had done him some large service, 'good man.' He pushed me firmly but not ungently out of the door. When I was on the pavement he leaned sideways and with two fingers gaily blessed me with the sign of the cross and produced a cracked cackle of laughter. 'God go with you, my son,' he said.

I stood listing slightly and watched as the big pink car slewed into Ormond Street and roared off with a great fart of exhaust smoke. I think I may even have waved, though feebly.

I decided at once that what I needed was more drink, and

set off for The Boatman. I found it eventually, after straying down a number of false trails. The pub was very dark and broody after the brightness of the afternoon streets. What month is it? October still? The barman was leaning on his elbows on the bar reading a newspaper and picking his teeth with a matchstick. I considered what would sit best with the remains of Gall's firewater and decided on vodka, a drink I do not like. I threw back three or four measures in quick succession and left.

There follows a period of confusion and distant tumult. I stumped along as if both my legs were made of wood from the thighs down, and there was a fizzing in my veins and my sight kept twitching distractingly with a regular, slow pulse. I remember stopping on a corner to speak to someone, a man in a cap – God knows who he was – but I could get no good of him and lurched on, muttering crossly. A patch of sky, delicate, deep and ardent, fixed like a great sheet of limpid blue glass between the tops of two high, narrow buildings, seemed to signify some profound thing. I saw again from childhood a path through winter woods and was preparing to weep but got distracted. I bought an ice cream cone and when I had greedily sucked up the ice cream I lobbed the soggy cone into a litter bin five yards away from me with such accuracy and aplomb that I expected the street to stop and break into applause. I met Francie and Gall shuffling along like dotards with Prince stalking carefully at their heels. The dog's fur seemed to crackle with a sort of electric radiance. Francie pawed my lapels and kept repeating something incomprehensible, his jaw making spastic move-ments as if his mouth were filled with stones. I do not know what I said to him but it must have been affecting, for he began to blubber and pawed at me with renewed fervour, until Gall gave a high whoop and clapped him on the back, which sent him into a fit of horrible, stringy coughing. They passed on. Prince lingered a moment, looking at me speculatively as if it thought I might somehow be the explanation for all this amazing behaviour, then padded off after its master. That dog is going to bite someone, I'm convinced of it.

When I got home (shortly I shall say a word about home) the telephone in the hall was ringing. It had a tone of vehemence that seemed to suggest it had been ringing for a long time. I held it gingerly to my ear. There is something avid and faintly hysterical about the telephone that makes me always wary of it. The voice on the line was already in mid-flow. I thought it was Mrs Haddon. I leaned against the wall and laid my throbbing brow against its clammy coolness. *This place. Trying to murder me. I have to. You must, you must.* Not Mrs Haddon. Someone else. With a sudden surge of alarm I recognised Aunt Corky. Her voice boomed and rattled as if she were speaking from the bottom of an enormous metal tank. I bade her calm down but that only made her worse.

I managed somehow to find a taxi, a large, ancient, wallowing machine that seemed to progress in a series of sliding loops, as if it were spinning with locked wheels along the surface of a frozen river. I sat in the middle of the back seat with my arms outstretched and my hands braced on the plastic seat-cover. Buildings rose and toppled in the windows on either side and strange, staring people reared up and then dropped away behind us like ragdolls. The driver was a squat man with a flattened hat set squarely on a large, loaf-shaped head; he bore a remarkable resemblance to a stand-up comedian of my youth whose name I could not remember. He crouched over the steering wheel with his nose almost touching the windscreen. He seemed to be very cross and I wondered uneasily if when I had first got in I had said something to offend him that I had since forgotten. We slalomed on to the coast road. The sun was muffled in strands of insubstantial cloud and there was an unearthly, creamy luminance on the sea. The effects of the alcohol were fading and the acid of dread began to eat into my befuddled understanding. Hesitantly my mind reached out a feeler and touched this and that fizzing contact point – the pictures, Inspector Hackett, the Da and the Da's musclebound minder – and at each place I experienced a sharp little shock of fright.

We laboured up the hill road, gears groaning, and came to a slipping stop outside The Cypresses. I got out and spoke into the microphone and heard the lock disengage. How high up here we seemed, almost airborne. A seagull hanging overhead made a raucous, cackling noise disturbingly reminiscent of the Da's cracked laugh. When we arrived at the house the driver objected when I asked him to wait, but in the end he capitulated and sat hunched over the wheel in a sulk and peered after me suspiciously as I went into the porch and knocked at the glass door. My eyeballs burned in their sockets like cinders and there was a taste of hot rust in my mouth. The Haddons were waiting for me, standing side by side in the hall, him stooped and watchfully diffident and she staring off rabbit-eyed and grimly chafing her wrist. I could not help admiring again those nice legs of hers. 'Mr Morrow,' she said. There are times when I regret having chosen that name.

'Yes yes,' I said majestically, holding up a hand to silence her, 'I have come to take my aunt away.'

This was as much of a surprise to me as it was to them, and the force of it stopped me in my tracks and I stood swaying. The Haddons looked at each other and Mrs Haddon gave her head a toss.

'Well,' she said, 'I don't think there's any need to talk to us like that.'

Like what? I must have been shouting. We all hesitated for a moment, seeming to turn this way and that uncertainly, then wheeled about, all three, and marched in the direction of Aunt Corky's room. When we got to the foot of the stairs, however, Mr Haddon deftly sloped off. His wife did not register his going but marched on ahead of me, her sensible shoes pummelling the stair-carpet. Those legs.

I discovered Aunt Corky in consultation with her priest. Father Fanning was a weary-eyed young man, tall and thin and somewhat stooped, with a plume of prematurely white hair that gave him the look of a startled, ungainly bird. He wore a clerical collar and a green suit and sandals with mustard-coloured socks. He bent on me a keen regard and shook my hand warmly. 'Your aunt has been telling me about you,' he said with a curious emphasis that smacked to me of effrontery. Aunt Corky clasped her hands. 'Oh, he has been so good, Father,' she cried. 'So good!' Father Fanning made a steeple of his hands under his chin and smiled and nodded and let fall his eyelids briefly, like a stage cleric. My aunt was wrapped in a tea-gown with elaborate flame-coloured designs leaping up at back and front. She sat on the edge of the bed with the priest standing beside her; they might have been mother and son. Her feet were bare; the sight of an old woman's toenails is hardly to be borne. I found myself struggling with a rising tide of impatience, treading water and bobbing about annoyingly. I greeted my aunt in a level, accusing voice, and Mrs Haddon, as if she had been awaiting this cue, darted out from behind me and shouted at Aunt Corky, 'Mr Morrow has come to take you away!' There was an expectant silence as they waited on me. I understood, my mind grimly clicking its tongue at me, that there was no way out of what I had got myself into. A headache started up like a series of hammer-blows and made it seem as if I were being forced to bend towards the floor in definite but imperceptible stages. I asked Aunt Corky brusquely if she was ready. She glanced at me wildly and a shadow of panic, I thought, passed over her face. Mrs Haddon was suddenly brisk. 'She's all packed and ready,' she said to me, and went to the wardrobe by the window and like a magician's assistant threw it open with a flourish to reveal empty hangers and bare rails and a bulging carpet-bag on the bottom shelf. 'We have only to pop her into her dress and she's all yours!'

Sharon the nurse was summoned and Father Fanning and I were banished to the landing, where we loitered uneasily in an ecclesiastical fall of light from the coloured window there. I felt aggrieved and sorry for myself. I would have liked to hit someone very hard; Father Fanning must have mistaken for self-congratulation the speculative glint in the eye with which I was measuring him, for he nodded again with his eyelids gently closed and said, 'Yes, you're doing the right thing, the decent thing.' I looked at my feet. The priest lowered his voice to a holy hush. 'You are a good man,' he said. Really, this was too much. I demurred, giving a sort of leonine snarl and baring my side teeth at him. With gentle firmness he grasped my arm and shook it a little. 'Yes, it's true,' he said, smiling wisely; 'a good man.' He lifted a finger, with which I thought for a moment he was going to tap the side of his nose at me; instead he pointed aloft and his smile turned faintly maniacal. 'The man above is the one who'll judge,' he said. 'Oh yes?' I said. 'Then God help me.' His brow buckled in puzzlement but he continued gamely smiling.

The door opened and Aunt Corky issued forth at a shakily regal pace, tottering between the nurse and Mrs Haddon, who supported her on their arms. She wore a bulky fur coat with bald patches and a rakishly cocked hat with a veil of stiff black net (yes, a real veil, not one I have imagined for her). In that raggedy fur she bore a striking and obscurely distressing resemblance to an ill-used teddy bear I had been much attached to as a child. She looked at Father Fanning and me and her lip trembled, as if she feared that we might laugh. We descended the stairs with funereal slowness, the women going ahead and the priest and I behind them with our heads bowed and our hands clasped at our backs. A vague and restive band of old women waited in the hall to bid Aunt Corky farewell. I spotted the silked and sashed Miss Leitch among them but she showed no sign today of imagining that she knew me. They were murmurously excited, being unused, I suppose, to the sight of one of their company making an escape from that place not only in a conscious but also a vertical state. On the step of the porch Aunt Corky halted with a surprised and even distrustful air and looked about her at the lawn and the trees and the sea view as if she suspected the whole thing was a false front put up to deceive and lull her. The taxi driver was unexpectedly solicitous and even got out and helped me to lever the old woman into the passenger seat; perhaps she reminded him also of some worn-out, treasured thing from the past. She took off her hat and veil and eyed the *no smoking* sign pasted to the dashboard and sniffed. Mr Haddon appeared, lugging Aunt Corky's bag, and the driver had to get out again and stow it in the boot. We started up with a cannonade of shudders and exhaust smoke, and Mr Haddon stepped away backwards from us slowly, like a batman pulling away the chocks. From the porch the gathering of ancient maenads waved wiltingly, while Mrs Haddon stood to one side looking angry and ill-used. Sharon the nurse ran forward and tapped on the window, saying something, but Aunt Corky could not get the window open and the driver did not see the girl, and we drove off and left her standing alone and uncertain, biting her lip and smiling, with the big, spindly, gruesomely festive house hanging over her. 'Don't look back!' my aunt said angrily in a shaky voice, and pulled her neck down into her fur collar. *Oh dear God*, I was thinking, mentally wringing my hands, *what have I done?*

How odd it is, the way the familiar can turn strange in a moment. Home, what I call home, took one look at Aunt

Corky and went into a sulk from which it has not yet fully emerged. I felt like an errant husband coming back from a night on the tiles with a doxy hanging on his arm. My flat is on the third floor of a big old crumbling narrow house on a tree-lined, birded street with a church at one end and a cream-painted, uncannily silent convent at the other. I inherited the place from another, real aunt, who died here, sitting alone at the window in the quiet of a summer Sunday evening. You will want to know these details, I hope. I have two big, gaunt rooms, one giving on to the street and the other overlooking an untended, narrow and somehow malignant-looking back garden. There is a partitioned-off kitchen, and a bathroom one flight down on the return. I should have brought you here, I should have brought you here once at least, so you could have left your prints on the place. The other tenants . . . no, never mind the other tenants. Brown light stands motionless on the stairs and everywhere there is the treacly smell of over-used air. We are a quiet house. By day despite the traffic noises we can hear faintly the tiny, dry staccato of typewriters in the offices on either side of us, though lately these lovely machines, which always make me think of the spoked car-wheels and cinema organs of my childhood, are being replaced increasingly by computers, whose keyboards produce a loose clatter like the sound of false teeth rattling. I like, or liked (your going took the savour from things), the vast, useless sideboard, the blue-black circular table with its breathed-on, plumbeous bloom, the dining chairs standing poised and wary like forest animals, the startled mirrors, the carpets that still smell of my dead aunt's dead cats. These rooms have a secret life of their own. There seems to be always something going on. When I walk into one or other of them unexpectedly – and who is there that would expect me? – I always have the impression of everything having halted in the midst of a stealthy and endless occupation that will quietly start up again as soon as

148

I am out of earshot. It is like living in the innards of a vast, silent and slightly defective clock. Aunt Corky, when we had finally negotiated the three flights of stairs – it is evening by now – looked about her in the half-light with a last reserve of brightness and said, 'Oh: Berlin!' and like a surly child the place turned its back on her, and on me.

By now I was sunk utterly in despondency and so weary I seemed to be melting into the ground, like a snowman. I turned on the gas fire (it uttered a resentful *Huh!*) and sat Aunt Corky by it swaddled in her furs and went into the bedroom and changed the linen on my bed; the starched sheets when I shook them rattled like distant thunder. When I was done I leaned by the window to rest my fevered brain for a moment. In the wintry twilight the garden stood gaunt and greyly adroop. I did not know myself (do I ever know myself?). That is what home is for, to still the self's unanswerable questionings; now I had been invaded and the outer doubts were seeping in like fog through every fissure.

Aunt Corky settled in straight away, calling up old skills, I imagined, from her refugee days. She made a nest for herself in the corner where her bed was, draping her things over the back of a chair and on a towel rack that she had fished out of some cupboard or other. I kept my eyes averted as best I could from this display of geriatric rags, for I have always been squeamish in the underwear department. She, of course, was undaunted by our enforced intimacy. There was the matter of the lavatory, for instance. On that first evening I had to joggle her back down the stairs on my arm, a step at a time, and stand outside the bathroom door humming so as not to hear the sounds of her relieving herself. When she came out and looked up at the climb awaiting her she shook her head and made that soft, clicking noise with her lips that I took for one of the signs of her foreignness, and I thought with foreboding of chamber pots, and worse. Next day, without consulting me, she commandeered from the kitchen a handleless saucepan which she kept under her bed and first thing each morning emptied through the window into the yard three storeys below. I waited in fear for the tenants on the ground floor to complain, but they never did; what did they think was the explanation for it, this tawny matutinal deluge landing with a splat outside their kitchen window? She managed in other ways, too. She liked to cook for herself, having a particular relish for scrambled eggs. She even did some of her laundry at the kitchen sink; I would come home of an evening and find pairs of satin bloomers with elasticated legs – heirlooms, surely – and soggy and lugubriously attenuated stockings hanging above the gas stove on a clothes-horse I had not noticed was there, and all four burners of the stove going full blast. (Her way with gas was something I could not let myself begin to worry about; ditto her habit of smoking in bed.) As for her illness, whatever it was, she showed scant sign of it. She coughed a lot – I pictured her lungs hanging in rubbery tatters, like burst football bladders – and behind the fogbank of her perfume there was detectable an acrid smell, like the smell of tooth decay, only worse, that seemed to me the very stink of mortality. She had a look that lately I catch sometimes myself in my mirror of a morning: the pinched, moist gaze, the slackness, the surprise and sad alarm at time's slow damage. She seemed hardly to sleep at all. At night, lying on my makeshift bed on the sofa in the front room with my head skewed at one end and my toes braced against the moulded armrest at the other, I would hear her in the bedroom, her mousy scrapings and fumblings, as she moved about in there for hours, waiting for the dawn, I suppose, for those first pallid, hopeful fingerings along the edges of the curtains. She never complained of feeling bad, though there were days when she did not get up at all but lay in the jumbled bed with her face turned to the wall, her hands clenched on the turned-down blanket as if it were the lid of something closing on her that required all her strength to hold ajar. On those bad days I would come sometimes in the afternoons, still quivering from you, with your smell all over me, and sit with her for a while. Although she did not acknowledge me I knew that she knew I was there. It was like being in the presence of a creature of another species, whose silent suffering was happening in a different sphere from the one I inhabited. I held her hand, or should I say she held mine. They were unexpectedly peaceful, these occasions, for me. The light in the room, the colour of tarnished tin, was the light of childhood. I would see again afternoons like this in the far past and myself as a child at a window watching the day fail and the rooks settling in the high, bare trees and the rain like time itself drifting down. That rain: when it grew heavy the drops danced on the shining tar of the road and looked to me like so many momentarily pirouetting little ballerinas; that must have been the very first simile I formulated.

Father Fanning came to visit, in his green suit and sandals, with his startled crest of young man's white hair standing up like a question mark (Tintin! – of course, that's who he reminded me of). Aunt Corky was not pleased to see him; her enthusiasm for God and godly things had not lasted long. She listened in silence, impatiently, blowing streamers of smoke past his head, as he spoke in his earnest and friendly way of the weather and the Lord's goodness; he might have been a tiresome stranger she had met on holiday and been polite to and who now had tastelessly turned up expecting to renew a seaside intimacy. After a little while he became discouraged and departed sadly. At the front door he tried to tell me again how good I was and in the guise of giving him a friendly pat on the shoulder I propelled him firmly into the street and shut the door on him.

And so Aunt Corky became another strand in the thick, polished, frightening rope into which my life was being woven. In the mornings I would wake with a knot of anxiety behind my breastbone, and for a minute or two I would lie stiff and staring as my mind strove laboriously to unpick this ganglion of hard-laid hemp. My days were a kind of breathless straining on tiptoe as I swung at the end of my fear between, on one side, Inspector Hackett and all he represented, and, on the other, Morden and the Da. Fear, yes, and something more than fear, a sense of there being another interpretation altogether of the things I thought I knew, of there being another world entirely, coterminous with this one, where another, wiser I grappled undaunted with terrible facts that this I could only guess at. And always there was the suspicion that for certain others I was a figure of fun, the one in the blindfold turning helplessly with outstretched arms in the midst of the capering crowd. Morden was at once evasive and scandalously blunt. 'I hear the cops are on to us,' he said to me one day with a shark's downturned grin. I stared at him, making a different kind of fishmouth. I had met him on Ormond Street sauntering through the morning crowds with the wings of his coat billowing and his crimson silk tie blowing back over his shoulder. I would often encounter him like this, going nowhere, relaxed and bored and faintly dangerous-looking, with a dead expression in his eyes. On such occasions he would drift to a stop and squint upwards at a corner of the roof of some distant building and begin to speak in a vague, distracted tone, as if we were already in the middle of a not very interesting conversation.

'Cops?' I said; it came out as a sort of frightened quack.

We walked down Rue Street. It was a blustery, brown day.

'Yes,' Morden said easily, 'Francie tells me you were accosted by a detective.' He glanced at me sideways with a bland expression. 'Fond of the boys in blue, are you?'

We came to the house and he looked on as I got out the

key and opened the door. I had a sense of silent derision. Dealing with Morden was like trying to get a grip on a big, soft, greased, unmanageable weight that had been dropped unceremoniously into my arms. He stood with his head cocked to one side and waited, considering me. The door stood open, the hall held its breath. He grinned.

'I hear you met the Da, too,' he said. He grasped me by the arm and gave it an eager shake. 'Tell us,' he said, 'what was he dressed as?'

I told him glumly and he laughed, a brief, loud shout.

'A priest?' he cried. Behind him an eddy of wind lifted dust and bits of paper on the pavement and swirled them in a spiral. 'What a character!' he said, shaking his head. 'He skinned a man alive one time, you know, and tanned the skin and sent it to the fellow's wife. In a parcel, through the post. True as God, he did.' He stepped past me and crossed the hall and started up the stairs. He halted with a hand on the banister rail and turned to me again. 'Don't mind the Da,' he said good-humouredly. 'Don't mind him at all.' He went on up, humming, then stopped a second time and leaned over the rail and grinned down at me. 'Cops and robbers,' he said, 'that's all it is, the whole thing.' He liked that. He laughed again and trudged on and laughing disappeared around a bend of the stairs. *'Cops and robbers, I'm telling you!'*

So you see how it was. Oh yes, as I have said, I was afraid, of course, but my fear was of that hot, fluttery variety that half the time feels like nothing more than a keen sense of anticipation. Something in me, a snickering goblin crouched and expectant, always wants the worst to happen. I remember once seeing in a newsreel report of some catastrophic flood somewhere an emaciated chap clad in turban and loincloth bobbing along on the torrent in a tin bathtub with his arms folded and grinning serenely at the camera. That's me, with my knees in my chest, helplessly being borne downstream in a trance of happy terror as the shattered tree-trunks and bloated bodies go swirling past. If the paintings were genuine they were stolen and I could go to jail for dealing with them. Simple as that. It was not prison, though, that I feared most, but the thought of losing you. (No, that's not true, why do I say such things – the prospect of prison filled me with boiling panic, at the very notion of it I had to sit down with a hand to my heart until I got my breath back.)

I have never been good at games, I mean the serious ones. I believe you really wanted to teach me how to play, I believe you did. There were times when I would catch you looking at me in a certain stilled, speculative way, with a smile that was hardly a smile, your head tilted and one eyebrow flexed, and I think now they were the moments when you might have taken pity on me and led me to the couch and sat me down and said, *All right now, listen, this is what is really going on* . . . But no, that is not how you would have done it. You would have blurted it out and laughed, wide-eyed, with a hand over your mouth, and only later, if at all, would I have realised the full significance of what it was you had told me. I never understood you. I walked around you, stroking my chin and frowning, as if you were a problem in perspective, a puzzle-picture such as the Dutch miniaturists used to do, which would only yield up its secret when viewed from a particular, unique angle. Was I very ridiculous? I say again, I don't care about any of the rest of it, having been cheated and made a fool of and put in danger of going back to jail; all that matters is what you thought of me, think of me. (Think of me!)

She it was who devised the games, she was mistress of the revels. I followed after her in my lumbering, anxious way, trailing my stick and pig's bladder, desperate to keep up. She was the initiator. She it was, for instance, who bought the fitting for the spyhole. It was the day that the third body was found, strung up by the heels on the park railings with throat cut so deeply the head was almost severed (the papers by now had found a name for the killer: the Vampire). When she came into the room, shaking rain-pearls from the hem of her black coat, I could feel her excitement – when she was like that the air around her seemed to crepitate as if an electric current were passing through it. She dropped her coat and handbag on the floor and plumped down on the couch and held out her upturned fist, smiling with her lips pressed shut, brimming and gleeful. My heart. 'Look,' she said, and slowly uncurled her fingers. I took the little brass barrel from her and peered at it in happy bafflement. 'Look through it,' she said impatiently, 'it's like a fish's eye.' I laughed. 'How will we fit it?' I said. She snatched the gadget from me and scanned the room through it, one eye screwed shut and a sharp little canine bared. 'With a drill,' she said. 'How do you think?'

I am not much of a handyman. She sat at my table smoking and watched me at work, offering facetious suggestions and snickering. After a long and bad-tempered search in the basement I had found a twist drill, an antique, spindly affair suggestive of the primitive days of surgery, and with this implement I bored a hole in the false wall, at knee level, as she directed. I asked no question; that was the first rule in all our games. When I had screwed the brass lens into place she went outside and knelt to test it. (By the way, what of that gap in the plaster through which I am supposed to have had my first glimpse of her? Must have been fixed.) She came back scowling. 'You've put it in the wrong way round,' she said. 'It's for looking in, not out!' She sighed. 'You're useless,' she said. 'Listen.'

She had it all worked out. This is how went. If we had an arrangement to meet at twelve o'clock, say, I was to come at eleven thirty and, without making a sound, kneel down at the spyhole and watch her for half an hour; then, at noon, I was to creep back out to the stairs and come tramping down the corridor as if I had just arrived. Sometimes, however, I was not to come early, and not to use the spyhole; nor was I to tell her which were the times I had been there unseen by her and which when I had not. In this way she would never know for certain if she was being spied on during the half hour before my arrival or if she was playing out her little charades for no one's benefit. I did as I was bidden, of course. What strange, shameful excitement there was in tiptoeing along the corridor – sometimes I went the entire distance on hands and knees – and putting my eye to that thrillingly cool glass stud and seeing the room beyond, radiant with silky light, resolve itself into a cup of swooping curves at the centre of which A. sat, a bulbous idol with pin-head and tiny feet and enormous hands folded in her swollen lap. This is how I always found her, sitting motionless and agaze, like tiny Alice waiting for the magic potion to take effect. Then slowly she would begin to stir, with odd, spasmic jerks and twitches. She would take a deep breath, drawing back her shoulders and lifting her head, carefully keeping her glance from straying in the direction of the spyhole; her movements were at once stiff and graceful, and touched with a strange, unhuman pathos, like those of a skilfully manipulated marionette. She would rise and take a step toward the window, extending one hand in a sweeping gesture, as if she were welcoming a grand guest; she would smile and nod, or hold her head to one side in an attitude of deep attention, and sometimes she would even move her lips in soundless speech, with exaggerated effect, like the heroine in a silent film. Then she would resume her seat on the couch with her invisible guest beside her and go through the motions of serving tea, handing him (there was no doubt as to this phantom's gender) his cup with a lingering smile and then demurely dropping her gaze and taking her lower lip delicately between her teeth and biting it until it turned white. Always the tableau began with these elaborate politenesses; gradually, however, as I shifted heavily from one knee to the other and blinked my watering eye, an atmosphere of menace would develop; she would frown, and shrink back and shake her head, pressing splayed fingers to her throat and lifting one knee. In the end, overwhelmed, her clothes undone, she would fall back slack-mouthed with breasts exposed and one arm outflung and a leg bared along its glimmering length to the vague dark hollow of her lap, and I would suddenly hear myself breathing. She would rest for a moment then, displayed there, her fingers idly playing with a strand of hair at the nape of her neck, and as the cathedral bell began to toll the noonday angelus I would get up stiffly and steal out to the landing and, composing myself as best I could (how the heart can hammer!), walk down the corridor again coughing and humming and breezily enter the room, by which time she would be sitting primly with knees pressed tightly together and her hands folded, looking up at me with a faint, shy, lascivious smile.

I wonder now if she devised all her scenarios beforehand or did she make them up as she went along? I was impressed always by how well she seemed to know what it was she wanted. Everything was at her direction, the words, the gestures, the positions, all the complex ceremonials of this liturgy of the flesh. *Tie my hands. Make me kneel. Blindfold me. Now walk me to the window.* How softly she stepped, like a sleepwalker, barefoot, with one of her own stockings bound tightly over her eyes, as I, half miserable and half excited, guided her across the room and stopped before the blank wall.

'Is this the window?'

'Yes.'

'Are there people in the street?'

'Yes.'

'Are they looking at me?'

'Not yet.'

The wall was pitted and scarred and there was the shadow of a dried-up water-stain shaped like a map of North America. Her hot little hand trembled in mine. Now, I told her, now they had seen her. And so powerful was the aura of her excitement that the scene began to materialise before me on the wall: the street and the stopped cars and the silent people staring up in the luminous grey light of the November day. She squeezed my hand; I knew what she wanted. Like a child being good she held up her arms and I bent and gathered her slip at the hem and lifted it slowly over her head, hearing the soft lisp of the silk as it grazed her skin. Now she was naked. The white wall reflected a faint effulgence on her breasts, her belly. She shivered.

'Have they really seen me?'

'Yes, they've seen you. They're looking at you.'

A sigh.

'What are they doing?'

'They're just pointing and looking. And some of them are laughing.'

A caught breath.

'Who? Who's laughing?'

'Two men. Two workmen, in their workclothes. They're pointing at you and laughing.'

She shivered again and gave a low gasp. I tried to take her in my arms but she stood rigid. Her greyed skin was cold.

'Why are you doing this to me?' she said softly. 'Why are you doing this?' And she sighed. And afterwards, when we were lying together slimed and sweating on the couch, she undid the stocking from her eyes and ran it thoughtfully through her fingers and said in the most matter-of-fact way, 'Next time, really take me to the window.'

She desired to be seen, she said, to be a spectacle, to have her most intimate secrets purloined and betrayed. Yet I ask myself now if they really were her secrets that she offered up on the altar of our passion or just variations invented for this or that occasion. One morning when I arrived at the house she was in the bathroom. I tapped on the door but she did not hear me, or did not choose to hear me. When I opened the door and slipped inside she was sitting on the side of the bath with a cracked mirror propped before her on the handbasin, cleaning her face with a pad of cotton wool. She did not look at me, only went still for a moment and drew in her lips to cut off the beginnings of a smile. She was wearing a loose shirt and her hair was wrapped in a towel. Her face without make-up was blurred, a clay-white, hieratic mask. I said not a word but stood with my hands behind me pressed to the door and held my breath and watched her. Steam swayed in the whitish light from the frosted window and there was the sharp tang of some unguent that made me think of my mother. A. finished with her face and stood up and unwrapped the towel and began vigorously to dry her hair, pausing now and then and shaking her head sideways as if to clear something from her ear. Our eyes met by accident in the mirror and immediately her gaze went blank and slid away from mine. Then, running her fingers through her still-damp hair, she hitched up her shirt and sat down on the lavatory and perched there for a minute, intent and still, her grey eyes fixed on emptiness, like an animal pausing on a forest track to drop its mark. A spasm of effort crossed her face and she was done. She wiped herself twice, briskly, and stood up. The cistern wheezed and gave its cataclysmic gasp. Her smell came to me, acrid and spicy and warm, and my stomach heaved languidly. She turned on the geyser then and glanced at me over her shoulder and said, 'Have you any matches?' I wanted to ask her if she always wiped herself with her left hand or was even that faked, too, but I did not have the heart.

But no, fake is not the right word. Unformed: that's it. She was not being but becoming. So I thought of her.

Everything she did seemed a seeking after definition. I have said she was the one who devised our games and enforced the rules, but really this seeming strength was no more than a child's wilfulness. In the street she would dig her elbow into my ribs and stare slit-eyed at some woman passing by. 'Hair,' she would say out of the corner of her mouth. 'Exact same shade as mine, did you not notice?' Then she would shake my arm and scowl. 'Oh, you're hopeless!' Poking among the drifts of immemorial rubbish in the corridors, one of our favourite pastimes, we came upon a mildewed volume of eighteenth-century erotic illustrations (suddenly it occurs to me: had she planted it there?) which she would pore over for hours. 'Look,' she would say, in a hushed, wondering tone, pointing to this or that indecorously sprawled figure, 'doesn't she look like me?' And she would turn from the page and search my face with touching anxiousness, my poor Justine, yearning for some sort of final confirmation of . . . of what? Authenticity, perhaps. And yet it was precisely the inauthentic, the fragile theatre of illusions we had erected to house our increasingly exotic performances, that afforded us the fiercest and most precious transports of doomy pleasure. How keen the dark and tender thrill that shot through me when in the throes of passion she cried out my assumed – my false – name and for a second a phantom other, my jettisoned self, joined us and made a ghostly troilism of our panting labours.

Will you laugh if I say I still think of us as innocents? No matter how dirty and even dangerous the games we played, something childlike always survived in them. No, that's wrong, for childhood is not innocent, only ignorant; we knew what we were doing. Paradoxical as it may sound, I think it was that knowledge itself that lent to our doings a lightsome, prelapsarian air. Like all lovers, we, I (for how do I know what *you* felt?) lived in the conviction that there were certain things that in us came into being for the first time in the world. Not great things, of course – I was no Rilke, and you were no Gaspara Stampa – yet between us always there was that which seemed to overleap the selfish flesh, that seemed to overleap even each other and, quivering, endured, as the arrow endures the bowstring before being transformed into pure flight. And still endures.

She told me her dreams. She dreamed of adventures, impossible journeys. Of a great dane that turned into a unicorn and ran away. Of being someone else. How solemn she would be, lying on her front with her chin on her hands and the cigarette lolling at the corner of her mouth and the swift smoke running up in a shaky line like the rope in a rope trick. The lilac shadows under her eyes. Her bitten fingernails. That flossed dip at the base of her spine. In these sleepless nights I go over her inch by inch, mapping her contours, surveyor of all I no longer possess. I see her turning slowly in the depths of memory's screen, fixed and staring, too real to be real, like one of those three-dimensional models that computers make. It is then, when she is at her vividest, that I know I have lost her forever.

I could feel it coming, that loss; from the start I could feel it coming. Intimations abounded: a word, a sly glance, a smile too quickly suppressed. In my arms one day she suddenly went still and put a hand to my mouth and said 'Ssh!' and I heard with a qualm of terror the faint, remorseless sound of a telephone ringing somewhere down in the depths of the house. A telephone! If a burst of gunfire had started up it would not have seemed more outlandish. Yet she was not surprised. Without a word she slipped from my arms and wrapped herself in my bathrobe and was gone. I followed after her, nimble with apprehension. The phone was in the basement, an ancient, bakelite model lost among jumbles of stuff on the workbench. I stopped in the doorway. She stood half turned away from me with one foot pressed on the instep of the other and the receiver cradled against her shoulder. She spoke to it softly as if to a child. I could sense that she was smiling. After a moment she hung up and turned and walked towards me with her arms tightly folded and her head lowered. Suddenly, acutely, I became aware of my nakedness. She folded herself against me and laughed with a low, tigerish rattle at the back of her throat. 'Oh,' she said almost gaily, 'how cold it is!' I stood mute with unfathomable anguish, and for a second the mist lifted and I was afforded a heartstopping view of a far and altogether different country.

It was she who discovered No. 23. She had been watching the place for ages, she said. It was supposed to be a solicitor's office (someone had a sense of humour) but the people she saw going in and out did not look as if they were on legal business. Then one day she arrived in the room and knelt excitedly on the couch without taking off her coat and tugged me by the hands and said I must come with her, that she had somewhere she wanted to take me. We hurried through the streets. It was mid-afternoon, there were few people about. Under an iron sky the pavements had a scrubbed, raw look and whoops of icy wind waited around corners. No. 23 presented a grimy, disused aspect. It had a big shop-window with a brown curtain pulled across it and a high, narrow front door. A. rang the bell and grinned and pressed herself against me with the crown of her head under my jaw; her hair was cold but her scalp burned. I heard dragging steps approaching inside and Ma Murphy in her cardigan and slippers opened the door and drew back her head and looked at us sceptically. 'He's not in,' she said. She had a strong moustache and a bosom that reached to where her waist had once been. A. sweetly explained that it was not the solicitor we had come to see. Ma Murphy continued to regard us with suspicion. 'Two of yiz,' she said. If it was a question we had no answer. After another interval of dour consideration she stepped aside and motioned us in. I hesitated, as if it were the portals to the Chapel Perilous that I was breaching, but A. excitedly tugged my arm and I followed her, my Morgana.

Ma Murphy's broad backside swayed ahead of us up a narrow stairs. The place was dim and there was a smell of stew. A. squeezed my hand gleefully and mouthed something at me that I could not make out. On the first floor we were shown into a sort of parlour, low-ceilinged, ill-lit and chilly, with an overstuffed sofa and net curtains and a table covered with oilcloth. Brownish shadows hung down the walls like strips of old wallpaper. Ma Murphy folded her hands under her bosom and resumed her sceptical regard. A. linked her arm more tightly in mine. I began to fidget.

'Yiz are not the Guards, are yiz?' Ma Murphy said with truculence.

A. shook her head vehemently. 'Oh no,' she said, 'no, we're not the Guards.' The woman fixed her eye on me. A. hurried on. 'We want a girl, you see,' she said.

I could feel myself blush. Ma Murphy remained impassive. Unable to sustain her colourless stare I turned with hands clasped behind me and paced to the low window and looked out; this was women's work, after all. Oh, I am a hound, and spineless, too. What was I feeling? Excitement, of course, the hot, horrible thrill of transgression; I might have been a sweaty little boy about to spy on his sister undressing. (Why do such moments always make me think of childhood? I suppose I am being reminded of first sins, those first, tentative steps into real life.) Outside, the grey was thickening; twilight already. A waft of melancholy rose in me softly, like a sigh. Below the window there was a narrow lane with dustbins and a jumble of lock-up sheds. A cat picked its way daintily along the top of a wall studded with broken glass. Why is it the detritus of the world seems to me always to signify some ungraspable thing? How could this scene mean anything, since it was only a scene because I was there to make it so? Behind me A. and the procuress were quietly discussing terms. I could have stayed there forever, glooming out of that mean little window as the winter day drew wearily to a close; not life, you see, but its frail semblance; that makes me happy.

Our girl's name was Rosie. She was a hard-edged twenty-year-old, slight but compactly made, with dyed yellow bangs and bad skin. She might have been the ghost of my daughter, if I had ever had a daughter. I addressed a pleasantry to her and in return was stared at coldly. She gave A. a cordial grin, however, and they struck up an immediate amity, and sat down side by side on the bed to take off their stockings, fags clamped identically in scarlet mouths and eyes identically averted from the smoke. The room was low and bare of everything except the bed and an office chair with a plastic seat. The bed had a disturbingly clinical look to it. Uneasily I took off my clothes and loitered by the chair in my drawers, feeling the small hairs rise on my skin, more from apprehensiveness than the cold. A.'s directions were simple: she and I were to make love while Rosie watched. That, Rosie said with a shrug, was all right by her; naked, she sauntered to the chair and, giving me an ironic glance, sat down and folded her arms and crossed her legs. Her shoulders were shapely, and her left earlobe was pierced by a tiny safety pin. A. lolled on the bed in her Duchess of Alba pose. The two of them considered me, quizzical and calm. I felt . . . perused. The consequences were inevitable. I muttered an apology, sprawled helplessly with my mouth crushed against A.'s neck. 'Don't worry,' she whispered breathily in my ear; 'just pretend.' She was pleased, I think. It was the way she would have wished it to be: not the act itself, but acting. And so for a quarter of an hour we toiled, miming passion, grinding and gasping and clawing the air. A. went at the task with especial energy, biting my shoulder and crying out foul words, things that she never did when we were alone and not pretending, or not pretending as much as we were now; I could hardly recognise her, and despite myself felt sad and faintly repelled. I avoided looking at Rosie – I could not have borne her disenchanted eye – but I was acutely conscious of her presence, and could hear the sound of her breathing and the tiny squeaks when she shifted her bare bum on the plastic seat. Halfway through our act she quietly lit up another cigarette. Afterwards, when she was putting on her clothes, I got up from the bed and tried to embrace her, in acknowledgement of something, I'm not sure what, and also, I suppose, as a rebuke to A. The girl went still and stood with her pants in her hands and one leg lifted, and sadly I released her. A. watched from the bed, and when Rosie was gone she stood up and laid her hand on my shoulder with a tenderness I had not known in her before that moment. 'We're just the same, aren't we, the two of us,' she said. 'Hardly here at all.' Or at least, might have said.

And that night I had the strangest dream, I remember it. You were in it. We were walking together through narrow, winding passageways open to the sky. It was our quarter, or an oneiric version of it – changed and yet the same – but also it was an open-air academy of some sort, a place of scholarship and arcane ritual: there was a hint of the Orient or of Arabia. No one was about save us. It was evening, overcast and darkly luminous, the sky low and smooth and flocculent above our heads. I was baffled but you knew our purpose there, I could feel you shivering with eagerness, your arm linked tightly in mine. We did not speak but you kept smiling into my face in that way you had, lips compressed and eyes shining with a kind of spiteful glee. We came to a pair of ornate doors, temple doors, they seemed, made of many intricately arranged interlocking blocks of polished wood through the interstices of which somehow a pallid daylight gleamed out from within. With a hieratic gesture and yet irreverently smiling and winking at me over your shoulder you reached up to the two wooden handles that were set very high, above our heads, and drew the doors open. Beyond was a narrow chamber, no more than another passageway, really, with a window at the end of it in which nothing was to be seen except a grey and glowing blankness that was a part of the sky or perhaps a clouded sea. Jumbled in this room and so numerous we hardly had space to make our way between them were what at first I took to be quarter-life-sized human figurines in contorted and fantastical shapes and poses, formed it seemed from a porous grey clay and stained with mildew or a very fine-textured lichen. As I walked here and there carefully amongst them, however, I discovered that they were alive, or animate, at least, in some not quite human way. They began to make small, sinuous stirrings, like things deep in the sea stirred by a once-in-a-century underwater current. One of them, a boy-shaped homunculus with a narrow, handsome head, perched on a high pedestal, smiled at me – I could see cracks forming in the mildew or lichen around his lips – smiled as if he knew me, or in some way recognised me, and, trying to speak but making only a mute mumbling, pointed eagerly past my shoulder. It was you he was showing me, standing with your strange smile in the midst of this magicked place. You. You.

6. **Revenge of Diana** 1642
J. van Hollbein (1595-1678)

Oil on canvas, 40 x 17½ in. (101.5 x 44.5 cm.)

The title, which is van Hollbein's own, will puzzle those unfamiliar with the story of Actaeon's ill-fortune in pausing to spy upon the goddess Diana at her bath, for which piece of mortal effrontery he was changed into a stag and torn to pieces by his own hounds. Van Hollbein himself was no scholar, despite the many classical references which appear in his work; like his great contemporary, Claude Lorrain, he came from a humble background, being the son of a corn-chandler from the town of Culemborg near Utrecht, and was largely ignorant of Latin and therefore had no direct access to the Virgilian world the poise and serene radiance of which he chose to ape in the work of his mature years. In this painting, the scene with which we are presented depicts the moment when Actaeon surprises the naked goddess (and, so it would seem from his expression, himself also), and therefore the action proper is yet to come; however, despite the limitations of his technique, the painter manages by a number of deft touches subtly to suggest the drama that will follow. Actaeon's stance, bent from the waist with arms lifted, has the tension and awkwardness of an animal rearing on its hind legs, while in the furrowing of his brow, where the drops of transfiguring water flung by the goddess still glisten, we seem to detect the incipient form of the antlers that presently will sprout there; and, of course, the dappled tunic that is draped about his thighs and chest and thrown over his left shoulder is obviously made of deerskin. Meanwhile the hounds milling at his heels are gazing up at their master in puzzlement and fierce interest, as if they have caught from him an unfamiliar, gamey scent. In the figure of Diana, too, turned half away and glaring askance at the gaping youth, we divine something of the violence that will ensue. How well the artist has caught the divine woman in her moment of confusion, at once strong and vulnerable, athletic and shapely, poised and uncertain. She looks a little like you: those odd-shaped breasts, that slender neck, the downturned mouth. But then, they all look like you; I paint you over them, like a boy scrawling his fantasies on the smirking model in an advertising hoarding. She is attended by a single nymph, who stands knee-deep in the shallows of the pool with the goddess's chiton and girdle folded over her arm and holding in her other hand, with curious negligence, Diana's unstrung bow. She maintains an odd, statuesque stillness, this figure, wide-eyed and impassive, her gaze fixed halfway between the goddess and the youth, as if she had been struck into immobility in the act of turning to look for the cause of Diana's startlement and dismay. Lowering over the entire scene and dwarfing the sylvan glade and the figures caught in their fateful moment are the wooded valley walls of Gargaphia, hazed and etherial in the golden light of afternoon and yet fraught with menace and foreboding. The temple built into the rocks on the right is unreal in its pale perfection and seems to gaze with stony sadness upon the scene that is being enacted under its walls. It is this stillness and silence, this standing aghast, as we might term it, before the horror that is to come, that informs the painting and makes it peculiarly and perhaps unpleasantly compelling. Just so the world must have looked at me and waited when

When she urged me to beat her I should have known the game was up, or at least that it soon would be. After such knowledge, and so on. There are moments – yes, yes, despite anything I may have said in the past, there are moments when a note sounds such as never has been heard before, dark, serious, undeniable, a strand added to the great chord. That was the note I heard the day she clutched my wrist and whispered, '*Hit me, hit me like you hit her.*' I stopped at once what I was doing and hung above her, ears pricked and snout aquiver, like an animal caught on open ground. Her head was lifted from the pillow and her eyes were filmy and not quite focused. Sweat glistened in the hollow of her throat. A vast, steel-blue cloud was sneaking out of the frame of the window and the rooftops shone. At just that moment, with what seemed bathetic discontinuity, I realised what the smell was that I had caught in the basement that first day when she brought me there. My heart now seemed to have developed a limp. In a frightened rush I asked her what she meant and she gave her head a quick, impatient shake and closed her eyes and took a deep breath and pressed herself to me and sighed. I can still feel the exact texture of her skin against mine, taut and slightly clammy and some-how both chill and hot at the same time.

In the closing days of November a false spring blossomed. (That's it, talk about the weather.) Bulbs recklessly sprouted in the parks and birds tried out uncertain warblings and people wearing half-smiles walked about dazedly in the steady, thin sunshine. Even A. and I were enticed outdoors. I see us in those narrow streets, a pair of children out of a fairy-tale, wandering through the gingerbread village un-aware of the ogres in their towers spying on us. (One of us, certainly, was unaware.) We sat in dank public houses and behind the steamed-up windows of greasy cafés. A. held on tightly to my arm, trembling with what seemed a sort of hazy happiness. I was happy, too. Yes, I will not equivocate or qualify. I was happy. How hard it is to say such a simple thing. Happiness for me now is synonymous with boredom, if that is the word for that languorous, floating sense of detachment that would come over me as I strolled with her through the streets or sat in some fake old-fashioned pub listening to her stories of herself and her invented lives.

It was she who first spotted Barbarossa. He was living in a cardboard box in the doorway of a cutler's shop in Fawn Street, a fat, ginger-bearded fellow in a knitted tricolour cap, that must have been left over from some football match, and an old brown coat tied about the middle with a bit of rope. We studied his habits. By day he would store his box down a lane beside the knife shop and pack up his stuff in plastic bags and set off on his rounds. Amongst the gear he carried with him was a mysterious contraption, a loose bundle of socketed metal pipes of varying thicknesses, like the dis-mantled parts of a racing bicycle or a chimney sweep's brushes, which he guarded with especial circumspection. Rack our brains though we might we could not think what use the thing could be to him, and though we came up with some ingenious possibilities we rejected them all. Obviously it was precious, though, and despite the considerable transportation problems it posed for him he lugged it everywhere, with the care and reverence of a court official bearing the fasces in solemn procession. His belongings were too much for him to carry all together and so he had devised a remarkable method of conveyance. He would take the pipes and three of his six or seven bulging plastic bags and shuffle forward hurriedly for fifteen yards or so and set down the bags in a doorway or propped against a drainpipe; then, still carrying the precious pipes, he would retrace his steps and fetch the remaining bags and bring them forward and set them down along with the others. There would follow then a brief respite, during which he would check the plastic bags for wear and tear, or rearrange the bundle of pipes, or just stand gazing off, thinking who knows what thoughts, combing stubby fingers through his tangled beard, before setting off again. Of all our derelicts – by the end we had assembled a fine collection of them, wriggling on their pins – Barbarossa was A.'s favourite. She declared she would have liked to have had him for a dad. I make no comment.

One afternoon we found ourselves, I don't know how, in a little square or courtyard somewhere near the cathedral – we could see the bell-tower above us, massive, crazy and unreal – and when we stopped and looked about, something took hold in me, a feeling of unfocused dread, as if without knowing it we had crossed invisible barriers into a forbidden zone. The day was grey and still. A few last leaves tinkled on the soot-black boughs of a spindly, theatrical-looking tree standing in a wire cage. There was no one about but us. Windows in the backs of tall houses looked down on us blankly. I had the sense of some vast presence, vigilant and malign. I wanted to leave, to get away from that place, but A. absently detached her arm from mine and stepped away from me and stood in silence, almost smiling, with her face lifted, listening, somehow, and waiting. Thus the daughter of Minos must have stood at the mouth of the maze, feeling the presence of her terrible brother and smelling the stink of blood and dung. (But if I am Theseus, how is it that I am the one who is left weeping on this desolate shore?) Nothing happened, though, and no one came, and presently she let me take her hand and lead her away, like a sleepwalker. Someday I must see if I can pick up the thread and follow it into the heart of that labyrinth again.

Often in the middle of these outings we would turn without a word and hurry back to the room, swinging along together like a couple in a three-legged race, and there throw off our clothes and fall on the couch as if to devour each other. I hit her, of course; not hard, but hard enough, as we had known I would, eventually. At first she lay silent under these tender beatings, her face buried in the pillow, writhing slowly with her limbs flung out. Afterwards she would have me fetch her the hand-mirror from my work-table so that she could examine her shoulders and hips and the backs of her flanks, touching the bruises that in an hour would have turned from pink to muddy mauve, and running a fingertip along the flame-coloured weals that my belt had left on her. At those times I never knew what she was thinking. (Did I ever?) Perhaps she was not thinking anything at all.

And I, what did I think, what feel? At first bemusement, hesitancy and a sort of frightful exultation at being allowed such licence. I was like the volunteer blinking in the spotlight with the magician's gold watch and mallet in his hands; what if I broke something ('*Go ahead, hit it!*') and the trick did not work and it stayed broken? From some things there is no going back – who should know that better than I? So I slapped at her gingerly, teeth bared wincingly and my heart in my mouth, until she became exasperated and thrust her rump at me impatiently like an urgent cat. I grew bolder; I remember the first time I drew a gasp from her. I saw myself towering over her like a maddened monster out of Goya,

174

hirsute and bloody and irresistible, Morrow the Merciless. It was ridiculous, of course, and yet not ridiculous at all. I was monster and at the same time man. She would thrash under my blows with her face screwed up and fiercely biting her own arm and I would not stop, no, I would not stop. And all the time something was falling away from me, the accretion of years, flakes of it shaking free and falling with each stylised blow that I struck. Afterwards I kissed the marks the tethers had left on her wrists and ankles and wrapped her gently in the old grey rug and sat on the floor with my head close to hers and watched over her while she lay with her eyes closed, sleeping sometimes, her breath on my cheek, her hand twitching in mine like something dying. How wan and used and lost she looked after these bouts of passion and pain, with her matted eyelashes and her damp hair smeared on her forehead and her poor lips bruised and swollen, a pale, glistening new creature I hardly recognised, as if she had just broken open the chrysalis and were resting a moment before the ordeal of unfolding herself into this new life I had given her. I? Yes: I. Who else was there, to make her come alive?

The whip was our sin, our secret. We never spoke of it, never mentioned it at all, for that would have been to tamper with the magic. And it was magic, more wand than whip, working transfigurations of the flesh. She did not look at me when I was wielding it, but shut her eyes and rolled her head from side to side, slack-mouthed in ecstasy like Bernini's St Theresa, or stared off steadily into the plush torture chamber of her fantasies. She was a devotee of pain; nothing was as real to her as suffering. She had a photograph, torn from some book, that she kept in her purse and showed me one day, taken by a French anthropologist sometime at the turn of the century, of a criminal being put to death by the ordeal of a thousand cuts in a public square in Peking. The poor wretch, barefoot, in skullcap and black pyjama pants, was lashed to a stake in the midst of a mildly curious crowd who seemed merely to have paused for a moment in passing to have a look at this free treat before going on about their busy business. There were two executioners, wiry little fellows with pigtails, also in black, also wearing skullcaps. They must have been taking the job in turns, for one of them was having a stretch, with a hand pressed to the small of his back, while his fellow was leaning forward cutting a good-sized gouge into the flesh of the condemned man's left side just under the ribcage with a small, curved knife. The whole scene had a mundane if slightly festive, milling look to it, as if it were a minor holiday and the execution a familiar and not very interesting part of the day's entertainments. What was most striking was the victim's expression. His face was lifted and inclined a little to one side in an attitude at once thoughtful and passionate, the eyes cast upward so that a line of white was visible under the pupils; the tying of his hands had forced his shoulders back and his knobbled, scrawny chest stuck out. He might have been about to deliver himself of a stirring address or burst out in ecstatic song. Yes, ecstasy, that's it, that's what his stance suggested, the ecstasy of one lost in contemplation of a transcendent reality far more real than the one in which his sufferings were taking place. One leg of his loose trousers was hitched up where the executioner – the one with the crick in his back, no doubt – had been at work on the calf and the soft place at the back of the knee; a rivulet of black blood extended in a zigzag from his narrow, shapely foot and disappeared among the feet of the crowd.

I asked her why she kept such a terrible thing. She was sitting cross-legged on the couch with the photograph in her lap, running a blindman's fingertips over it. I took it from her. The once-glossy surface, cross-hatched with a fine craquelure, had the flaky, filmed-over texture of a dead fish's eye.

'Are you shocked?' she said, peering at me intently; when she looked at me like that I understood how it would feel to be a mirror. Her gaze shifted and settled on the space between us. What did she know? The penumbra of pain, the crimson colour of it, its quivering echo. She did not know the thing itself, the real thing, the flash and shudder and sudden heat, the body's speechless astonishment. I handed her back the photograph. It struck me that we were both naked. All that was needed was an apple and a serpent. Light from the window gave her skin a leaden lustre.

'Tell me about that man you knew,' she said. 'The one that killed the woman.'

She was so still she seemed not even to breathe.

'You know nothing,' I said.

She nodded; her breasts trembled. She found her cigarettes and lit one with a hand that shook. She resumed her cross-legged perch on the end of the couch and gave herself a sort of hug. A flake of ash tumbled softly into her lap.

'Then tell me,' she said, not looking at me.

I told her: midsummer sun, the birds in the trees, the silent house, that painted stare, then blood and stench and cries. When I had recounted everything we made love, immediately, without preliminaries, going at each other like – like I don't know what. '*Hit me*,' she cried, '*hit me!*' And afterwards in the silence of the startled room she cradled my head in the hollow of her shoulder and rocked me with absent-minded tenderness.

'I went to No. 23 the other day after you were gone,' she said. I knew that dreamily thoughtful tone. I waited, my heart starting up its club-footed limp. 'I went to see Rosie,' she said. 'Remember Rosie? There was this fellow there who wanted two women at the same time. He must have been a sailor or something, he said he hadn't had it for months. He was huge. Black hair, these very black eyes, and an earring.'

I moved away from her and lay with my back propped

against the curved head of the couch and my hands resting limply on my bare thighs. A soft grey shadow was folded under the corner of the ceiling nearest the window. Dust or something fell on the element of the electric fire and there was a brief crackle and then a dry hot smell.

'Did you open your legs for him?' I said. I knew my lines.

'No,' she said, 'my bum. I lay with my face in Rosie's lap and held the cheeks of my bum apart for him and let him stick it into me as far as it would go. It was beautiful. I was coming until I thought I would go mad. While he was doing it to me he was kissing Rosie and licking her face and making her say filthy things about me. And then when he was ready again I sucked him off while Rosie was eating me. What do you think of that?'

I could feel her watching me, her little-girl's gloating, greedy eye. This was her version of the lash.

'Did you let him beat you?'

'I asked him to,' she said, 'I begged him to. While he was doing me and Rosie he was too busy but afterwards he got his belt and gave me a real walloping while Rosie held me down.'

I reached out gropingly and took one of her feet in my hand and held it tightly. I might have been one huge raw rotten stump of tooth.

'And did you scream?'

'I howled,' she said. 'And then I howled for more.'

'And there was more.'

'Yes.'

'Tell me.'

'No.'

We sat and listened to the faint, harsh sound of our breathing. I shivered, feeling a familiar blank of misery settle on my heart. It was an intimation of the future I was feeling, I suppose, the actual future with its actual anguish, lying in wait for me, like a black-eyed sailor with his belaying-pin.

I am not good at this kind of suffering, this ashen ache in the heart, I am not brave enough or cold enough; I want something ordinary, the brute comfort of not thinking, of not being always, always . . . I don't know. I looked at the photograph of the execution where she had dropped it on the floor; amongst that drab crowd the condemned man was the most alive although he was already dying. A. squirmed along the couch, keeping her eyes averted, and lay against me with her knees drawn up and her fists clenched under her chin and her thin arms pressed to her chest.

'I'm sorry,' she said, a sort of sigh, her breath a little weight against my neck. 'I'm sorry.'

We parted hurriedly on those occasions, not looking at each other, like shamefaced strangers who had been forced for a time into unwilling intimacy and now were released. I would stop on the doorstep, dazed by light, or the look of people in the street, the world's shoddy thereness. Or perhaps it was just the sense of my suddenly recovered self that shocked me. As I set off through the streets I would skulk along, wrapped up in my misery and formless dismay, a faltering Mr Hyde in whom the effects of the potion have begun to wear off. Then all my terrors would start up in riotous cacophony.

Aunt Corky said there were people watching the flat. She had rallied in the unseasonably vernal weather. The brassy wig was combed and readjusted, the scarlet insect painted afresh but crooked as ever on her mouth. In the afternoons she would get herself out of bed, a slow and intricate operation, and sit in her rusty silk tea-gown at the big window in the front room watching the people passing by down in the street and the cars vying for parking spaces like bad-tempered seals. When she tired of the human spectacle she would turn her eyes to the sky and study the slow parade of clouds the colour of smoke and ice passing above the rooftops. Surprising how quickly I had got used to her presence. Her smell – her out-of-bed smell, compounded of face powder, musty clothes, and something slightly rancid – would meet me when I came in the door, like someone else's friendly old pet dog. I would loiter briefly in the porch, clearing my throat and stamping my feet, in order to alert her to my arrival. Often in the early days I was too precipitate and would come upon her lost in a reverie from which she would emerge with a start and a little mouse-cry, blinking rapidly and making shapeless mouths. Sometimes even after I had noisily announced my arrival I would enter the room and find her peering up at me wildly with her head cocked and one eyebrow lifted and a terrified surmise in her eye, not recognising me, this impudently confident intruder. I think half the time she imagined the flat was her home and that I was the temporary guest. She talked endlessly when I was there (and when I was not there, too, for all I know); now and then I would find myself halting in my tracks and shaking my head like a horse tormented by flies, ready to hit her if she said one word more. She would stop abruptly then and we would stare at each other in consternation and a sort of violent bafflement. 'I am telling you,' she would declare, her voice quivering with reproach, 'they are down there in the street, every day, watching.' With what a show of outraged frustration she would turn from me then, fierce as any film goddess, swivelling at the waist and tightening her mouth at the side and lifting one clenched and trembling fist a little way and letting it fall again impotently to the arm of her chair. I would have to apologise then, half angry and half rueful, and she would give her shoulders a shake and toss her gilt curls and fish about blindly for her cigarettes.

As it turned out, she was right; we were being watched. I do not know at what stage my incredulity changed to suspicion and suspicion to alarm. The year was darkening. The Vampire was still about his fell business and another mutilated corpse had been discovered, folded into a dustbin in a carpark behind a church. The city was full of rumour and fearful speculation, clutching itself in happy terror. There was talk of satanism and ritual abuse. In this atmosphere the imagination was hardly to be trusted, yet the signs that I was being stalked were unmistakable: the car parked by the convent gates with its engine running that pulled out hurriedly and roared away when I approached; the eye suddenly fixed on me through a gap in a crowd of lunchtime office workers hurrying by on the other side of the street; the figure behind me in the hooded duffle-coat turning on his heel a second before I turned; and all the time that celebrated tingling sensation between the shoulder-blades. I was I think more interested than frightened. I assumed it must be Inspector Hackett's men keeping an eye on me. Then one morning I arrived home still shivery with the afterglow of an early tryst with A. and found the Da's big mauve motor car double-parked outside the front door. Young Popeye was at the wheel. I stopped, but he would not turn his eyes and went on staring frowningly before him through the windscreen, professional etiquette forbidding any sign of recognition, I suppose. He was growing a small and not very successful moustache of an unconvinced reddish tint, which he fingered now with angry self-consciousness as I leaned down and peered at him through the side window. I let myself into the house and mounted the stairs eagerly. I pictured Aunt Corky bound and gagged with a knife to her throat and one of the Da's heavies sitting with a haunch propped on the arm of the couch and swivelling a toothpick from one side of his mouth to the other. Cautiously I opened the door of the flat – how it can set the teeth on edge, the feel of a key crunching into a lock – and put in my head and listened, and heard voices, or a voice, at least: Aunt Corky, spilling invented beans, no doubt.

She was sitting by the fire in her best dress – you should have seen Aunt Corky's best dress – balancing a teacup and saucer on her knee. Facing her, in the other armchair, the Da sat, arrayed in a somewhat tatty, full-length mink coat and a dark-blue felt toque with a black veil (another one!) that looked like a spider-web stuck with tiny flies. He was wearing lumpy, cocoa-coloured stockings – who makes them any more? – and county shoes with a sensible heel. A large handbag of patent leather rested against the leg of his chair. Tea-things were set out on a low table between them. A half-hearted coal fire flickered palely in the grate. 'Ah!' said Aunt Corky brightly. 'Here he is now.'

I came forward hesitantly, feeling an ingratiating smile spreading across my face like treacle. What would be the rules of comportment here?

'I was just passing,' the Da said and did that cracked laugh of his, making a sound like that of something sharp and brittle being snapped, and his veil trembled. Dressed up like this he bore a disconcerting resemblance to my mother in her prime.

'I believe you're working together,' Aunt Corky said and gave me a smile of teasing admonishment, shaking her head, every inch the *grande dame*; she turned back to the Da. 'He never tells me anything, of course.'

The Da regarded me calmly.

'Is Cyril still out there?' he said. 'The son,' he told Aunt Corky; 'he's a good lad but inclined to be forgetful.'

'Oh, don't I know!' Aunt Corky said and cocked her head at me again. 'Will you take off your coat,' she said, 'and join us?'

I drew up a chair and sat down. I kept my coat on.

Cyril.

The Da took a draught of tea. He was having trouble with his veil.

'He was to blow the horn when you arrived,' he said. 'Did he not see you, or what?'

I shrugged, and said he must not have noticed me; I felt

suddenly protective toward young Popeye, now that I knew his real name, and had seen that moustache.

There was a silence. A coal in the fire whistled briefly. The Da stared before him with a bilious expression, pondering the undependability of the young, no doubt. Really, it was uncanny how much he reminded me of my mother, God rest her fierce soul; something in the stolid way he sat, with feet apart and planted firmly on the rug, was her to the life.

Aunt Corky's attention had wandered; now she gave a little start and looked about her guiltily.

'We were discussing art,' she said. 'Those pictures.' She smiled dreamily with eyes turned upward and sighed. 'How I would love to see them!'

The Da winked at me and with mock gruffness said, 'Why don't you take your auntie down to that room and let her have a look?' He turned to Aunt Corky. 'They're all the same,' he said, 'no regard.' He put down his cup and heaved himself from the chair with a grunt and walked to the window, stately, imperious and cross. 'Look at him,' he said disgustedly, glaring down into the street. 'The pimply little get.'

While his back was turned I looked at Aunt Corky with an eyebrow arched but she only gazed at me out of those hazed-over eyes and smiled serenely. Her head, I noted, had developed a distinct tremor. I had a vision of her dying and the Da and me carrying her downstairs to the ambulance, I at the head and the Da, his hat raked at a comical angle and his veil awry, clutching her feet and walking backwards and shouting for Cyril.

The Da came back and resumed his seat, arranging his skirts deftly about his big, square knees. His fur coat fell open to reveal a black velvet dress with bald patches. He eyed me genially.

'Have you seen our friend at all?' he said. 'Mr Morden.' I

shook my head. He nodded. 'They seek him here, they seek him there,' he said.

I considered for a moment and then asked him if he realised that the police were on to him. He only beamed, lifting his veil to get a better look at me.

'You don't say!' he said. 'Well now.'

I mentioned Hackett's name.

'I know him!' he cried happily, slapping his knee. 'I know him well. A decent man.'

'He asked me about the pictures,' I said.

His shoulders shook. 'Of course he did!' he said, as if this were the best of news.

Aunt Corky had been following these exchanges like a spectator at a tennis match. Now she said, 'A headache for the police, I am sure, such valuable things.' We looked at her. 'Guarding them,' she said. 'And then there would be the question of insurance. I remember dear Baron Thyssen saying to me . . .'

The Da was watching her brightly, with keen attention, like Prince the dog.

'Oh, we don't need that,' he said, 'the Guards, or insurance, any of that. No, no. We can look after our own things by ourselves.' He turned to me again. 'That right, Mr M.?' M for Marsyas, slung upside-down between two bent laurels with his innards on show and blood and gleet dripping out of his hair. 'By the way,' he said, 'I had a dream about you last night.' He lifted a finger and circled it slowly in the air above his head. 'I see things in my dreams. You were in a little room with your books. You weren't happy. Then you were outside and this fellow came along and offered you a job. He knew you were a man he could trust.'

I think of fear as a sort of inner organ, something like a big pink and purple bladder, that suddenly swells up and squeezes everything else aside, heart, liver, lights. It is always a surprise, this sudden, choking efflorescence, I can't say why; God knows, I should be familiar with it by now. The Da's pale eye in its pachydermous folds was fixed on me, and now something in it flashed and it was as if his face were a disguise within a disguise and behind it someone else entirely had stepped up and put a different eye to the empty socket and looked out at me with casual and amused contempt, taking the measure of me, and I flinched and heard myself catch my breath sharply.

The doorbell rang, two short bursts and then a long, and Aunt Corky's teacup rattled. The Da, become his genial self again, grasped his handbag and stood up, grunting. 'There's my call,' he said. Aunt Corky smiled up at him sweetly, her faltering mind elsewhere by now. He took her hand and shook it solemnly. 'Goodbye now, missus,' he said. 'And remember what I say – water, that's the thing for you. Take five or six good big glasses of water a day and you'll be right as rain. I'm a great believer in it.' He nodded slowly, still shaking her hand, his head and arm moving in unison; then he turned and stumped to the door. On the way he paused and peered at himself in the mirror above the sideboard and adjusted his hat and veil. He winked at me over his shoulder and said, 'Are my seams straight?' I opened the door for him. It felt as massive as a bulkhead. My hand on the latch would not be steady. 'Well, ta ta for now,' he said, and wiggled his broad rump and went off cackling down the stairs.

When I came back into the room Aunt Corky gave me a roguish little grin and shook her head.

'The company you keep!' she said.

That was to be her last levee. She sat on for a while gazing vacantly before her and when she stood up she took a tottery step backwards and I was afraid she would fall into the fire. I held her arm and she looked through me with an expression of vast, vague amazement, as if everything inside her had been suddenly transformed and she could no longer recognise the features of this internal landscape. 'I think,' she said with a shake in her voice, 'I think I would like to lie down.' Her meagre forearm – a stick in a brown-paper bag – quaked where I held it. She leaned her weight on me and looked at the morning light in the window and gave a fluttery sigh. 'How bright the evenings are becoming,' she said.

I left her and fled back to the house in Rue Street, but you had left. I lay down in my coat again on the couch. Our stain on the sheet had gone cold but was still damp; I took some of the pearly slime on my fingertip and tasted it. Sometimes after we had made love and were walking through the streets she would give an involuntary shiver and make a face, turning her mouth down at the corners, and say accusingly, 'I'm leaking.' These small vicissitudes amidst the logistics of love were always my fault. 'Look at me!' she would cry, showing me this smear, that bruise, 'look what you've done to me!' And then a sullen flush would spread up from her throat and her face would go fat with resentment, and I would have to spend a quarter of an hour abasing myself at her feet before she would unbend and let me touch her. But afterwards how she would leap under me, lithe as a fish, her ankles locked behind my back and her poor bitten nails searching for a purchase in the quivering muscles of my shoulders. She smelled of brine and bread and something excitingly musty and mushroomy. Her spit tasted of violets, whatever violets taste of. She licked my hands, took my fingers one by one into her mouth and softly sucked them. In the street she would stop suddenly and draw me into a doorway and make me put my hand inside her dress; 'Feel me,' she would say, her breath booming in my ear, 'feel how wet I am.' But most affecting of all, I think, were the times when she forgot about me altogether, standing by the window in afternoon light with her arms folded, looking out vague-eyed over the roofs, or in a shop beadily scanning the magazine racks, or just walking along the leaf-strewn pavements, with her head down, thinking; what moved me, I suppose, was that at those moments she was most nearly herself, this stranger every inch of whose flesh I knew better than I knew my own. She could change from one second to the next, now child, now crone. She had a short-sighted way of peering into her purse, the tip of her grey-pink tongue stuck in the corner of her mouth, while she rummaged for her lipstick or a cigarette lighter, and crouched thus she would look like one of those ancient little bird-like women you see in off-licences buying their nightly naggin. I told her so once, thick-throated with emotion, thinking of her old and of me gone. She said nothing, only considered me for a beat or two in silence and then decided – I could see her doing it – that she had not heard me.

Despite the physical attentions that I lavished on her – the demented gynaecologist, speculum in hand – there were areas into which I did not venture. I never knew, for instance, what precautions she took, if she took any. I never thought about it; I could not conceive of her conceiving. She was already her own child, a frail, suffering creature to be nursed and fondled and cooed over. She would speak of herself – her health, her looks, her desires – with the transparently false off-handedness of a doting mother holding up her little girl for general admiration. There were things she must have, especially if they belonged to others, whose relinquishing of them was an added savour. My past was a place for her to plunder: my childhood, my family, my school friends (that one was quickly exhausted), first loves, the gradual disaster of adulthood, all was a playground for her imagination. She would have stories, she insisted on stories. She had a particular craving for the lore of life in prison (have I mentioned my prison days, I wonder?), and would sit rapt as I described – not without embellishing them for her sake – the sexual transactions, the rituals of punishment and reward, the fevered excitement and alarm of visiting-day, the strange torpor of afternoons, the nights restless with sighs and whisperings, the silence of those interminable, louse-grey dawns. It might have been the lost world of the Incas I was describing. How passionately, with what gentle abandon, she would give herself to me at the end of these narratives, sinking against me with her face lifted and pale throat exposed and her shadowed eyelids twitching.

These memories. Where is she in them? A word, a breath, a turning look. I have lost her. Sometimes I wish that I could lose all recollection of her, too. I suppose I shall, in time. I suppose memory will simply fall away from me, like hair, like teeth. I shall be glad of that diminishment.

We never spoke of the pictures, or Morden, or any of that, yet it was always there. It was as if at some immemorial time we had discussed everything and then put it aside, never to be mentioned again. Sometimes this feeling was so strong that I would wonder confusedly if there really had been such a conversation and that somehow I had forgotten it. On the rare occasions when I did let slip this or that reference to my predicament – for by now it had become a predicament – she would turn aside vaguely and her eyes would swim and her face become slack, as if she were suppressing a yawn. Yet I seemed to feel too an awareness in her, a sort of steady, perhaps resentful yet vigilant wakefulness, such as a fitful sleeper would sense in one sitting all night unmoving by his bedside. Did you betray me, my love? Well, I don't care if you did. If we had it all to do over again I would not hesitate, not for a second.

Now I fell asleep, huddled there on the couch in my coat with my knees drawn up and my arms clenched around myself. I had a dream of you. We were here together, but now there was a third with us, a great pale naked woman, majestic and matronly, with broad hips and narrow shoulders. Her white breasts were tipped with pink and her eyes, fixed dreamily on nothing, were of a washed-blue shade. She was sprawled between us where we sat on either side of the couch, unfettered and yet our prisoner. I touched her rosebud mouth and she made a vague, lost sound deep in her throat. You smiled at me with great sadness and I guided your hand and laid it on her breast; my own hand was buried in the thick fleece of her lap, which felt warm and dry and inexplicably familiar. She was us and yet not us, our conduit and ourselves. You leaned down and kissed that red, pursed mouth, and your blue-black hair fell over her face like a bird's wing.

When I woke the day was already failing. I was cold and there were pins-and-needles in my fingers. Something had followed me out of that dream, a dark, slow, dragging something. I lay blank and unmoving for a while with my eyes open, clutched in fear. I had thought, before Morden and the pictures and you, that I would never be afraid again, that I had been immunised against it. I got myself up and stood by the window lost in a kind of unfocused anguish. Around me the house squatted sullenly in silence. I wanted to put my face into my hands and howl. Something was moving under me, I felt it, the first, infinitesimal shift of the glacier.

I left the house. On the doorstep the cold air filled my mouth like water and made me gag. The false spring had ended and the air was bruised and darkened by the first of winter's winds. Why is it, I wonder, that certain brownish, raw, late days like this make me think of Paris? Is that where you are? I can see you in your black coat and needle heels clicking along one of those mysteriously deserted, teetering little streets – rue de Rue! – off the Luxembourg Gardens. You stop on a corner and glance up at a window. Who is waiting for you in that shuttered room, with his smouldering Gauloise and smoky eyes and his air of moody insolence? Big hand-shaped leaves scrabble along the pavement.

Children are at play in the Gardens under the shedding planes, their voices come to you like memories. You think you will live forever, that you will be young forever. I hope he abandons you. I hope he breaks your heart. I hope that one day without a word he will walk out of your life and destroy you.

Why do I goad myself like this? I am so tired, so tired.

In Hope Alley a man in a raincoat and a pixie's woollen cap with a bobble walked along sobbing harshly and wiping his raw and reddened eyes with the heel of his hand.

As I passed through those wind-haunted streets I had again that creepy sense of being followed, and felt again that tingling target-point between my shoulder-blades. I kept stopping to look in shop windows or tie my shoelaces and covertly scanned the streets. It is remarkable how strange people come to seem when you are searching anxiously amongst them for a particular face. They turn into walking waxworks, minutely detailed yet not quite convincing copies of themselves, their features blurred to anonymity, their movements stiff and curiously uncoordinated. Yet when at last Inspector Hackett's grinning, globular head and cubist countenance materialised out of the crowd I did not recognise him until he spoke. I had been expecting Popeye or the Da or someone even worse. He was standing under the archway in Fawn Street with his hands in the pockets of his buttoned and belted raincoat. He looked more than ever like a life-sized toy man, overstuffed, and tacky with too many coats of varnish. We shook hands; always that odd, impressive formality. 'How is it going?' he said, another of those ambiguous openers that he and the Da both favoured.

We went through the archway and turned on to the quays. The wind whistled in the spumy air above the river and the water heaved and tumbled like a jumble of big square brown boxes. 'Winter coming on,' Hackett said and stuck his hands deeper into the pockets of his rat-coloured mac and gave himself a shivery squeeze with his elbows. 'I suppose,' he said musingly, 'it takes a lot of work to become an expert? Lot of reading and so on?' He glanced at me sideways with his jester's grin. 'Of course, you had plenty of time for it, didn't you.'

We stopped. He leaned on the river wall and watched the jostling water for a while. Cold spits of rain were falling at a steep slant. I told him how the Da had come to the flat dressed in his fur coat and velvet dress. He laughed.

'That's the Da, all right,' he said, 'mad as a hatter. He writes to me, you know. All sorts of topics: how to cure cancer, the Pope is a Jew, that kind of thing. Stone mad. He knows I know he has those pictures. The question is, where are they?'

Sometimes I think all of the significant occasions of my life have been marked only by misery and fright and a sort of disbelieving slow sense of shock as I step outside myself and stare aghast at what I am doing. Your face appeared and hung in my head like a Halloween mask, gazing at me with lips pressed shut, warningly.

'Morden has them,' I said, in a voice so faint I hardly heard it myself, and immediately had a dismaying urge to weep. 'There is a room . . .' And in my head you slowly turned your face away from me and I remembered you lifting your hand and floating it on the air and saying, *Free*.

Hackett kept his gaze fixed on the river, frowning, as if he were idly doing calculations in his head.

'Is that so?' he said at last, mildly. 'And you'd say they're the real thing?'

'Yes,' I said, 'it's them; they're genuine.'

A wash of watered sunlight from somewhere briefly lit the emerald moss on the river wall and made it glisten. Hackett blew into his hands and rubbed them together vigorously.

'The only question, then,' he said, 'is how will he get them out of the country.'

We walked on. A bus bore down on us suddenly out of nowhere with a swish of huge tyres. In its wake a ball of air and rain churned violently. I was thinking, *What have I done, what have I done?* But I knew, I knew what I had done.

'By the way,' Hackett said, 'I told you he'd do it again, didn't I?' I looked blank and he gave me a playful nudge. The fellow with the knife, he said. 'That's three now.' He squeezed himself again with his elbows. 'And more to come, I'd say.'

When I got home the house was silent. The bathroom door stood open, I saw the light from the bare bulb as I climbed the stairs, an expressionist wedge of sickly yellow falling across the landing and broken over the banister rail. What I took at first for a bundle of rags heaped on the floor in the open doorway turned out on closer inspection to be Aunt Corky. She lay with her head pressed at a sharp angle against the skirting board, and with one leg and an arm twisted under her. I thought of a nestling fallen from the nest, the frail bones and waxen flesh and the scrawny neck twisted. I assumed she was dead. I was remarkably calm. What I felt most strongly was a grim sense of exasperation. This was too much; really, this was too much. I stood with my hands on my hips and surveyed her, saying something under my breath, I did not know what. She groaned. That gave me a start. I became even more irritated: think of a stevedore, say, faced with an impossibly unhandy piece of cargo. I should not even have thought of touching her, of course, I had seen enough screen dramas to know better (*Don't try to move her, Ace, better wait for the doc!*). Impetuous as ever, though, I crouched down beside her and got her by an elbow and a knee and hoisted her across my shoulders in what I believe is called a fireman's lift. She seemed so light at first that for a second I thought that her limbs must have come clean out of their sockets and left the rest of her lying on the floor. The silk of her teagown felt like very fine, chill, slippery skin. She had soiled herself, but only a little, her old-woman's leavings being meagre; I was surprised not to mind the smell. I started up the stairs. It was a little like carrying an uprooted tent with the poles still tangled in it. I thought of Barbarossa and his precious contraption. I could feel Aunt Corky's bird-sized heart throwing itself against the cage of her ribs. 'Oh Jesus, son!' she said, and I was so startled to hear her speak so clearly so close to my ear that I almost dropped her. At least, I think that is what she said. It may have been something entirely different.

It was a long way up the via dolorosa of that flight of stairs. What at first had seemed an easy burden grew heavier with each step and by the time I got to the top I was bent double and sweat was trickling into my eyes. I worried about getting the key to the flat out of my pocket – should I set her down or keep her balanced precariously on my back while I fished about for it? – but luckily she had left the door on the latch. Going through, I bumped her head on the door-frame and she groaned. Later on, Dr Mutter could not understand how she had survived the ordeal of that climb, with a broken hip and what must have been an incipient aneurysm. I meant well, Auntie, really I did. For those few minutes you were my life and all I had left undone in it, not to mention one or two things that I had done but should not have. I wanted to save you, to bring you back into the world, to knit up your poor shattered bones and make you whole. While all I managed to do was hasten your dying. I wish you had not left me your money.

I got her into the bedroom and unloaded her on to the bed as gently as I could; stevedore first, then fireman, and coal deliverer now. Aunt Corky and the bedsprings complained in unison. Her eyelids flickered open but her eyes were absent, trying to see into some impossible distance. I stood back, breathing; I knew what must come next. I got the teagown off easily enough (those stick arms!) but underneath she was bound in various strapped and tethered things which took a lot of tugging and swearing to remove. What a mysterious and compelling object the human body is. It struck me that this was the first time in my life, within remembering, at least, that I had looked at a naked woman without desire. I thought of you, and shivered, and hastily covered Aunt Corky's withered flesh with a blanket and went out to the kitchen to fetch a bowl of water and a rag. My movements were those of a frantic automaton. I knew that if I paused now to reflect for a second my nerve would fail me and I might slam shut the bedroom door and flee the house altogether and never come back. I returned to the bedroom and was faintly surprised to find my aunt still there, though how or where I might have expected her to have gone I don't know. I switched on the bedside lamp and then switched it off again; the glimmer from the window was ample illumination for the task awaiting me. I lifted the blanket and, holding my breath, removed the bundle of soiled rags from under her hips and cleaned her with soap and water as best I could. When I was lifting one of her legs aside I heard a gristly, cracking sound that must have been, I realised later, the broken ends of her hip-bone shifting against each other. When I was done I covered her up again – she felt frighteningly cold – and went down to the telephone in the hall on the ground floor to call for help. I had brought no coins for the phone and had to bound upstairs again. In my memory of that afternoon I am constantly on the move, covering the distances between bedroom and kitchen and stairs in great, mad leaps, like a demented ballet dancer.

I called The Cypresses. I was not aware it was that number I had dialled until Mrs Haddon came squawking on the line. I began shouting back at her at once, in agitation and furious hilarity. 'I need a doctor!' I cried, and kept repeating it, and she kept answering me with the same phrase over and over, which I could not make out; she seemed to be insisting that she had *told me so*; perhaps it was Dr Mutter's name she was yelling – Kehoe, Devereaux, something like that? – for in a lull in the uproar she informed me in a small, hard voice that the doctor in fact was there, was standing at her elbow, no less, and that he would call in on his way home, if he had time. This last addition started me off shouting again, until the retired hangman who lived in the ground-floor flat put out his bristly head and glared at me. I took a breath and looked into the black, breathed-on hole of the receiver and said quietly that my aunt was dying. More than the words, it was the sudden calm in my voice, I think, that had an effect. There was a pause, and Mrs Haddon put her hand over the mouthpiece, making a squashing sound that gave me the sensation of being pushed in the face, and then came back and said sulkily that the doctor would set out right away.

Trembling after this exchange, I hurried upstairs again. As I neared the open door of the flat I paused, hearing my aunt's voice, and a crawling sensation passed up my back and across my shoulder-blades. Who was she talking to? Quakingly I went inside and shut the door behind me and approached the bedroom on tiptoe. I decided that if it was the Da, who had somehow got in again without my seeing him, I would kill him. I even pictured myself coming up behind his broad back with a poker in my hand and . . . But there was no one, only Aunt Corky lying on her back talking to the ceiling. Her eyes were open but they still had that distant, preoccupied expression. The wind had slammed the door, she was saying, a dreadful wind had sprung up in the night and slammed the door shut. She spoke in awed tones, as if of some great and terrible event. Eerily the scene rose before me: the shadowed furniture crouched in stillness, a gleam of light on a polished wooden floor and a Biedermeier clock softly clicking its tongue, then a wary stirring as if something had been heard and then the great gust and the door swinging shut like a trap. Her big hand lay on the blanket, twitching; I took it in mine: it was chill and dry yet somehow slippery. I seemed to have been here for hours yet day still lingered in the window and the sky was a high dome of muddied radiance. I went and looked down into the tangled shadows in the garden and thought of the myriad secret lives teeming there. Rooks wheeled and tumbled in the wind-tossed sky like blown bits of black crape. I put my forehead to the coolness of a stippled pane and felt the soft throb of the world in the glass. Night was creeping up the garden. I did not know myself. Behind me the old woman whimpered. I began to pace the room and heard myself counting my steps. One two three four five six, turn. Time seemed to have faltered here; day surely was dead by now but still the sky clung to its tawny glimmer. Aunt Corky lay motionless with her eyes closed, like an effigy of herself, there and yet not there. I wanted to speak a word aloud and hear my own voice but I could not think what to say and anyway I was embarrassed; this was a special manner of being alone. One two three four five six, turn.

I recall that half hour with a strange and potent clarity. Nothing happened – precisely nothing happened: it was like time spent in a lift or waiting to hear news that will not come – yet I have the sense of an event so vast as to be imperceptible, like the world itself turning towards night. It was as if I were undergoing a ritual test or rite of purification: shadows, solitude, cawing rooks, the sleeping ancient, and I in the dimness pacing, pacing. When at last the doorbell rang, a sustained and somehow unfamiliar, harsh trilling, it sounded in my ears an urgently liturgical note.

When I opened the front door to him Dr Mutter stepped in quickly with a sideways motion, like a spy, or a man on the run. He was tall and awkward with a small, rather fine head set upon a long stalk of neck. He reminded me of those unfortunates who in the last year of school would suddenly turn into six-footers, all wrists and knees and raw-boned anguish. When he spoke he had a habit, picked up from Mrs Haddon, perhaps, of gazing off intently to one side, as if he had just been struck by a terrible thought to do with something else entirely. He shook my hand gravely, his eye fixed on a patch of wall beside my shoulder, and followed me up the stairs with weary tread, sighing and softly talking, whether to me or to himself I did not know. In the bedroom I switched on the light and he stood a moment contemplating Aunt Corky with his bag in his hand and his shoulders stooped. He hooked a finger under his shirt-collar and – shades of Hackett, this time – tugged it vigorously, throwing up his chin and sliding his mouth sideways, while his adam's apple bounced on its elastic. 'Hmm,' he said uncertainly. Aunt Corky was an ashen colour and she seemed to have shrunk appreciably in the minutes that I was away answering the doctor's ring. Her wig of yellow curls was still incongruously in place. Dr Mutter laid a bony hand on her forehead. 'Hmm,' he said again, hitting the tone of gravity with more success this time, and frowned in what he must have thought was a professional way. I waited but nothing more came. I said I thought she must have broken something when she fell; I could not rid my voice of a note of impatience. He seemed not to have heard me. He turned to me but looked hard at the window. 'We'll have to have an ambulance, I think,' he said.

The telephone again, and another lip-gnawing wait. I paced while Dr Mutter muttered. Then the ambulance and the blue light in the street, and two jolly ambulance men with a stretcher, and at the door of each flat on the way downstairs a face peering out in eager sympathy. On the pavement I hung back while they stowed my aunt. The lighted interior of the ambulance reminded me of a nativity scene. The night roundabout this moving crib was wild and raw, with a black sky full of struggle and tumult. The blanket under which my aunt lay strapped was the colour of half-dried blood. One or two bundled passers-by slowed their steps and craned for a look. An ambulance man came to the open back door and held out a hand to me. 'There's a seat here,' he said. For a second I did not know what he meant. Dr Mutter was already seated beside Aunt Corky with his bag on his knees. In the neon glare both patient and doctor had an identical pallor. Reluctantly I climbed up to join them, queasily feeling the big machine tilt under my weight and then right itself.

The hospital . . . Must I do the hospital? A windy porch faintly illumined by the swaying light of what my memory insists was a gaslamp; within, a corridor the colour of phlegm where my aunt on her trolley was briefly abandoned like a railway wagon shunted into a siding. There was a warm, gruelly smell that brought me straight back to infancy. Somewhere unseen what sounded like a doctor and a nurse were listlessly flirting. Then a flurry of starched uniforms and rubber soles squealing on rubber floors and Aunt Corky was briskly wheeled away.

When I saw her again, in the aquatic hush and glow of a dark-green room somewhere underground, I hardly recognised her. They had taken off her wig; the few wisps of her own hair that remained were the same shade of rusty red as mine. How pale her scalp was, white and porous, as if it were the bone itself that I was seeing. They had removed her teeth, too; I wonder why? I touched her cheek; very firm, cool but not yet cold, and slightly clammy, like recently moulded putty. I stepped back and heard it again, more distinctly this time, that black wind sweeping through the stillness of the European night and the dark door slamming shut.

A hand touched my shoulder. I jumped in fright. First my heart was in my mouth and then I seemed to have swallowed it. Dr Mutter hung behind me at a pained angle. 'Have a word?' he said softly. I followed him to another subterranean room, a windowless cell with a metal table and two metal chairs and a bare lightbulb that shivered on its flex in time to the beat of some vast motor silently throbbing at the core of the building. We sat. The chairs gave out prosthetic creaks. Dr Mutter leaned down sideways suddenly as if to lay his cheek on the table, but he was only reaching into his black bag. He produced a dog-eared form and looked at it grimly in silence for a long, unhappy moment. Then he shifted his gaze to a far corner of the room and sighed.

'They're insisting she must have died before the ambulance came,' he said. His troubled eyes met mine briefly. 'I didn't think she was gone, did you?' I looked at my hands on the table; in the shivery glow from the bulb above my head they had a greenish cast. He sighed again, crossly this time, and stuck a finger under his collar and did that thing with his chin and sideways sliding mouth. 'I think they're just avoiding paperwork, myself,' he said crossly. 'Anyhow, it means I have to do the cert. Now . . .' He peered with misgiving at the paper before him and began to ask me questions about Aunt Corky that I could not answer. I told him I had hardly known her. He paused and nodded and sucked his pen. 'But she was living with you,' he said. I had no answer to that, either. It was an awkward moment. What could I do? Shamelessly I made it all up, dates and places, whatever he asked for; an invented life. I felt Aunt Corky would not mind. He wrote it all out happily; I would not have been surprised if he had started to whistle. Then we got to the tricky question of the cause of death and he became depressed again and sucked his pen and shifted in his chair, sighing and blinking, like a student sitting an examination for which he had not sufficiently prepared. He turned to me again hopefully. With diffidence I suggested heart-failure. He thought it over briefly and shook his head. 'Needs to be more specific,' he said. We brooded. He considered the ceiling while I stared at the floor. Next, I suggested stroke. He was doubtful but I persisted. 'All right,' he said, 'stroke it is.' Still he hesitated, then frowning he bent over the document and, having dithered for a final second, inscribed the word and sat back with an air of dissatisfaction and faint resentment, as if it were a crossword puzzle he had been doing and I had solved the final clue for him. He flourished the paper in my face, like something he was about to palm; I tried to read his signature but could not make it out. Then he stowed it in his bag and we stood up awkwardly, patting our pockets and looking about at nothing. I could sense him working up to something. Suddenly he took my hand in both of his and gave it a sort of anguished shake. 'I'm sorry,' he blurted, looking desperately past my shoulder, 'I'm sorry for your trouble,' as if . . . well, as if I had suffered a real bereavement; as if, indeed, I were in pain. How had he come by such an idea? I stared at him, shocked, and inexplicably dismayed, then turned away without a word. Amazing, as Morden would have said.

Outside, the night set upon me with a vengeance. Black rain fell across the shaking lamplight in the porch and the carpark was awash with wrinkled water. On the road the wind was smacking its huge hands on the streaming tarmac and passing cars dragged white-fringed tailfins in their wake. It took me a long time to find a taxi. The driver, humped and hatted, reminded me of the fellow who had taken me to fetch Aunt Corky from The Cypresses; maybe it was the same one, I would not be surprised. In the suddenly, definitively empty flat I threw myself on the couch – would I be able to get myself into that bed ever again? – and slept fitfully, hearing the nightwind keening for Aunt Corky. She came to me in a dream and sat beside me calmly with her labourer's big square hands folded in her lap and told me many things, none of which I can remember. I woke into an exhausted dawn. The world outside looked tousled and awry after the night's riotous gales. I was prey to an odd, fevered exhilaration; I felt buoyant and hollow, like a vessel that had been emptied out and scoured. The bedroom I avoided; the bathroom was not much better. I shaved with a shaky hand, and cut myself. I wanted to see you. That was all I could think, that I must see you.

7. **Acis and Galatea** 1677
Jan Vibell (1630-1690)

Oil on canvas, 18 x 27½ in. (45.8 x 69.9 cm.)

How calmly the lovers . . . I can't. How calmly the lovers
lie. (As you lied to me.) How calmly the lovers lie embow-
ered in bliss. In blissful unawareness of the watcher in the
woods. Polyphemus the cyclops loves Galatea the nereid
loves Acis the shepherd. The one-eyed giant plies the faith-
less nymph with gifts (see Ovid, *Metamorphoses*, Book XIII),
to no avail. Acis, son and lover of a sea nymph, Acis must
die, crushed by a rock the giant hurls, and then will be
transformed into a river (presently Odysseus with his burning brand will settle in turn the cyclops' hash). Vibell's is a
subtle and ambiguous art; is the subject here the pain of
jealousy or the shamefaced pleasure of voyeurism or, again,
the triumphant female's desire to be spied on by one lover
while she lies in the arms of another? In this painter's dark
and sickly world nothing is certain except suffering. The
glorious, sunshot landscape against which the little triangular
drama is played out, reminiscent of the landscapes of Watteau
and Vaublin, is at once a stately pleasure park and a portrait
of Nature rampant and cruelly supreme. The feral profusion
of plants and animals seems a token of the world's indifference to human affairs. Polyphemus himself is dwarfed by

the overarching surroundings amongst which he lurks: it is not he who is the giant here. See him crouching in the depths of the greenery (do you see?), his single eye staring, mad with grief and rage; is he merely hunched in pain or is he engaged in an act of anguished self-abuse? The artist's dirty little joke. I feel a strong and melancholy affinity with the lovelorn giant. The lions and bears, the bulls and elephants (it is apparent Vibell has never seen a real elephant), which are the cyclops' unavailing gifts to the uncaring nereid, roam the landscape as if lost in vague amaze, incongruous in this northerly clime, amidst these tender greens, soft umbers, limpid blues; soon, we feel, very soon they shall throw off puzzlement's restraint and then the slaughter will start. Under their great mossy rock the lovers lie entwined like twins in the womb. The pool of blue waters at the feet of Acis prefigures the transformation that awaits him, while the jagged point of rock above his head seems poised to shatter him. Galatea. Galatea. She is the daughter of Nereus. She will make a river of her slain lover. The rock will split and from the crevice will spring a sturdy reed, slender, wet, glistening. I am Acis and Polyphemus in one. This is my clumsy song, the song the cyclops sang.

I should not have gone to Rue Street in that raw and shaken, deludedly eager frame of mind. The morning had an air of aftermath, with fitful gusts of wind and torn clouds scudding and leaves and litter flying everywhere. I stepped along as if on springs, snuffing up the chill air through lifted nostrils and contemplating the mystery of death. This was a world without Aunt Corky in it. What had been her was gone, dispersed like smoke. Forgive me, Auntie, but there was something invigorating in the thought; not the thought that you were no more, you understand, but that so much that was not you remained. No, I do not understand it either but I cannot think how else to put it. I suspect it was a little of what the condemned man must feel when the last-minute reprieve comes through and he is led away rubber-kneed from the scaffold: a mingling of surprise and left-over dread and a sort of breathless urgency. *More, more* – it is the cry of the survivor – *give me more!* I stopped at the Ptomaine Café in Dog Lane and sat down amid the coughs and the fag-smoke and ate a monstrous breakfast, sausages and black pudding and a rasher sandwich and a fried egg singed brown around the edges and floating in a puddle of hot fat. *Che barbaro appetito, lalala la!* I even bought, from a dispenser the size of a coffin ('Give it a kick,' one of the regulars advised me with a sepulchral wheeze of laughter), a packet of cheap cigarettes, and though I have never been a smoker I sat there puffing away and smiling about me hazily. Sometimes I really think I must be mad.

In Rue Street three cars were parked crookedly outside the house, one with a plastic dog in the back window. The front door of the house was open wide, hanging by a hinge, though it gave an impression more of gaiety than violence, as if the damage were the result of a carnival crowd having forced its way through. A lumpy man in grubby but sharply pressed grey slacks and a blue blazer loitered in the hall with a cigarette ill-concealed in a cupped hand that was the size of a small ham. He gave me an uncertain look and said something that I did not catch as I swept past him and started up the stairs. On the first landing I came upon two more henchmen, standing about with the vacant, slightly peeved air of callers who had already been kept waiting an unconscionable time. They were wearing anoraks, and one of them had what at first I did not recognise as a snub-nosed submachine-gun resting negligently in the crook of his arm. They regarded me with interest. This pair also I disdained and went on up the stairs. At the door of the atelier yet another anorak stood guard; he too was armed. He was menacingly polite. He wanted to know who I was. I told him I lived here, which was almost true, after all. He frowned, and made an uncertain gesture with the snout of his machine-gun, waving me on. I swept past him haughtily with nostrils flared and head thrown back. I had an extraordinary feeling of invincibility. I could have walked through the wall if necessary.

I paused in the doorway, though, struck as always by the glare of white light falling from the tall, sky-filled windows. Morden was standing as he had been the first time I saw him, posed in profile against the backdrop of the draped sheet, his big flat face lifted to the light and his hands thrust deep in the pockets of his long overcoat. He did not turn. In the middle of the floor Inspector Hackett stood looking at his left hand, which was bleeding; he was subjecting it to a close and what seemed admiring scrutiny, turning it this way and that in front of his face. A little way off from him Prince the dog sat stiffly to attention, in an attitude at once defiant and abashed and licking its lips rapidly and noisily, its forelegs trembling. Francie squatted beside the dog with a hand on its scruff. He gave me an impassive glance.

'Ah, Mr M.' said Hackett. 'Come in, come in. You're just in time, as usual.' He seemed in high good humour, and was polished to a particularly bright shine today. He extended his hand proudly for my inspection; a drying trickle of blood led down his wrist and under his shirt-cuff. 'Will you look what the towser did to me?' he said. Together we contemplated the wound. 'More of a rip than a bite,' he said. 'See?'

There was a step behind me in the doorway and a tall, thin, skull-faced man in a three-piece suit of houndstooth tweed came in drying his hands on an enormous, snowy handkerchief. His small, bony head was broad at the brow and narrow at the chin, and he had a peculiarly prominent upper lip that made it seem as if he were wearing a set of stage teeth over his own. Blue eyes, very keen and watchful and spitefully amused. He had the manner, at once sleek and brisk, of a medical man – that handkerchief, those hands – and for a second I saw you sprawled on the chaise-longue in a tangle of blood-soaked sheets, one shoe off and one white hand dangling to the floor.

'Mr Sharpe!' Hackett said genially and pointed his wounded hand at me. 'Here's Mr . . . what is it again? . . . Mr Morrow. Mr Morrow – Mr Sharpe.'

Sharpe looked me up and down quizzically and sniffed.

'You are the art expert, are you?' he said. His blue glance glittered and I could see he was suppressing a snicker.

'Mr Sharpe is over from England,' Hackett said, his voice dropping a curtsey. 'I thought it would be a good thing to get another expert in.' Gently he smiled an apology. 'A second opinion, so to speak.'

Sharpe finished with the handkerchief and deftly tucked it into his breast pocket, then paced to the window with one hand in the pocket of his jacket and stood for a moment in thoughtful contemplation of the street. Still Morden had not turned. All waited. Inspector Hackett delicately cleared his throat.

'Yes,' Sharpe said, as if in answer to a question. He turned with a quick movement, suddenly brisk. He looked at Hackett, at Morden and at me. 'They are all copies,' he said. 'Every one of them.'

There was a beat of stillness, as if everything everywhere had halted suddenly and then slowly, painfully, started up again. Sharpe, gratified at the effect he had made, looked about at us with a faint, death's-head leer. Morden turned his face and gazed at me without expression. Hackett stood with his head tilted, faintly frowning, as if he were listening to something ticking inside his skull. He gestured vaguely at Sharpe with his bloodied hand. 'Here, give us a lend of that hankie,' he said. Sharpe drew back, startled. He hesitated, and reluctantly, with an expression of deep distaste, drew out the handkerchief and relinquished it. Hackett with thoughtful deliberation wrapped the cloth around his torn hand and then stood looking at the loose ends helplessly, until I stepped forward and tied them for him, and remembered as I did so a woman in a flower shop I used to frequent, in the days when I did that sort of thing, who could tie a ribbon into an elaborate bow with a deft twist of one hand. I could hear Hackett breathing; he exuded a hot, moist, constricted smell, the same smell a crippled uncle in my childhood used to leave behind him when he was lifted out of his wheelchair. Strange the things the mind remembers at a time like that.

'Yes,' Sharpe said again, pleasurably chafing together his pale, long-fingered hands, 'they are copies, no doubt of it. One or two are not bad, in their way. Done from photographs, I should think, probably those rather muddy ones in Popov's so-called *catalogue raisonné* of the Behrens collection.' A faint, sour smirk and Popov was dismissed. 'Two copyists were involved, I believe. Amateurs. The canvases and frames are Victorian, the pigments were supplied by the grand old firm of Messrs Winsor and Newton.' He frowned pleasantly and looked at his finger-nails. 'Such a quintessentially English name, I always think.' He allowed a sly, almost flirtatious glance to slide over me. 'I cannot imagine how anyone could have mistaken such daubs for the real thing.'

The dog detached itself from Francie and trotted forward silently and sat down beside me, folding itself into position with a deft, subsiding sweep of its haunches. I put my hand on its head. Its fur had the bristly, polished texture of plastic and smelled, not unpleasantly, of old carpets; the feel of it – how shapely that skull – imparted to my hand an incurious, companionable warmth. They say dogs can smell fear; perhaps this one could smell . . . what? Shock? But I was not shocked, not really. There had been an odd, unidentifiably familiar ring to Sharpe's announcement; it was like news so long awaited that when it came at last it was no longer news. My brain had slowed to an underwater pace. I wanted to sit down. I wanted to sit down in some dim, deserted corner and think slowly and carefully for a long time. There was much to be pondered.

Morden turned his head at last and spoke. 'I told you,' he said to Hackett, 'I told you they were copies.'

'Fakes,' Hackett said.

The dog growled softly and Francie slapped it on the snout.

'Copies,' Morden said again, with soft emphasis, and smiled.

Gall, I was thinking; Gall the painter and the piss-artist Packy Plunkett.

Hackett was examining his bandaged paw again. I admired his self-possession.

'They're signed,' he said mildly, in a faraway tone, as if he were thinking of something else altogether.

Morden gave a start of mock astonishment. '*Just what is it you're driving at, Inspector?*' he said in an Ealing-comedy accent, and Sharpe, who had been leaning against the window-frame with an expression of supercilious amusement, arms folded lightly on his prominent little chest, laughed. Morden came forward slowly, smiling at the floor and shaking his head. He stopped beside Hackett and contemplated him almost with compassion. Hackett frowned at the window.

'Have I tried to pass the pictures off as the genuine article?' Morden said. 'Have I tried to flog them to anyone? No. They're copies. I had them made. I'm an art-lover. I'm going to hang them in my house. In my house in France. My villa on the Riviera. Is that a crime?'

Hackett turned to him and—

Ah, I am tired of this. Shall I have Prince bite someone else, take a lump out of Morden's pinstriped calf or turn on Francie and tear out his throat? No, I suppose not. I stood stroking the dog's head and listened to them sparring, their voices coming to me buzzingly, as if from a long way off. I had sunk into a dulled, sleepwalking state, not unpleasant, really, and almost restful. The rug had been pulled from under my feet with such skill and swiftness that I had hardly noticed myself tumbling arse over tip and banging the back of my head on the floor.

Presently I found myself in the street with Hackett; we walked to his car in a shared, thoughtful silence. His men, silent also, had already packed up their guns and driven away. He got behind the wheel and started up the engine and let it idle. I stood beside him at the open door with my hands in the pockets of my mac. It had begun to rain, a faint, pin-like stuff that swayed and swirled in the gusting air. November. I told him that my aunt had died. He nodded seriously but said nothing and went on gazing through the windscreen. Could he have known about Aunt Corky? Was he so intimate with the details of my life? The thought was almost comforting. I have always wanted to be watched over. He heaved a sigh and put the car into gear. 'They'll have to do something about that dog,' he said absently. His hand was still bandaged with Sharpe's handkerchief, stiff now with drying blood. I shut the door on him and he crept the car away at the speed of a hearse.

I met Morden coming down the street with Francie and the dog behind him (Sharpe by now has been wrapped up in his tissue paper and safely stowed away). Morden had the look of a schoolboy who has pulled off a glorious prank. Full of himself, as my mother would have said. He was buried in his big coat with his hands in the pockets and the collar turned up against the rain. When they drew level he stopped and fixed me with his blankest look; yes, trying not to laugh, as always. 'Sorry about the pictures,' he said. 'Just a joke.' He nodded once brusquely and they passed on in file, the three of them, satrap and vizier and heraldic hound. Francie and the dog cast a backward look, both grinning. I shall miss old Prince.

Since I am no longer speaking to anyone except myself (and maybe some dazed survivor of Armageddon, in foot-rags and squashed top-hat, idly turning over these scorched pages in his bomb-shelter of a night), I do not know why I should go on fussing over niceties of narrative structure, but

I do. It troubles me, for instance, that at about this point I have a problem with time. After that Day of Revelation there is a hiatus. A day and night at least must have passed before Aunt Corky's interment but I have no recollection of that interval. Surely I would have tried to see you; surely, knowing all that I now knew, and with so much more still to know, my first thought would have been to confront you? But I stayed clear of Rue Street, where the gin-trap and the men with the guns were, and instead laid low in my hole, licking my wounds.

The sun shone for Aunt Corky's funeral, weak but steady, though the day was cold. The Da turned up. God knows how he knew the time and place. I was surprised at how glad I was of his presence. Aunt Corky too would have been pleased, I'm sure. The big mauve car came swarming up the cemetery drive, incongruously gay amid the sombre yews and gesticulating marble angels, and drew to an abrupt stop, its front parts nodding. Popeye in his outsized suit shot out from behind the wheel in his whirling way and snatched open the rear door, and with a heave and a shove the Da emerged and stood and looked about him with an air of satisfaction. Today he was wearing a plain dark suit and dark overcoat; the absence of a costume I took for a mark of respect for the deceased, unless this sober outfit were another, subtler form of disguise. Spotting me he advanced in stately fashion, breasting the air like an ocean liner through the waves, chest stuck out and the wings of his coat billowing, and gravely shook my hand. 'She was a grand woman,' he said, pursing his lips and nodding, 'grand.' Then he stood aside and gave slow-witted Popeye a glare and the young man awkwardly stepped forward and offered me a surprisingly delicate, fine-boned, fat-fingered little hand (where . . . ? whose . . . ?) and looked at my knees and muttered something that I did not catch. The three of us walked together to the graveside over the still-lush grass in a not uncomfortable silence; nothing like a funeral for promoting a sense of fellowship among the quick. The sky was very high and still and blue. The priest and the under-taker were there, and also, to my surprise, with his hands clasped before his flies and his head bowed, dark-suited Mr Haddon; in the open air his round, smooth face had a pinkish tinge and his fair hair seemed transparent. He gave me a studiedly mournful glance and lowered his gaze again. The ceremony was brief. The priest stumbled over Aunt Corky's consonantal surname. As soon as the prayers were done a canary-yellow mechanical digger trundled forward and set to work with strangely anthropomorphic, jerky movements, like an idiot child eating fistfuls of clay. I turned and made off at once, fearing to be spoken to by Haddon. The Da stuck with me, however.

We went to a pub close by the cemetery for what he called a funeral jar. I like pubs in the morningtime, with that stale, jaded, faintly shamefaced air they have, as if a night-long debauch has just stumbled exhaustedly to an end. This was one of those brand-new antique places with fake wood and polished brass and a great many very clean and curiously blind-looking mirrors. The sun coming in at the tops of the windows suggested strong spotlights banked up outside on the pavement. We sat in a pool of shadowed quiet at a table in the corner and Popeye was sent to order our drinks. The Da watched him with a gloomy eye and sighed. 'Have you any children yourself?' he said to me. 'I thought I heard you too had a son . . .'

Popeye returned, hunched in popeyed concentration with three glasses perilously clasped between his small hands, and the light caught his face and something leaped out at me for a second, something that was him and not him, and that I seemed to know from somewhere else (this is all with the benefit of shameless hindsight, of course). He set the drinks on the table. The Da lifted his glass in silent tribute to the dead. He drank deep of his pint and set it down and licked a moustache of froth from his upper lip. Then he leaned back at ease with his arms folded and began to tell me of the techniques he had developed for dealing with police interrogations, to which he had been subjected frequently over the years. 'The thing is not to say a word no matter what,' he said. 'Drives them mad. Do you know what the best trick is? Tell him, Cyril.' Popeye rolled an eye and chuckled and began to jerk a hand up and down in his lap with fingers and thumb joined in a ring. The Da nodded at me. 'That's it,' he said. 'Just take out the lad and sit there in front of them waggling away. Puts them off their bacon and cabbage, I can tell you.' He cackled. 'I'll try it on Hackett,' he said, 'when he has me in to help him with his enquiries.' He laughed again and slapped his knee, and then, bethinking himself and the occasion, he turned solemn again, and coughed and buried his nose in his pint glass. A restive silence settled on the table and Popeye began to fidget, looking about the bar in a bored fashion and whistling faintly through his teeth. The Da sat back and eyed me with an amused and speculative light.

'Where are they,' I said, 'the pictures? I mean the real ones.'

Popeye stopped whistling and sat very still, looking at nothing. The Da gazed at me for a moment, considering, then laughed and shook his head and held up a commanding hand. 'No: no shop,' he said. 'Respect for the dead. I'm in the export business now. Have another drink.' He went on watching me with a mischievous smile, playfully. 'Did Morden pay you for the work you did?' he said. 'Present him with a bill, that's the thing. List it all out: *to expert advice, such-and-such.* You earned it.' He paused, and leaned forward and set his face close to mine. 'Or did you get what you wanted?' he said. He watched me for a moment with a sort of stony smile. 'She's the genuine article, all right,' he

214

said. 'A real beauty.' And he took up his glass and drained it and gave me a last, lewd wink.

The thinned-out sunlight seemed charged and sharpened as I ran through the streets to Rue Street: I have always lived in the midst of a pathetic fallacy. She was gone, of course. So were the pictures, my table, books, instruments, everything; the chaise-longue had been stripped, the sheets and pillows taken away. We might never have been there. I swarmed through the house, up and down the stairs like a maddened spider, muttering to myself. I must have been a comic sight. I had lost her, I knew, yet I would not stop searching, as if by these frantic spirallings through the empty house I might conjure some living vision of her out of the very air. In the end, exhausted, I went back to our now emptied room and sank down on the chaise-longue and sat for a long time, I think it was a long time, with shaking hands on shaking knees, staring at the roofs and the still sky beyond the window. I know the mind cannot go blank but there are times when a sort of merciful fog settles on it through which things blunder in helpless unrecognition. Far off on a rooftop a workman in a boiler suit had appeared and was clambering laboriously among the chimney-pots; he seemed impossibly huge, with bowed arms and a great blunt head and tubular legs. I watched him for a while; what was he doing out there? Idly and with a grim sense of exhilaration I considered what it would be to fling myself from a high place: the receiving air, the surprise of such speed, and everything whirling and swaying. Would I have time to hear the slap and smash before oblivion came? Presently I rose to go, and it was then that I found her note, scribbled in pencil on a piece of grey pasteboard torn from a matchbox and attached to the arm of the couch with a safety pin. It spoke in her voice. '*Must go. Sorry. Write to me.*' There was no signature, and no address. I sat down again suddenly, winded, as if I had been punched very hard in the midriff. I have not got my breath back yet.

If only I could end it here.

I do not know for how long the noises had been going on before I noticed them. They were not noises, exactly, but rather modulations of the silence. I crept downstairs, pausing at every other step to listen. The basement was dark. I stopped in the doorway in the faint glow falling darkly from the high lunette at the far end of the corridor. Linseed oil, turpentine, old-fashioned wood glue. I remembered A. bringing me here that first day, my arm pressed in hers, a shimmer of excited laughter running through her. She had shown me what I could not see, what I would not understand.

In the dark before me Francie laughed quietly and said, 'You too, eh? Where Jesus left the Jews.' His voice was blurred. I switched on the light and he put up a hand to shade his eyes from the weak glare of the bare bulb. He was lying on the floor beside the workbench on a makeshift pallet of rags and old coats. 'You wouldn't have a fag, I suppose?' he said. In fact, I had: the packet I had bought in the café that breakfast time an aeon ago was still in my pocket, battered but intact; the coincidence, or whatever it was, struck me as comical. He sat up and fished about in his pockets for a match. Had it not been for the ginger suit (lining lolling like a tongue from a torn lapel) and wispy red hair I might not have recognised him. His face was bruised and swollen, a meat-coloured puffball with rubber lips and purple and honeysuckle-yellow eye-sockets. One of his front teeth was gone, and each time before he spoke he had to organise his tongue to the new arrangement of his mouth. He held the cigarette in a shaking hand, the swollen index finger of which stuck out stiffly at an oblique angle. I sat down on the floor beside him with my arms around my knees. He smelled warmly of blood and pounded flesh. He

216

squinted at me, and chuckled, and coughed. I asked him what had happened to him and he shrugged. 'Your friend Hackett,' he said. 'Brought me in for a chat. What could I tell him? Morden forgot to leave a forwarding address.'

I saw a long straight road with poplars and an ochre- and olive-green mountain in the distance. Paysage. My demoiselle.

There is an interval, I have discovered, a little period of grace the heart affords itself, between the acknowledgment of loss and the onset of mourning. It is effected by a simple, or impossibly complicated, piece of legerdemain by which a blocking something is inserted between the door-frame and the suddenly slamming door, so that a chink of light remains, however briefly. In my case curiosity was the wedge. Suddenly I was agog to know how they had done it, and why, to be told of the forger's art, the tricks of the trade, to be admitted to the grand arcanum. Not that I was interested, really. What I wanted, squatting with Francie there in the gloom of that Piranesian vault, was to have it all turned into a tale, made fabulous, unreal, harmless.

'Gall and Plunkett painted them,' Francie said with a shrug, 'and I did the framing.' He waved a hand, and winced. 'Down here. Day and night for a week. And what did I get for my trouble?' He contemplated his torn coat, his broken finger. 'We dried them under the lamps,' he said, 'they were still sticky when he showed them to you and you never noticed.'

Tarraa!

'What were they for?' I said.

He fixed me with a bloodied eye and seemed to grin.

'You'd like to know, now, wouldn't you,' he said.

Then he leaned his head back against the leg of the bench and smoked for a while in silence.

There really was a man called Marbot, by the way. Yes, he was real, even if everything else was fake. Amazing.

Francie sighed. 'And Hackett had poor Prince destroyed,' he said.

The world when I stepped back into it was immense, and hollowed out somehow. I saw myself for the rest of my days rattling about helplessly like a shrivelled pea in this vast shell. I walked homeward slowly, taking cautious little steps, as if I were carrying myself carefully in my own arms. The day was overcast, with a greasy drizzle billowing sideways into the streets like a crooked curtain. Things around me shimmered and shook, edged with a garish flaring like a migraine aura. In the flat I spent what seemed hours wandering abstractedly from room to room or sitting by the window watching the winter evening glimmer briefly and then slowly fade. I dragged Aunt Corky's bag from under the bed and went through her things. It was something to do. Lugubrious rain-light slithered down the window. I unrolled her yellowed papers; they crackled eagerly in my hands, like papyrus, they couldn't wait to betray her. She had been no more Dutch than I am. Before the war she had been married briefly to an engineer who had come from Holland to build a bridge and who abandoned her as soon as the last span was in place (the bridge later fell down, as I recall, with considerable loss of life). I sat on the floor and would have laughed if I could. What an actress! Such dedication! All those years keeping that fiction going, with foreign cigarettes and that hint of an accent. I wish I could have shed a tear for you, Auntie dear. Or perhaps I have?

In the days that followed I could not be still. I walked the streets of the quarter, peering into remembered corners. Everything was the same and yet changed. It was as if I had died and come back. This is how I imagine the dead, wandering lost in a state of vast, objectless bewilderment. I lurked in Rue Street watching the house. No one; there was no one.

When the story at last came out in the papers I was filled

with indignation and proprietorial resentment; it was as if some painful episode of my private life had been dug up by these pig-faced delvers (*our reporter writes . . .*) and spread across eight columns for the diversion of a sniggering public. I did not care that my name appeared; it was my old name, and the mention was purely historical (*Previous Theft at Whitewater Recalled*), and I was grateful to Hackett for keeping me out of it; no, what galled me, I think, was the way the whole thing, that intricate dance of desire and deceit at the centre of which A. and I had whirled and twined, was turned into a clumping caper, bizarre, farcical almost, all leering snouts and horny hands and bare bums, like something by Bruegel. How could they have reduced such complexity to a few headlines? *Daring Robbery – Priceless Cache – Mystery of Pictures' Whereabouts – Security Man Dies.* It was all so impersonal, so . . . denatured. Morden was not named, though you could almost see *our reporter* squirming from buttock to buttock, like a boy in class with the right answer, dying to blurt it out. He was *a leading businessman with underworld connections*; far too dashing a description, I thought, for the distinctly loutish conman I had known. He and A. became *the mystery couple*. The Da was *a notorious criminal figure*. A Detective Inspector Hickett was quoted as saying that the police were following a definite line of inquiry. The butcher and the knave and the butcher's daughter linked hands and stumbled in a ring . . .

I saw A. everywhere, of course, just as I had done in the first days, after that first kiss. The streets were thronged with the ghost of her. The world of women had dwindled to a single image. There were certain places where I felt her presence so strongly I was convinced that if I stood for long enough, shivering in anguish, she would surely appear, conjured by the force of my longing. In Swan Alley there was a narrow archway beside a chip shop, it must at one time have been the entrance to something but was bricked off now, where buddleia grew and feral cats congregated, and where one dreamy November twilight we had made awkward, desperate, breath-taking love, standing in our coats and holding on to each other like climbers roped together falling through endless air locked in a last embrace. There I would loiter now, obscurely glad of the squalor, trying to make her appear; and one evening, huddled in the shadows under the archway, racked by sobs, I opened my coat and masturbated into the chip shop's grease-caked dust-bin, gagging on her name.

This is all confused, I know, unfocused and confused and other near-anagrams indicating distress. But that is how I want it to be, all smeary with tears and lymph and squirming spawn and glass-green mucus: my snail-trail.

Barbarossa was still living in his box. I was surprised he had survived so far into the winter, huddled there in the cutler's doorway. I suppose he was pickled by now, pre-served, like a homunculus in its jar of alcohol. How even the frailest things could endure, as if to mock me! It was surprising too that the owner of the shop had not had him shifted; it could not have been good for business, to have a character like that living on your doorstep, even if he was careful to absent himself discreetly during business hours. But the derelicts in general, I noticed, seemed to be getting more impudent every day, encroaching more and more upon the city, moving out of the back alleyways into the squares and thoroughfares, bold as brass, colonising the place. At the cocktail hour they would gather with their bottles around an oily, dangerous-looking fire on that bit of waste ground by the bus depot and sing and fight and shout abuse at passers-by. Even when they approached me individually they could be surprisingly truculent. One of them accosted me in Fawn Street one evening, big strapping young fellow with a mouthful of crooked teeth, planted himself in my path with his hand stuck out and said nothing, just glared at

me with one eye rolling like the eye of a maddened h
and would not let me pass. There was no one else about a
for a minute I thought he might haul off and take a swing
at me. Breath like a furnace blast and the skin of his face
glazed and blackened as if a flaming torch had been thrust
into it. Alarming, I can tell you. Why is it so hard to look
a beggar in the eye? Afraid of seeing myself there? No; it's
more a sort of general embarrassment, not just for him but
for all of us, if that does not sound too grand. I gave him a
coin and made a feeble joke about not squandering it on
food and heard myself laugh and hurried on discomfited and
obscurely shamed. Instead of which, of course, I should have
taken him tenderly in my arms and breathed deep his noxious
stink and cried, '*My friend, my fellow sufferer!*' as the misan-
thropic sage of Dresden recommends.

Barbarossa had abandoned the tricolour cap A. had liked
so much in favour of a much less picturesque, imitation-
leather affair with ear-flaps. Also he sported now a rather
natty pair of pinstriped trousers, the kind that hotel porters
wear or ambassadors when they are presenting their creden-
tials. I should very much like to know the history of that
particular pair of bags. By the way, that beard of his: it did
not seem to grow at all, I wonder why; or perhaps it did
and I just did not notice it because I saw him every day? His
girth was steadily increasing, I noticed that. On what was
he growing so rotund? I never saw him eating anything, and
the rotgut wine or sherry or whatever it was that he drank
– always demurely jacketed in its brown-paper bag – surely
could not be so nourishing that it would make him into this
roly-poly, Falstaff figure? Perhaps, I thought, he was like
those starving black babies one sees so many distressing
pictures of these days, their little bellies swollen tight from
hunger. He had a fixed course that he followed daily, squar-
ing off the quarter in his burdened, back-tracking way: down
Gabriel Street, across Swan Alley into Dog Lane, then along

Fawn Street and under the archway there on to the quays, then into Black Street and Hope Alley and down the lane beside The Boatman and so back into Gabriel Street, as the day failed and the shops began to shut and lights came on in uncurtained upper windows, though never in ours, my love, never in ours.

I have a confession to make. One night when I was passing Barbarossa's doorway I stopped and gave him a terrible kick. I can't think why I did it; it's not as if he were doing me any harm. He was lying there, asleep, I suppose, if he did sleep, wrapped up in his rags, a big, awful bundle in the shadows, and I just drew back my foot and gave him one in the kidneys, or kidney, as hard as I dared. He had a dense, soggy feel to him; it was like kicking a sack of grain. He hardly stirred, did not even turn his head to see who it was that had thus senselessly assaulted him, and gave a short groan, more of gloomy annoyance, I thought, than pain or surprise, as if I had done no more than disturb him in the midst of a pleasant dream. I stood a moment irresolute and then walked on, not sure that the thing had happened at all or if I had imagined it. But it did happen, I did kick the poor brute, for no reason other than pure badness. So much violence in me still, unassuaged.

What *are* those damn pipes for? I cannot say. Not everything means something, even in this world.

One afternoon I witnessed a touching encounter. Iron-grey weather with wind and thin rain like umbrella-spokes. Barbarossa on his rounds turns a corner into Hope Alley and finds himself face to face with Quasimodo and rears back in obvious consternation and displeasure. They must know each other! I halt too, and skulk in a doorway, anxious not to miss a thing. The hunchback gives the burdened one an eager, sweet, complicitous smile, but Barbarossa, clutching to him his fistful of pipes, pushes past him with a scowl.

Quasimodo, rebuked and near to tears, hurries on with head down. *Compagnon de misère!*

In those terrible weeks I spent much of my time by the river, especially after nightfall. I liked to feel the heave and surge of water – for in the dark of course one senses rather than sees it – coiling past me like a vast, fat, undulant animal hurrying to somewhere, intent and silent, the slippery lights of the city rolling swiftly along its back. I'm sure I must have seemed a potential suicide, hunched there staring out haggard-eyed from the embankment wall with my misery wrapped around me like a cloak. I would not have been surprised if some night some busybody had grabbed me by the arm, convinced I was about to throw a leg over and go in. *Do not do it, my friend*, they would have cried, *I beseech you, think of all that you will be losing!* As if I had not lost all already.

But I knew I must not give in to self-pity. I had nothing to pity myself for. She had been mine for a time, and now she was gone. Gone, but alive, in whatever form life might have taken for her, and from the start that was supposed to be my task: to give her life. Come live in me, I had said, and be my love. Intending, of course, whether I knew it or not, that I in turn would live in her. What I had not bargained for was that this life I was so eager she should embark on would require me in the end to relinquish her. No, that was the wrinkle I had not thought of. Now there I stood, in the midst of winter, a forlorn Baron Frankenstein, holding in my hands the cast-off bandages and the cold electrodes and wondering what Alpine fastnesses she was wandering in, what icy wastes she might be traversing.

When I heard Aunt Corky had left me her money I bought champagne for the girls at No. 23 to celebrate my windfall. Yes, I had begun to go there again, but mostly for company, now. I saw myself as one of Lautrec's old roués, debouching from a barouche and doffing my stovepipe to the pinched faces watching with feigned eagerness at the windows. I liked to sit in the parlour chatting in the early evening while business was still unbrisk. I think the girls looked on me as their mascot, their safe man. In their company I glimpsed a simpler, more natural life: does that seem perverse? And of course there were the memories of you there, flickering in the dimness of those mean rooms like shadows thrown by a wavering candle-flame. That day after the reading of the will, when I arrived with my clanking bag of bottles, the place did its best to stir itself out of its afternoon lethargy and we had a little party. I got skittishly drunk and thus fortified had the courage at last to approach Rosie again, our Rosie. She is, I realise, beautiful, in her ravaged way; she has wonderful legs, very long and muscular, with shapely knees, a rare feature, in my admittedly limited experience. Also her skin has that curiously soiled, muddy sheen to it that I find mysteriously exciting (perhaps it reminds me of the feel of you?); this skin tone is the effect of cigarettes, I suspect, for she is a great smoker, unlike you a real addict, going at the fags like billy-o, almost angrily, as if it were an irksome task that had been imposed on her along with the rest of her burdens. At first she was guarded; she remembered me, and asked after you; I lied. She was still wearing that safety pin in her ear; I wondered idly if she took it out at night. Presently the bubbly began to take effect and she told me her story, in that offhand, grimly scoffing way they adopt when speaking about themselves. It was the usual tale: child bride, a drunken husband who ran off, kids to rear, job at the factory that folded, then her friend suggested she give the game a try and here she was. She laughed phlegmily. We were in what Mrs Murphy calls the parlour. Rosie looked about her at the cretonne curtains and lumpy armchairs and the oilcloth-covered table and expelled contemptuous twin steams of smoke through flared nostrils. 'Better here than on the streets at least,' she said. I put my hand on her thigh.

She was a raw, hard, worn working girl, your opposite in every way, and just what I thought I needed at that moment. But it was not a success. When we went upstairs and lay down on the meagre bed – how quickly these professionals can get out of their clothes! – she ground her hips against mine in a perfunctory simulacrum of passion and afterwards yawned mightily, showing me a mouthful of fillings and breathing a warm, sallow fug of stale tobacco-fumes in my face. She had been better as a witness than a participant. Yet in the melancholy afterglow as I lay on my stomach with chin on hands and the length of her cool, goosefleshed flank pressed against mine – I think she had dropped off for a moment – and looked out through the gap under the curtain at the shivery lights along Black Street I felt a pang of the old, fearful happiness and gave her a hug of gratitude and fond fellowship, to which she responded with a sleepy groan. (None of this is quite right, of course, or quite honest; in truth, I remain in awe of this tough young woman, cowering before her breathless with excitement and fright, trembling in the conviction of enormous, inabsolvable transgression; it might be my mother I am consorting with, as Rosie wields me, her big baby, with a distracted tenderness that carries me back irresistibly to the hot, huddled world of infanthood. Deep waters, these; murky and deep. She has a scar across her lower belly knobbled and hard like a length of knotted nylon string; caesarean section, I presume. What a lot of living she has done in her twenty years. I hope, by the way, I have made you jealous; I hope you are suffering.)

How powerfully affecting they are, though, these reflexive moments when you not only feel something but also feel yourself feeling it. As I lay on that frowsty bed in Ma Murphy's gazing down at that strip of windswept night street I had a kind of out-of-body experience, seeming to be both myself and the trembling image of myself, as if my own little ghost had materialised there, conjured out of equal measures of stark self-awareness on one side and on the other the fearful acknowledgment of all there was that I was not. Me and my ectoplasm. And yet at the same time at moments such as this I have the notion of myself as a singular figure, a man heroically alone, learned in the arts of solitude and making-do, one with those silent, tense characters you come across of a night standing motionless in the hard-edged, angled shadows of shop doorways or sitting alone in softly purring parked cars and who make you jump when you catch sight of them, their haunted eyes and glowing cigarette-tips flaring at you briefly out of the dark. *Esse est percipi.* And vice versa (that is, *to see is to cause to be*; how would I put that into bog Latin?) You see what you have done to me by your going? You have made me an habitué of this flickering, nocturnal demi-monde I was always afraid I would end up in at the last. Oh, I know, at heart I was ever a loner – who, at heart, is not? – but that was different to this. This is another kind of isolation, one I have not experienced before.

Yet I am not what you could properly call alone. There is a sort of awful, inescapable intimacy among us solitaries. I know all the signs by now, the furtive, involuntary signals by which the members of our brotherhood recognise each other: the glance in the street that is quickly averted, the foot tensely tapping amid the straggle of pedestrians waiting on the windy corner for the lights to change and the little green man to appear (the emblem of our kind, our very mascot!), the particular presence behind me in the supermarket queue: a pent, breathy silence at my shoulder that seems always about to break out into impossible babblings and never does. Children of the dark, we make diurnal night for ourselves in the bare back rooms of pubs, in the echoing gloom of public libraries and picture galleries, in churches, even – churches, I have noticed, are for some reason especially popular when it rains. Our favourite haunt, however, our happiest home, is the afternoon cinema. As we sit star-scattered there in that velvety dark, the lonely and the lovelorn, the quiet cranks and mild lunatics and serial killers-in-waiting, all with our pallid faces lifted to the lighted screen, we might be in the womb again, listening in amazement to news from the big world outside, hearing its cries and gaudy laughter, watching huge mouths move and speak and feed on other mouths, seeing the gun-barrels blaze and the bright blood flow, feeling the beat of life itself all around and yet beyond us. I love to loll dreamily there, lost to all sense, and let the images play over me like music, as you materialise enormously in these moving sculptures with their impossible hair and bee-stung lips and rippling, honeyed flanks. Where are you. Tell me. Where are you. What we see up there are not these tawdry scenes made to divert and pacify just such as we: it is ourselves reflected that we behold, the mad dream of ourselves, of what we might have been as well as what we have become, the familiar story that has gone strange, the plot that at first seemed so promising and now has fascinatingly unravelled. Out of these images we manufacture selves wholly improbable that yet sustain us for an hour or two, then we stumble out blinking into the light and are again what we always were, and weep inwardly for all that we never had yet feel convinced we have lost.

What shall I do with myself? I could get a job, I suppose. Often I think it might be something as simple as that that would be the saving of me. Nothing serious, of course, nothing to do with science or art, none of that old pretence, that worn-out fustian. I could be a clerk, say, one of those grey, meek men you glimpse in the offices of large, established firms, padding about in the background furtive as mice, with dandruff on their collars and their suits worn shiny. I can see myself there, bleakly diligent, keeping myself to myself, suffering the banter of the younger clerks with a thin unfocused smile and going home in the evening to cold cuts and the telly. Dreams, idle dreams; I wouldn't last a wet week. The junior partner would be given the task of talking to me. *Ahem, yes, well* – frowning out of the window at the rain and jingling coins in his trouser pocket – *Oh, the work is fine, fine, very satisfactory. It's your manner, you see; that's the problem. A bit on the gloomy side. The girls complain, you know what they're like, and Miss McGinty says you're inclined to stare in a way she finds unnerving . . . Had a bereavement recently, have you?* Yes, sir; sort of.

I went to see Hackett. His office was in a big grey mock-Gothic fortress with wire mesh on the windows and a pillared porch where I waited meekly, trying to look innocent, while a bored young policeman in shirt-sleeves phoned the Inspector's office, leaning on his counter with the receiver tucked under his chin like a fiddle and looking me up and down with a gaze at once bored and speculative. Flyblown notices warned of rabies and ragweed. Two detectives in padded jerkins went out laughing, leaving behind them a mingled smell of cigarette smoke and sweat. Police stations always remind me of school, they have the same dishevelled, sullen, faintly desperate air. A billow of wind bustled in from the street, bringing dust and the smell of approaching rain. The young policeman's voice made me start. He slung down the phone. 'Third floor, first on the left.' Brief pause, a sour smirk. 'Sir.' They can always recognise an old gaolbird.

Hackett's office was a partitioned-off corner of a large, low-ceilinged, crowded room where angry-looking men walked here and there carrying documents, or sat with their feet on their desks or hunched over and glaring at big, old-fashioned typewriters. That schoolroom smell again: dust, stale paper, rotten apple-cores. Through the glass of his door Hackett motioned me to enter. He stood up awkwardly, smiling his shy smile. He wore a broad, greasy tie with a windsor knot, and his too-tight jacket was buttoned as always, the gaps between the buttons pulling agape like vertical, fat, exclaiming mouths. On the floor beside his incongruously grand mahogany desk an electric fire was tinily abuzz; the sight of it almost made me sob. In the corner, at a smaller, metal desk, an elderly policeman in uniform was poking with the smallest blade of a penknife at the innards of a half-dismantled pocket-watch; he was balding, and had the leathery look of a countryman; he gave me a friendly nod and winked. Crêpe paper decorations were strung across the ceiling, and there were sprigs of holly, and Christmas cards pinned to a notice board. One of the cards was inscribed *To Daddy* in tall, wobbly lettering. I would not have taken Hackett for a family man; I pictured two scale-models of him, globe-headed and chicken-eyed, one in britches and the other in a gym-slip, and had to think of death to keep from laughing. He saw me looking at the card and gave what I realised was a sympathetic cough. 'And you buried your poor auntie,' he said, and lowered his eyes and shook his great head slowly from side to side.

Despite everything I know, despite all the things I have seen, and done, I persist in thinking of the world as essentially benign. I have no grounds for this conviction – I mean, look at the place – yet I cannot shake it off. Even those – and I have encountered a few of them, I can tell you – who have perpetrated the most appalling wickednesses, can seem after the event as mild and tentative as any of . . . of you (*us*, I almost said). This is what is known, I believe, as the problem of evil. I doubt I shall ever solve it to my satisfaction. Hackett, now, with his shy smile and buttoned-up look of sorrow and sympathy, seemed the soul of harmlessness.

'I saw Francie,' I said.

Hackett beamed as if I had mentioned an old, fond friend of his.

'Yes,' he said. 'Had to give him a tap or two. The Sergeant there couldn't hear him and I had to keep asking him to speak up. That right, Sergeant?' The elderly policeman, without looking up from the intricacies of his watch, delivered himself of a rich, low chuckle. 'Brought the Da in too,' Hackett said. 'Couldn't get a thing out of him. Do you know what he does when—

'I know,' I said. 'He told me.'

'Dirty bugger,' Hackett said, but laughed, rueful and admiring. He sat back on his swivel chair and laced his fingers together on his chest and contemplated me. 'I'd have had you in, too,' he said, 'but I knew you knew nothing.' He waited, smiling with fond contempt, but I did not speak. What was there for me to say? I was beginning to have an inkling of his sense of humour. 'Any word?' he said. 'Of your friends, I mean. Morden, and . . .' He raised his eyebrows. I shook my head. 'Oh, by the way,' he said as if he had just remembered, 'you were right about the pictures. Or about one of them, at least.' He leaned forward and searched among the papers on his desk and handed me a postcard. A crease ran aslant the coloured reproduction on the front like a vein drained of blood. The butcher's art. *Birth of Athena: Jean Vaublin (1684-1721)*. I turned it over. *Behrens Collection, Whitewater House*. It was addressed to Hackett. The message was scrawled in a deliberately clumsy hand: '*Who's the daddy of them all?*' 'He's fond of a joke,' Hackett said. He watched me with that gentle smile. He pointed to the postcard. 'They wanted to get that one out,' he said. 'They must have had a buyer for it. Some moneybags somewhere. The rest will be in store, for another day.' Brown light of the winter afternoon pressed itself against the meshed windows, the electric fire fizzed. In the office outside someone laughed loudly. Hackett gave himself a sort of doggy shake, and turned aside in his chair and set one shiny brown brogue on the corner of the desk and shut an eye and took a sighting along the toe. 'Seven fakes,' he said dreamily. 'Who would have thought the eighth would be the real thing? Not our friend Sharpe, anyway. Not when he had you to laugh at.' He looked at me again with that lopsided stare, that saddest smile. His eyes seemed crookeder than ever. A muscle in his jaw was jumping. 'We've been at this for years, the Da and me. It's like one of them long-distance chess games. He'll make a move, send it to me, I'll make a move, send it to him.' He swung his leg to the floor and leaned forward and shifted the invisible pieces before him on the desk. He smiled. 'He wins, I lose; I win, he loses. This time it was his turn. He stuck that real one in with the duds and gambled that we'd all miss it. And we did. But he wouldn't have cared if we had spotted it. He doesn't care about anything, only the game. I'm telling you, mad as a hatter.'

'What about the other seven?' I said.

He shrugged, and shifted bunched fingers this way and that over the desk-top again. 'He'll wait, then make another move. We'll see who'll win next time. It's a great match we have going.' He gazed toward the window with an almost happy sigh. 'Yes,' he said, 'yes: the daddy of them all.'

The Sergeant at the desk pressed something in the recesses of his timepiece and the mechanism returned a tiny, silver chime.

Hackett and I walked down the echoing stairs. Below us men were talking loudly, their voices came to us in a blare. There had been another murder, the last, as it turned out. 'Bled her white,' Hackett said. 'It's a bad world.' On the last step a young detective sat staring at a splash of vomit on his shoes, grey-faced and breathing deeply, while two older men stood over him shouting at each other. They did not look at us as we sidled past. In the porch we paused, not knowing quite how to part. Outside, the grimed December dusk was flecked with rain.

'And the daughter,' Hackett said, 'you haven't heard from her?'

I looked at the rain drifting in the light at the doorway. Behind us the two detectives were still arguing.

'Daughter?' I said, and was not sure that I had spoken. 'What daughter?'

Hackett looked at me. I wonder what it was *he* thought of in order to keep himself from laughing?

'The girl,' he said. 'Morden's sister. The two of them; the Da is their . . .' He touched my arm with a sort of solicitude, awkwardly, like a mourner offering comfort to one bereaved. 'Did you not know?' he said.

What I thought of immediately was her telling me one day how in her bored childhood she used to spend hours alone hitting a tennis ball against the gable end of a house. At the time of course I pictured a tranquil suburb in the hills above some great city, dappled sunlight in the planes and a chauffeur in shirt-sleeves and leggings polishing the ambassador's limousine. Now what I saw was a mean terrace with defeated scraps of garden and a woman leaning out of an upstairs window raucously calling her name, while a toddler on a tricycle upends himself into the gutter and begins to whinge, and *pock!* goes the ball as the girl swings her racquet with redoubled fury. It was no dead twin that walked beside her always, but the ghost of that ineluctable past.

Birth of Athena. Behrens Collection.

Consider these creatures, these people who are not people, these inhabitants of heaven. The god has a headache, his son wields the axe, the girl springs forth with bow and shield. She is walking towards the world. Her owl flies before her. It is twilight. Look at these clouds, this limitless and impenetrable sky. This is what remains. A crease runs athwart it like a bloodless vein. Everything is changed and yet the same.

I saw her yesterday, I don't know how, but I did. It was the strangest thing. I have not got over it yet. I was in that pub on Gabriel Street that she liked so much. The place is fake, of course, with false wood panelling and plated brass and a wooden fan the size of an aeroplane propeller in the ceiling that does nothing except swirl the drifting cigarette smoke in lazy arabesques. I go there for the obvious reason. I was in the back bar, nursing a drink and my sore heart, sitting at that big window – I always think of windows like that as startled, somehow, like wide-open eyes – that looks down at the city along the broad sweep of Ormond Street. The street was crowded, as it always is. The sun was shining, in its half-hearted way – yes, spring has come, despite my best efforts. Suddenly I saw her – or no, not suddenly, there was no suddenness or surprise in it. She was just there, in her black coat and her black stilettos, hurrying along the crowded pavement in that watery light at that unmistakable, stiff-kneed half-run, a hand to her breast and her head down. Where was she going, with such haste, so eagerly? The city lay all before her, awash with April and evening. I say *her*, but of course I know it was not her, not really. And yet it was. How can I express it? There is the she who is gone, who is in some southern somewhere, lost to me forever, and then there is this other, who steps out of my head and goes hurrying off along the sunlit pavements to do I don't know what. To live. If I can call it living; and I shall.

Write to me, she said. Write to me. I have written.

A NOTE ON THE TYPE

This book was set in a version of the well-known Monotype face Bembo. This letter was cut for the celebrated Venetian printer Aldus Manutius by Francesco Griffo, and first used in Pietro Cardinal Bembo's *De Ætna* of 1495.

The companion italic is an adaptation of the chancery script type designed by the calligrapher and printer Lodovico degli Arrighi.

Composed in Great Britain
Printed and bound by Quebecor Printing,
Fairfield, Pennsylvania